The Key Lime Crime

The Key Lime Crime

KEY WEST FOOD CRITIC MYSTERY

Lucy Burdette

CROOKED LANE

NEW YORK

Published in the United States by Crooked Lane Books, an imprint of The Quick Brown Fox & Company LLC.

Crooked Lane Books and its logo are trademarks of The Quick Brown Fox & Company LLC.

Library of Congress Catalog-in-Publication data available upon request.

ISBN (paperback): 978-1-64385-951-4
ISBN (hardcover): 978-1-64385-308-6
ISBN (ePub): 978-1-64385-329-1

Cover design by Griesbach/Martucci
Book design by Jennifer Canzone

Printed in the United States.

www.crookedlanebooks.com

Crooked Lane Books
34 West 27th St., 10th Floor
New York, NY 10001

Paperback Edition: July 2021
Hardcover Edition: July 2020

10 9 8 7 6 5 4 3 2

For my Uncle Don, whose relationship with my dad showed us what friendship could be.

Chapter One

. . . no, everybody is not a critic. What most of you are doing out there, online and in three dimensions, is complaining.
—Pete Wells, "The Art of Complaining," *The New York Times*, February 6, 2019

To whom does our island belong? I found myself wondering that as I sat on my scooter in the rain, late for my pricy-but-absolutely-necessary-for-a-person-who-eats-for-a-living personal trainer, attempting to cross a massive traffic jam on Eaton Street. Underneath the beads and the beer and the outdoor burgers and music on Duval Street where the tourists found their "happy place," there was a struggle for ownership. I'd seen this on Instagram and Facebook when I posted something especially beautiful about our little knob of coral. Outsiders craved a piece of paradise as much as the locals—the insiders—wanted them gone.

This week between Christmas and New Year's, Key West was bursting at the seams. Even my general practitioner had confessed he wouldn't leave his condo complex unless going to work; he'd never seen the island this busy. People wouldn't stop for anyone—on a bicycle, walking, on a scooter, in a car. Old folks, children, chickens, residents, visitors—we were all in the cross hairs of holiday-crazed motorists. Already since Monday there had been five accidents, including two couples airlifted to a Miami trauma center, outcomes unknown.

And that pointed to one of the drawbacks of living on a small island and getting sick, with the way to mainland being a four-hour drive to Miami. You could get by fine visiting local doctors with a garden-variety cold or to get a few stitches or an eye exam, but detach a retina or bash your head on the pavement, and you had an expensive helicopter trip to Miami ahead of you.

Because of the congestion, I seemed to be running late for everything. Adding to the chaos of the holiday season, key lime pie aficionado David Sloan had persuaded the city to host his key lime extravaganza and contest this busy week, rather than waiting for the slower summer months, I couldn't avoid the additional madness because my bosses had assigned me to cover the event. Every pie purveyor in Key West (and there were a ton of them) was determined to claim the key lime spotlight—and win the coveted Key Lime Key to the City. My bosses at *Key Zest* magazine wanted me to get a jump on other foodie journalists by reporting on as many pies as possible before the contest even began, along with writing an article about Sloan's contest, not to mention my regularly featured restaurant roundup, this time a review of fast but delicious island options. Call me Hayley Snow, food critic and frantic foodie fanatic.

I dashed through a slight break in the traffic and whizzed across Frances Street, nearly slamming into a golf cart loaded with tourists.

"Even in Key West on vacation, a stop sign is not a suggestion," I hollered.

They waved their beer cans and hooted with laughter.

"Chill, baby," the driver yelled back. "Anger isn't an aphrodisiac."

Idiots.

Several blocks later I noticed blue lights in my rearview mirror. I pulled over to the curb. It had to be Nathan. My new husband, a Key West police detective, was not usually a prankster. But we'd had a little kerfuffle this morning—about nothing important, really—and he'd stormed off mad. He must finally be getting over his annoyance with me and lightening up. I took off my helmet, fluffed my sure-to-be-wayward auburn curls, blotted the skin under my eyes where my mascara had no doubt smudged because I was always in a hurry, and smiled warmly.

But it wasn't Nathan who emerged from the cruiser; it was two police officers I did not know, one tall and lanky with a shaved head, the other shorter, with the smallest smirk on his face. He stood about ten feet away from the tall man and watched him approach my scooter.

"Did you mean for *me* to stop?" I asked, feeling confused and annoyed. I tipped my head back to look him in the eyes— he had to be at least a foot taller than me.

"Yes. Were you aware that you ran through that stop sign without even looking? Do you have a medical reason to be in a hurry?"

How should a person answer a question like that if she isn't nine months pregnant, clutching her contracting belly, or staunching an obvious blood flow? Maybe *Give me the freaking ticket and let's get on with it?*

Nathan would be furious.

"No. I've got nothing. I'm late for the gym. That's the best I can do." I shrugged my shoulders and grinned, trying to communicate that I was admitting to being in the wrong, that I promised never to do this again, and that I hoped we could settle on a warning.

He did not smile in return. "I like going to the gym, too, but this is a matter of safety—your safety and the safety of the people you might have hypothetically mowed down."

That made me mad. And since I hadn't slept well in weeks, it was hard to tamp down a rising head of steam. "What about those lunatics in a golf cart who blew right through the stop sign on Southard and almost laid me out? I assure you, that was not hypothetical."

"I didn't see them run a stop sign, I saw you," he said, his lips and chin setting like hardening cement.

"You didn't see them? Maybe that's your problem right there," I said, sorry almost as soon as the words came out of my mouth.

The cop watching my officer frowned and nodded, his hands now on his hips, near the equipment on his belt.

"License and registration," the rookie cop said.

Chapter Two

"You can train someone to use a knife, but it's hard to train someone who doesn't have heart," the chef *Masayoshi Takayama* wrote in an email.
— Julia Moskin, "Where the World's Chefs Want to Eat," *The New York Times*, February 25, 2019

O n the way back home from the gym, I wrestled with whether to confess the cop stop incident. I decided I had to tell Nathan about the citation, police-speak for ticket, because he'd find out sooner or later. Worst of all would be if the brand-new officer chose to show him the video of our transaction before he'd heard anything about it. As the partying tourist had suggested, anger in general, and angry arguments with the police in particular, were not an aphrodisiac. Nathan abhorred uncooperative citizens who thought they knew better about everything. Best to get ahead of the situation and admit I'd made an error in judgment. And beg him not to look at the damning video.

Lucy Burdette

I zipped over First Street, crossed Route 1, and lurched into the parking lot for Houseboat Row. Seemed like everyone in our little blended family was irritable lately. Even my octogenarian roommate Miss Gloria's usual cheeriness was sagging. Probably the adrenaline that had carried us through Nathan's on-the-job injury and dramatic rescue and slow recovery and the wedding and multiple visiting family members had evaporated, leaving us tired and sore and crabby. The renovations on our houseboat next door to Miss Gloria's place were not yet completed. Our contractor, Chris, had taken the week off to enjoy his family—and who could complain about that? But with Nathan installed in Miss Gloria's adorable houseboat along with two ladies, two cats, one hyperactive dog, and one small bathroom, our home felt tiny and cramped. Like too many rats jammed into a cage, we were beginning to turn on each other.

No one was sleeping well. I knew Nathan was suffering from the aftermath of his injuries, though damned if he'd say so. Evinrude, my gray tiger cat, was incensed about being upstaged by Nathan's dog. And I felt crowded by my brand-new husband. Considering that I'd been married only three weeks, this seemed like an unfortunate time to lose the glow.

As I reached the finger of dock that led to our houseboat, my phone burred. Nathan's name came up on the screen.

"I'm sorry," I said, before he could get a word in edgewise.

"Me too." He chuckled. "Of course, I was calling to apologize if I was a heel in any way, but I had another matter to discuss with you as well. My mother's coming to town."

"That's fabulous!" I said. His mom had declined to attend our wedding, real reasons unknown. I was pretty sure they related to her disappointment over Nathan's divorce and her reluctance to embrace a second daughter-in-law when she'd adored wife number one.

"I am so looking forward to meeting her," I added, though the idea of his mom in Key West scared the pants off me. "Let's get it on the calendar so we don't book anything else that might conflict with her visit. What kinds of things does she like to do? Do you think she'd be interested in a food tour or a cooking class? I can start looking for what's happening in the next couple weeks at the Tennessee Williams and the Waterfront Playhouse and—"

He broke in. "Tomorrow. That's when she's coming."

"Tomorrow?" I gulped. "Where will she be staying?"

"I'm hoping with us."

I could feel my inner harridan rising up, ready to shriek. *Deep breath, Hayley.* "Hmm," I said. "I would adore hosting her, but I can't imagine how that's going to work exactly. Would she find sleeping on the couch acceptable? Or I could sleep on the couch, but that leaves you sleeping with your mom. He-he." No return chuckle from Nathan. "I could call around, see if there might be a room in any of the bed-and-breakfasts in Old Town." Which there wouldn't be—during the week between Christmas and New Year's, even the dodgiest lodging options were full. "Maybe my mother knows someone."

"Sorry about the notice," he said. "She only called this morning. And I couldn't say no."

"Of course not," I said. "She's your mother; apology accepted. We'll figure something out."

"But what were *you* apologizing for?" he asked.

So I had to explain my stop sign transgression and the ensuing citation, babbling longer than I probably should have. "Okay, I did run the stop sign, but I'm certain I looked both ways, and honestly he was more grim than he needed to be. If he had smiled even a little tiny bit, this never would have gone as far as it did. I'm not exactly the kind of criminal they're looking for, right?"

"If you broke the law, they had every reason to stop you. I can review the video of the incident and see if the rookie did something wrong, but it's a little early to be pulling strings—"

"Please don't pull the video. How about those guys giving me the benefit of the doubt? Shouldn't the more experienced cop have known who I was? Everyone knows you just got married, right?"

"So, what, the police department is supposed to let every cute girl with a smart mouth off the hook because she might be my wife?"

"Not funny," I said.

"I don't think it is funny," he said. "Look at it this way. New cops have to learn to follow procedure in every way. If he lets you off for a traffic citation because you're married to me, next time does he let another cop's family member go scot-free after a felony assault? Entitlement can creep in before anyone notices, and then the rot starts in the department."

I couldn't argue with his reasoning. With cops in the news in all kinds of trouble, he took training the new guys very seriously. He wanted them to do their jobs with compassion, gravitas, and the right amount of discipline. And humanity, too. I loved and admired him for that.

"Besides," he added, "this stop may very well have saved your life." I could hear someone rapping impatiently at his door, and his desk phone was ringing, too. "Look," he said. "I'm going to spend the night at my apartment tonight, to pack up my kitchen. I'd love to have you join me, but maybe with my mother coming, we should all get a good night's sleep?"

"Problem solved," I said brightly. "Your mother can stay at the apartment."

"The movers are coming tomorrow to pick up the furniture and put it in storage. So no bed, no couch, no table, nothing." He sighed. "Listen, it's going to be a late night, and if I expect to have any time off at all while my mother is here, I've got to dig in. Four of our incoming reinforcements for New Year's Eve have already canceled, and none of our regulars want to fill in. And why should they? We've had the schedule made out for weeks."

"That sounds so stressful," I said, remembering Miss Gloria's wisdom about calming an agitated husband—show that you understand and appreciate him, even if at that very moment, you don't. "Call me later?"

I hung up and went inside to stretch out on my bed next to my cat. He circled around and wedged himself in the little curve between my neck and the pillow. I had a whirling mixture of feelings—irritation with Nathan for bailing out, embarrassment that I was failing this first test of our relationship. And sadness, too. This evening, I would miss his warmth and the soft sounds of him breathing in the night, and his good-morning kiss. And the way he smiled at me early in the day, before he'd donned his cop armor to face the world, when he wore an expression that said he was the luckiest guy alive.

I flapped my arms and legs like a snow angel. On the other hand, the bed felt gloriously roomy—it wasn't intended for two people full-time, one of them a muscular six-footer. And I hadn't heard Evinrude purr like this in days. Face it, we'd both be relieved to have a night alone. If there was a Guinness world record for shortest marriage ever, I was deeply afraid Nathan and I were in contention.

I buried my face in the cat's striped fur and tried to channel his calm. Purr . . . breath in . . . purr . . . breath out. After a few minutes, I got up and went out to the kitchen and living area, imagining I was seeing it for the first time as Mrs. Bransford would. The windows were fogged from salt spray, the grout around the sink was trending gray, the flooring at the edges of the kitchen where linoleum met paneling was faded and starting to curl.

It's not that Miss Gloria and I were dirty people, but we weren't the obsessive deep-cleaning types either. The houseboat was funky; that's what Mrs. Bransford would see. And she wouldn't be looking around with eyes rosy from the idea of having added a beloved daughter-in-law to her family. She'd already had her beloved daughter-in-law, and it wasn't me. For whatever reason, Mrs. Bransford had adored Nathan's first wife, and she probably always would. I felt as though

nothing I could do to curry her favor would ever be enough—
and I hadn't even met the woman.

Twenty phone calls later to all the bed-and-breakfasts
I could imagine she might find palatable, I decided the couch
was the only choice. My mother called when I was on hands
and knees in the bathroom, scrubbing the baseboard behind
the toilet.

"What's wrong?" my mother said. "I hear something in
your voice."

Which under ordinary circumstances might have annoyed
me, because what girl wants her mother sensing her every
mood? But she was right in this case—something was wrong,
and I needed support. I told her about the police stop and the
little argument with Nathan. "He's going to spend tonight at
his place to finish his packing. Or so he says," I couldn't help
adding. "But that's okay, that's all good; what's more stressful
is that his mother is arriving tomorrow. Spur-of-the-moment
plans. And I'm late for the opening salvo of this silly key lime
extravaganza." I could hear my voice breaking, and I was sure
she could too.

"How long is she staying?" my mother asked.

"I didn't even ask. Once he mentioned that he hoped she
would stay with us, I kind of lost track of the details because
I was so busy freaking out. The place looks cleaner than it
ever has, but it's not going to get any bigger no matter how
much I scrub. I wondered if Nathan and I could sleep on our
boat next door on a blow-up mattress, but we're still in the
wall-studs stage with no bathroom and no electricity." The
longer I talked, the more desperate I felt.

"That problem is easily solved," she said. "She'll stay with us. We have a perfectly lovely guest room with a private bath—both of which I offered to you and Nathan, remember?—and it will be perfect. You can spend all the time you want over here, and bring her to your place for delicious treats and local color, and when you've had enough, you deliver her back to us."

"This is your busiest—"

"Don't even start on how Sam and I don't have time to entertain a stranger. Almost all the parties I'm catering this week are low-key. I have most of the prep work done already. I insist. We'll go about our business, and it will be so much fun to get to know her!"

It seemed a little like cheating, foisting her off on my mother. But on the other hand, I could breathe again.

Chapter Three

I put pie energy out into the universe. And it sends pie information my way.

—David Sloan, Facebook

An hour later, I buzzed down Southard Street and then over on Elizabeth to the opening of David Sloan's key lime pie event at the Key West Library. The lovely pink stucco building was not known as a venue for culinary events, but the price to rent the space for the afternoon would have been right. As in zero. Mr. Sloan was not only an astonishing self-promoter; he had an expertise in eliminating unnecessary expenses. I climbed the concrete steps to the front door, passing several homeless men and tourists using the library's Wi-Fi. The auditorium was packed, and I knew exactly why. Sloan had managed to land front-page articles in the *Key West Citizen*, the *Florida Keys Weekly*, *Konk Life*, and several of the glossy magazines regularly distributed to the most expensive hotels around the island.

I was a few minutes late. I paused, looking into the little auditorium. Almost every metal folding seat was occupied, and our newish library administrator, Michael Nelson, had taken the stage and begun the introductions. He had his short hair gelled into a ridge, like a dog with hackles raised, though he had a quiet voice and a shy smile, giving the impression he'd be a man whose book recommendations you could trust. "We're honored to host this talented group of local bakers," he said. "Christopher, our new library assistant, will be working with me on today's event." He gestured to a thin, fair-haired man leaning against the wall to my left. One seat remained right behind him, so I hurried in to snag it. Michael continued to speak.

"Though Mr. Sloan has taken cooking classes at Florida International University and written a cookbook on the subject of key lime pie, he is more widely known as the developer of the Key West Ghost Tours, the brains behind the zero-K Cow Key Channel Bridge run, and a writer. His bucket-list books about visiting and living in the Keys are extremely popular and will be on sale at the back of the room after our event."

I harrumphed to myself. I'd thumbed through his books, even bought a couple. None of them were deep, but they were clever and funny. And he was smart enough to have made "buy a drink for an author" one of the items on his things-to-do list. I'd seen this in action in Facebook photos of Keys-obsessed tourists desperate to purchase him a cocktail. And it didn't hurt that he was personable and even handsome. And maybe I was a bit envious of how far ahead of me he was, both as a culinary author and as an all-round Key West celebrity.

David Sloan moved forward to take the podium on the little stage. He thanked Michael for his introduction and the audience for coming.

"Many people don't believe key lime pie was developed by a sailor," he said. "But this is not folklore; it's the truth. The magic happened when they mixed cans of condensed milk with key lime juice. This combination helped the filling set up as though it had been made with eggs, which of course were not available on ocean voyages—unless from a random pigeon."

Snickers from the audience.

"In addition to tasting delicious, the pie had the side benefit of helping prevent scurvy. But enough about history. Key lime confections are ubiquitous in this town, and we are determined this week to identify and crown the king or queen of key lime pie."

He walked across the stage to a box at the back of the area and extracted a headpiece. At first glance, it glittered in the spotlights like a bejeweled crown. But the base had been constructed to resemble a key lime pie, with peaks of faux meringue standing up around the edges like the points of a real crown. He placed it on his own head, vamping to the left and then to the right, receiving much applause. He pointed to the people watching. "And you, our esteemed audience of chefs, foodies, and critics, will be our assistant judges. The final decision, of course, will be made by me." He tucked the crown back in its box.

"Today we will introduce our participants, and on Friday we'll hold the official tasting. Don't miss that event, which will culminate in the coronation, accompanied by key-lime-pie martinis. I predict many local celebrities will be on hand, including our own Mayor Teri Johnson and bookstore celebrities Suzanne Orchard from Key West Island Books and Judy Blume from Books and Books."

Then he called up the bakers who would be participating in the contest, representatives from about fifty percent of the restaurants and bakeries around town. They settled into a row of metal chairs behind the podium. None of them looked very happy to be here, but it was a command performance. Sloan was so good at drumming up publicity that any restaurant or shop relying on sales of this citrus confection to help with its bottom line could not afford to miss his event, and thereby miss getting featured in local media.

"Each chef will come to the microphone and describe what makes their creation stand out from the others. Every one of these talented bakers has brought a pie to illustrate their skill. We are not asking them to reveal trade secrets"— he turned to wink at the lineup—"but we'd love a description of why you believe your pie is the most outstanding example of our iconic dessert on this island."

The pastry chef from Blue Heaven restaurant, a funky tourist favorite because of the outdoor seating, consistently good food, and resident chickens, introduced herself as Bee Thistle. She was tall and willowy, with a long braid of shiny dark hair down her back. She wore a colorful tiered skirt that fell almost to the floor, a handful of necklaces, and a blue apron. She extracted a pie from the cardboard box she'd brought to the podium and held it up to a smattering of oohs and aahs.

"As you can see," she said, "what distinguishes us from the competition is our mile-high meringue."

She walked out from behind the podium to the front of the stage, holding the pie out so the audience could see more clearly. The meringue stood at least three inches above the lip of the pan, shaped into peaks that glistened firm and golden in the overhead spotlight.

"I'm not authorized to give away our recipe," she said, "nor do I wish to illuminate trade secrets to benefit our competitors. We at Blue Heaven are famously known for our key lime pie, and we plan to win this week." She grinned and smoothed her apron. "But I will share one secret: hot sugar syrup."

The people in the audience tittered and rustled, and I heard a woman at the end of the row nearest me ask a friend if she'd written that down. I hated to tell her that, even supposing hot sugar syrup was the key to the key lime kingdom, if we had no idea how much to use and when and how to add it, we risked a lot of collapsed meringue in our futures.

Next Sloan called Sigrid, manager of the Key Lime Pie Company on Greene Street, to the center of the stage. A small, dark-skinned woman with velvet brown eyes and a wide smile, she posed alongside the podium with her pie held high. Probably, I thought, so she and her pie could be properly admired without being swallowed by the podium.

"No meringue for us," she said. "We have the creamiest pie in town, and that explains precisely why we are flooded with requests to ship our pies all over the country. And what other version of this delicacy has been featured on the TV show *The Profit?*" She explained that Marcus Lemonis, entrepreneur and star of the CNBC show known for resuscitating struggling businesses, had ended up buying the company, with the caveat that only the original recipe be utilized.

"Whipped cream, key limes, condensed milk, and a homemade graham cracker crust. Extra-creamy, homemade everything—those are our secrets." She settled her pie on the table next to the Blue Heaven confection and smiled sweetly.

Two more contestants followed, both classically trained pastry chefs from bakeries that produced not only key lime pie but also bread and pastries, in the case of Old Town Bakery, and cakes and cupcakes, in the case of Key West Cakes. Both chefs appeared slightly stiff, perhaps feeling a whiff of resentment about their command performances at the pie celebration. But again, I thought, skipping this Sloan event would have been bad for business.

"We use very few ingredients, all fresh and organic," said Niall Bowen, the chef at Old Town Bakery. "That is our motto: plain and simple; the best ingredients produce the best pie. And PS: we finish our pies with a dollop of real whipped cream, no meringue."

One of the owners from Key West Cakes gave a similar minimalist presentation. He was followed by the pastry chef from the Moondog Cafe and Bakery, a newly opened restaurant within spitting distance of the Hemingway Home and its cats.

He mugged an unhappy face. "Really? No meringue?"

Was he talking with a slight French accent? Was he French? Or was he pretending?

He held up a section of his pie so we could see the layers, the bottom pale yellow in color, topped by a frosting of meringue that had been sprinkled with green zest and broiled so that only crests of the egg whites were browned.

"While we don't go to the point of ridiculous heights"—he did not glance in the direction of the Blue Heaven chef, but it was obvious who he meant—"we do like meringue, and we especially like it made with bits of lime zest. Meringue is constructed of whipped egg whites—the result is beautiful and showy but usually not very flavorful. This bit of extra zest is what helps our pie rise above the crowd." He kissed the tips of his fingers, took a little bow, and deposited his pie on the table.

Last, Claudette Parker, who had opened the brand-new pastry shop Au Citron Vert in the fall, came forward on the stage with an assistant, a dark-complected man with a round face and a nice smile whom she introduced as Paul Redford. She had blonde curls and red lips and wore a fitted white jacket several eons more fashionable than the baggy coats and aprons the other contestants had shown up in. She also wore high heels—black patent leather with a gold toe—that looked expensive and uncomfortable. Paul hovered behind her like a worried mom.

"Key lime pie is passé, and that is precisely why I've replaced it in my establishment with a key lime napoleon. My contribution today is our best-selling confection. I believe our fans understand the difference between a true French pastry and a plate of green glop." She waved her hand dismissively at the lineup of pies from the other cooks and bakers. "I would like to present to you a handmade pâtisserie with layers of homemade puff pastry drizzled with a glaze containing local honey and key limes and stuffed with pastry cream scented with a whisper of lime. Key limes are no bigger than a walnut," she explained.

Her assistant, Paul, held up one of the small green fruits to show the audience.

"Unfortunately," she continued, "they are not too common on our island, in spite of what our host claims. And so we source them from further up the Keys." She opened a small white pastry box and produced a napoleon that made my stomach groan with anticipation. "Flaky layers brushed with organic butter, tart glaze, and a handcrafted cream pastry kissed with lime," she added as she held up the pastry. Her sous-chef stood behind her nodding and smiling. "All of this is homemade in my new shop on Greene Street, Au Citron Vert."

But David Sloan strode to the podium and snatched the microphone away from her. "I am sorry to do this publicly, but as was clearly stated in our entry forms and communicated in a phone call, we are accepting only pies in this contest. No cookies, no martinis, no flaky pastries, regardless of how delightful the chef insists they might taste."

Claudette's face grew stony, and she seemed to freeze in place. But her assistant pushed forward and grabbed the mic back from Sloan. "We deserve to be here. You cannot do this," he shouted.

"Oh, but I can," said Mr. Sloan, retrieving the microphone, a smile on his lips that looked anything but friendly.

"This is my event, and I make the rules. Please step down from the stage." He shooed at the two of them as if they were dogs begging at a table.

Off to the left of the stage, I saw a flash of movement. Before my brain could fully register what was coming, Claudette Parker marched to the display table and picked up the pie from the Key Lime Pie Company, the one that had been touted as extra-creamy, with whipped cream piped joyfully around the edges. She slammed it into David Sloan's face. The pie tin slid off his nose and chin and clattered on the floor in a puddle of filling. Sloan's eyes blinked like windshield wipers in heavy snow, working holes in the whipped cream.

There was a collective noise of sucking air from the audience, followed by a few snickers. The room felt suddenly tight with tension. David Sloan said nothing in response, and the roomful of people fell silent too. He looked clownish, with the pale-green filling dripping off his hair, his eyebrows, and his carefully shaped goatee and running in rivulets down his collar and across his starched chef's coat with *Sloan's Key Lime Pie Key to the City* written across the chest pocket in green script.

I stuffed a sudden urge to burst into laughter as I heard a smattering of giggles burst out around me. It *was* sort of funny, like in a million sitcoms where something ridiculous happens to the main character. On the other hand, David Sloan was not laughing. In silence, he began mopping his face with a red bandanna. The more pie he cleared from his skin, the angrier he looked.

His mouth began to work, and finally he hissed out, "You bitch."

The librarian, Michael, rushed up the steps, grabbed the mic, and thanked people for attending. Christopher, the library assistant, approached David Sloan with a wad of brown paper towels. Sloan pushed him and the scratchy towels aside, looking as though he was prepared to strangle Claudette. The din in the room rose as the attendees milled about, some pushing to get out, others rushing up toward the row of pastry chefs who sat stunned on the stage.

"Please pick up a flier on your way out, which will list the other events for the key lime extravaganza," shouted the librarian, looking apoplectic. "And don't forget the lecture series sponsored by the Friends of the Library, beginning in January."

I had been planning to chat with Sloan after the event to get some quotes for my article, but clearly now was not the time to gather pithy and cheerful comments about key lime pie recipes. I'd have to check in with him later. I found myself standing next to Christopher, who was watching Claudette storm away from David Sloan.

"Do you have a minute to chat?" I asked, after introducing myself.

He agreed, and I shook my head. "I sure didn't see that coming, but I was running a bit late. How about you? Did you notice any friction between them while you were setting up?"

"Not exactly," he said, "but put two divas in the room at your peril."

"Divas?" I prodded, thinking he might have some juicy background information to offer.

His attention shifted from Claudette's face to mine. "I don't have hard facts, but I do have a hypothesis. I imagine she thought she could come down here from New England and break into this food scene without a murmur and rise like cream right to the top. Key West looks so open-minded from the outside, right? Loosey-goosey, welcome everyone, we are all one human family and all that good stuff. But people still get hyped up about competition on their turf. And today Claudette ran right into David Sloan's buzz saw."

He laughed, and it appeared he had enjoyed the altercation more than felt stressed out by it, as I had. And for a new guy, he understood a lot about our city. "The look on his face was priceless, though, wasn't it?"

"More like scary," I said, glancing at Christopher again. Michael, his boss, was signaling furiously for his attention from across the room.

"Excuse me," he said. "I'd better go help mop up the mess."

* * *

I spent the rest of the afternoon in my cubby at the office writing up the event, describing the contestants and the pies and wondering whether it would be acceptable to mention the pie in David's face. Or should I limit myself to describing the bakers and their products? I didn't want to come across as gossipy, or seem to be reveling in the disaster as Christopher had. I finally wrote two versions: one straightforward, listing all the pies and leaving out Claudette and her pastry, and the other describing the whole story as it had unfolded. I sent them both to Wally and Palamina. They were making the big bucks; let them make the hard decisions.

That done, I buzzed up the island, stopping at Fausto's to pick up a rotisserie chicken and a couple of sweet potatoes for supper. I tucked them into the basket of my scooter and drove home.

As I came up the dock, I waved to my friend Connie, who was playing with her daughter on the deck of her boat. "Do you have time for a tiny glass of wine?" I asked.

Within minutes, I'd popped the sweet potatoes into the oven, and my friend arrived with her baby and a basket of toys to keep her occupied while we chatted. I hugged each of them and supplied baby Claire with a sippy cup of organic apple juice and Connie with a glass of rosé from Provence.

"How was your day? You look exhausted," said Connie. She glanced around the deck and peered into the living room. "Something looks different."

"What's different is we've been scrubbing everything to within an inch of its life to get ready for Nathan's mother arriving tomorrow. Unexpectedly," I added.

"Cheers," said Connie, lifting her glass to tap it gently against mine. "Here's to adding to the family. The unexpected part doesn't sound so great, but it's good news that she's coming, right?"

Which shut me up instantly, as Connie had lost her own mother to cancer while we were in college, and lost her father to bad behavior right after her wedding. I knew she relied on Ray's parents as her only familial connections. She loved my mother and Sam dearly too, and envied my easy access to maternal support.

"You're totally right," I said. "I'm just a little wound up about what she'll think of the place. And with all our animals crammed into the boat and our close neighbors, I'm afraid she's going to find it claustrophobic. When you take a step back, Houseboat Row is a little funky, don't you think?"

"Absolutely," she said, and let loose a big belly laugh. "And that's why we all love it here. Either she'll love it or she won't, but she isn't the one living here, right? What else were you up to today?"

"I spent the afternoon at David Sloan's key lime extravaganza at the library. It deteriorated into a true rhubarb." I explained about the high-powered pastry chefs and the ending frenzy with pie in the face of the organizer.

"I can't really figure that guy out," I said. "How can a person specialize in and make a career out of key lime pie? There simply isn't that much to it. Lime, milk, crust, ta-da! But he had all these talented chefs up on the stage waxing on about their sugar syrup and their lime zest and flaky puff pastry as if this was a summit of world leaders addressing sea-level rise or gun violence."

Connie took a sip of her wine and studied my face. "Do you mind if I say that you sound a little sour? No pun intended. Like this guy rubs you wrong for some personal reason?" She paused. "Was he the one who dissed your article when you first got the job?"

I'd written an article for *Key Zest* after I was first hired—the thesis was that there wasn't any truly remarkable food on the island. It was tourist fare, plain and simple. And greasy. Wally, who'd been my sole boss at the time, had urged me not to play too safe with my pieces. *Be controversial; stake out extreme positions when you can,* he'd said. So I'd dissed our island's cuisine. The truth was, I wasn't familiar enough with Key West chefs and restaurants to make a generalization like that. Sloan had noticed and published a scathing rebuttal. He'd been correct, but it had still stung. And I'd kept my distance ever since.

I could feel my face getting red and hot. "You're right. Same guy."

Chapter Four

But even as Ms. Cadbury was teaching us the proper way to fold butter into puff pastry and the technique for making silky bearnaise sauce, I made a silent vow to myself: I would follow the rules, and then I would break them.

—Kathy Gunst, "The Epiphany That Turned Me Into a Good Baker," *The Washington Post*, March 28, 2016

By noon the next day, Miss Gloria and I had done everything possible to make the little houseboat shine. I'd also been through every recipe in my files, both paper and electronic, looking for the perfect supper dish. Nathan had called early this morning to let me know he'd be picking his mother up at three PM. Did I want to ride over to the airport with him? Or meet them at my mother's place?

Chicken that I was, I chose my mother's place. I'd have all my troops marshaled for backup support. And I wouldn't have to yammer all the way to the airport about how worried

I was, and thereby show my new husband in full living Technicolor that I was terrified about meeting his mother.

Once we got past the initial awkward hellos, the evening should go by quickly. Nathan reported that Mrs. Bransford wanted to see the Christmas lights of Key West. So he had made a reservation for three of us on the last Conch Train that would ferry guests around the island to see the holiday displays. We'd have a cocktail and snacks at my mother's place, then drive over to New Town to catch the train at the high school. Nathan was pretty sure he could meet us back at the houseboat for a light supper. Miss Gloria would attend all the festivities, including the train ride, and Mom, Sam, and Nathan would join us for dinner.

"What does she like to eat?" I'd asked him. "Even more important, what does she not like?"

"She'll like anything you make," he said. "Food isn't that important to her."

Which meant we were starting out light-years apart. Not only was I the food critic for *Key Zest*, but I came from a long line of foodies whose lifelong obsession was the next great meal. Food was love—that was our language. Obviously, she spoke some other dialect altogether. I'd already made repeat visits to both Fausto's markets and the Restaurant Store, where I'd bought an array of unusual cheeses plus crackers, Key West's best smoked fish dip, some pricy but delish artichoke dip, and wine and fruit. I had no idea whether Mrs. Bransford was gluten-free or sugar-free or carbohydrate-free or heaven help the chef, salt-free, so I wanted to have something for any and all possibilities.

In the end, I opted for a hominy and shrimp stew for supper that we'd tried last week, with hominy from a mail-order bean company I'd recently become enamored with. I could make the broth ahead of time and add fresh Key West pink shrimp when we got back to the houseboat. I also whipped up a recipe of cheese puffs, filling half of them with hot pepper jelly and the rest with fig jam, in case she didn't do spicy.

I chopped onions and celery and began to sauté them in a large pot with smoked paprika and other spices, and our home soon filled with the comforting scents of something delicious. While the flavors melded, I shucked and cleaned three pounds of Key West pinks, which we could add to the hominy mixture when we got back after our tour of the lights. I was banking on Nathan's mother enjoying food with a southern twist, coming from the outskirts of Atlanta. As Miss Gloria had pointed out earlier when I vacillated about what to cook, she'd never eaten a bad dish at my table. I was clinging to that.

"And even if Nathan's mother hates the food, she can push it around in her bowl and exclaim about the unusual flavors. It's never killed anyone to miss a meal. Maybe you," she'd conceded with a giggle.

As I finished the stew and washed vegetables for a salad, I tried to concentrate on my second of three assignments for *Key Zest* this week: a pre-contest roundup of key lime pie from the bakeries of Key West. Palamina, though she'd never touch a bite of the stuff herself, wanted our magazine to get a jump on describing the plethora of pies across the island.

For dessert tonight, I planned to serve the first wave of pie samples I'd collected from the Moondog Cafe, Blue

Heaven restaurant, and Old Town Bakery (voted best key lime pie in the Keys by *New Times*.) These had all been presented at the library event yesterday, but I wanted to try them myself before the amateurs attending the contest started clogging my mind with their opinions. I'd also snagged a few coconut macaroons from Cole's Peace, in case Mrs. Bransford despised key lime pie. (Seemed impossible to me, but if I didn't plan for this, I was superstitious enough to be sure it would happen.) And a key lime napoleon from the newest sensation, Au Citron Vert, which David Sloan had ejected from the judging yesterday. The place had dominated Yelp and OpenTable and TripAdvisor reviews since it opened in November. A recent full-page article in the *Key West Citizen* had irritated other local bakeries to no end with its declaration that Claudette Parker's key lime napoleon had rendered key lime pie obsolete. And yesterday afternoon, I'd seen the rancor in the food community in person. I couldn't help chuckling as a vision of David Sloan's pie-covered face came to mind.

Miss Gloria watched my preparations, staying well out of my way. She hunkered on the couch with the cats, who also seemed to sense something big in the works.

"You realize she's going to love you no matter what you serve her, right?" she asked, after I'd finished furiously chopping green onions and pimentos for the cheese spread I'd bring to my mother's place.

"I don't exactly realize that," I said. "Why would she? She loved the first wife. And from what I can tell, Trudy and I are not anything alike. But I certainly remember seeing my husband hanging all over her when she came down here to reclaim him—"

"Which she failed at, am I right? Because correct me if I'm wrong, but didn't he marry you about a month ago?"

Of course he had, but plenty of supposedly happily married people still had regrets about the loss of their first true love. "Even after knowing him for three years, I've never managed to squeeze much out of Nathan on the subject of his first wife and whether it was her who chucked him out or him her. But it happened not long after their home invasion, that's for sure. I got the idea he pretty much freaked out and wanted to lock her up for safekeeping. And maybe she dumped him and then panicked and wanted him back? He'll never say. It's so complicated, and who knows what side Mrs. Bransford was on."

Miss Gloria chuckled and said again, "But Nathan's not married to his ex. He divorced her several years ago, and then he chose you. His mother will love you because Nathan loves you. Even if you have a rocky introduction, she'll understand that after she's been here a while."

"So you admit that this visit is going to be rocky," I said, pouncing on the scariest part of her calming explanation.

Miss Gloria rolled her eyes. "She'll see that you are funny and quirky and warm and loyal, even if you are nutty as a fruitcake sometimes. And she'll see that because you're a loving person with a good sense of humor, you have more friends than you could count on fingers and toes." She stroked Sparky, her black cat, who had curled up on her lap. "And she'd be a fool not to be one of them."

Now it felt as if she'd pressed the off button on my neurotically spinning mind. "You're the best," I said, crossing the room to give her a hug.

When I'd finished the dinner preparations, I packed up my cocktail snacks and we walked up the dock to the parking lot. I still couldn't help seeing the things I thought Mrs. Bransford would notice on her first visit to our neighborhood and our lives: the disaster that was our future home in progress, the boat toward the end of the walk that was tented for termites and posted with a prominent sign declaring *Danger! Hazardous Poisons!*, the trash that stunk to high heaven accumulating near the laundry room for garbage pickup tomorrow.

Miss Gloria said, "By the time we get back here, it will be dark, and all the fairy lights will be shimmering up and down the dock. And you know how magical that makes this place. And then she'll smell the luscious stew you're making, and she will fall in love with the possibilities of Houseboat Row. The same way you did when you first arrived, and me before that."

I felt myself tear up with the love I got from this little old lady. I settled all the food on the floor behind the front seats and gave her another big hug.

"And even if she doesn't love me, Nathan does and that's what matters, right?"

"Right," she said, climbing into the passenger seat and fastening her lap belt. "Didn't I already say that?"

The rest of the way down the island on Southard, I concentrated on navigating Miss Gloria's oversized old car along the narrow, one-way street lined with a bike path and many parked cars, toward the Truman Annex at the bottom of the island. We stopped at the light on Duval and watched cup-carrying tourists stream by, tattooed with their sunburn of the day. The light changed to green and the rush of humanity continued, as if the traffic laws meant nothing in this town.

"I honestly don't know how many more people they can cram into this island," I said. "I would never suggest that anyone come to visit during this week. It feels a little bit like the *Titanic* right before that big tub sank." Which I knew was overdramatic, but still . . .

We whisked by the Green Parrot and the Courthouse Deli, both packed to the point of people spilling out on the sidewalks, and drove through the gates of my mother's community. I parked the car in the small space behind her home, and we went inside. Even though Sam and my mother were catering a cocktail party this afternoon, the house was in impeccable shape. They'd left enough lights on to make it look cheerful and welcoming, and arranged a bouquet of bright tropical flowers on the table inside the door. I set the groceries on the big granite counter island in the middle of the kitchen and began to arrange snacks on the pretty plates my mother had left out.

Finally we heard the familiar sound of Nathan's SUV cruiser pulling into the drive. My heart clenched with a surge of anxiety. Greet her inside? Greet her outside? Hugs? Handshakes? My overworked brain kicked into high gear and swirled with the possibilities.

Miss Gloria gave me a friendly push from behind. "Let's go show her a warm Key West welcome."

Nathan was already out of the car, extracting two suitcases from the back of his vehicle. He hurried around to open the passenger's side door. His mother stepped out. She was beautiful: tall and slender, with broad shoulders for a woman, just like his, and wavy salt-and-pepper hair without one strand misplaced. And the same stunning gray-green eyes as my husband.

I hurried toward her with my hands out. "Mrs. Bransford, I am so thrilled to meet you. Thank you for reproducing my incredible husband."

What an idiotic thing to say. I could feel my face pulsing with heat and wished I could magically drop through a trapdoor into the coral underneath the tropical vegetation. "That was so awkward. What I meant was, we are so happy you're here."

We exchanged a stiff hug-pat, and over her shoulder I could see Nathan smirking.

"It's kind of your mother to put me up," Mrs. Bransford said. "I suppose I hadn't really thought this visit through. I assumed you and Nathan had a guest room. And if not, that you could rent me a room. Then he explained the houseboat limitations and how there's not an empty hotel bed on the island."

"Not a problem," I said, gesturing for her to follow me into my mother's home. "She adores having houseguests, especially VIPs."

Nathan came along behind with her luggage, and he gave me a quick peck on the lips on his way upstairs to the spare bedroom.

"Are you hungry? Thirsty? Maybe you'd like to clean up after your trip?"

Oh gosh, what a rude thing to say, suggesting that she needed mopping up as if she were a toddler. Nathan trotted back down the stairs as I was explaining the night's plan to his mother.

"I need to finish up a few things at the station," he said apologetically. He glanced from me to his mother. "Hopefully I will be able to join you after the train tour for supper. Text me when you are almost back to the boat?"

"Will do," I said, smiling cheerfully, although I'd really hoped he would stay for a bit to oil our first interactions. I carried the tray of hors d'oeuvres out to the porch, and Miss Gloria followed with a bottle of sparkling water and one of white wine.

Food and wine would have to do the lubrication job instead.

Chapter Five

The stainless steel kettle reminds me of Claire: polished to a gleam on the outside, boiling within.
—Ann Mah, Kitchen Chinese

After we had exhausted all our chitchat subjects—the weather, mostly, and my mother-in-law's flight—Miss Gloria launched into a rundown of the details of my wedding.

"It might have been the most touching ceremony I've ever witnessed," she said. "Perfect clear night and beautiful music and food and flowers. And we were all so relieved that Nathan was alive and out of the hospital—you could feel the love between those two and amongst all our friends and relations. It was like someone threw the coziest, fuzziest blanket in the world over our pier and tucked us in."

Which I thought was the sweetest description ever, but my mother-in-law barely reacted.

"I'm sorry I wasn't able to be there," Mrs. Bransford said. She took a tiny sip of sparkling water and a nibble of celery.

I had recommended that she load it up with either pimento cheese or smoked fish dip, but she'd done neither. "I'd like to hear more about the rescue before the wedding and his recovery from gunshot injuries. He doesn't tell me much, as he knows I worry."

"Sounds familiar," I said, with a grin. At last something we had in common. But before I could begin to report the details of all that, the phone alert I'd set sounded with the warning that we needed to leave for the tour of holiday lights. I collected the dishes and glasses from the porch, carried them to the kitchen, and quickly stowed away the food.

We drove out to the high school on Flagler, Miss Gloria pointing out sites of interest along the way, though not the ones I would have chosen.

"There's Bobby's Monkey Bar, voted best karaoke in Key West this year, and that's Better Than Sex restaurant, which serves only desserts and fancy drinks. They get a lot of traction because of their name." She giggled. "And here's the Salvation Army thrift shop. They are loaded with great bargains," she announced, as if we knew it well, as if we'd shopped for all our household furnishings there. Not that that wouldn't have been perfectly fine, and even contributed to saving the planet by recycling stuff—but Nathan's mother didn't seem like the kind of person to browse in thrift stores.

I parked, and we got out of the car. I locked the doors behind us. The Conch Train, which took passengers on tours of the island, consisted of four bright yellow and red cars outfitted with bench seats pulled by a jeep disguised as the engine of a train. We snagged the last three seats on the last car, the red caboose. Mercifully, we'd be facing out toward the road behind us, which put a tiny amount of space between us and the other train riders.

As the conductor welcomed passengers over a crackly audio system and distributed blankets for our journey in case we felt a chill, I considered how things were going so far. Mrs. Bransford had been pleasant but cool. There was nothing I could put my finger on as evidence that she disliked me on sight, other than the fact that aside from the celery stalk, she'd nibbled on only one piece of the mildest cheese in my display. I knew I needed to give this relationship time. Lots of time.

All the cars were strung with blinking holiday lights, and Christmas music began to pipe out of speakers right above our heads. The rest of the customers, many wearing Santa hats or fuzzy antlers, appeared extremely well lubricated, some already warbling "Grandma got run over by a reindeer" in full voice. The train driver, dressed in an elf hat with a string of lights around his neck, explained that we should all keep our feet and hands inside the ropes strung across the door to each seat. Then a tinny rendition of "Rudolph the Red-Nosed Reindeer" began to blare over the PA system, and the visitors in front of us cheered and sang along.

"You have very enthusiastic tourists in this town," Mrs. Bransford said.

"You haven't seen the half of it," Miss Gloria shouted over the music. "Since you'll be here for New Year's, you'll get the whole picture."

I flinched at the mention of New Year's—Nathan hadn't told me how long his mother was planning to stay, and honestly, three to four days under this kind of strain felt a bit like a life sentence. Not that she was terrible; it was just that I felt so tense in her presence, afraid I'd do or say the exact wrong thing that would alienate her and convince her I was too dizzy to be married to her precious Nathan for life.

"Though you are definitely enduring the worst Christmas songs ever written," Miss Gloria was saying. "We should have warned you in case you were allergic."

The train lurched across Flagler Street and into a small New Town neighborhood that tourists seldom saw. We drove by small concrete block houses decked out with lights of all colors, blow-up Christmas figures from *The Grinch, Charlie Brown, The Polar Express.* We saw fake-snow machines, home-owners having cocktails in lawn chairs and enjoying our enjoyment, and finally the first-place home, which we'd heard through the grapevine belonged to our brand-new mayor. She and her wife had decorated the front of the house as the North Pole, with enough lights to power every home on the Keys all the way up to Miami.

"It's quite beautiful, isn't it?" asked Miss Gloria.

"Very enthusiastic," said Nathan's mother.

"Wait'll you see the way the drag queens dress up for Christmas," Miss Gloria told her. "And if you can stay up that late on New Year's Eve, you won't want to miss Sushi the drag queen dropping from the heavens in a giant sparkly red shoe."

"Sounds quaint in a truly bizarre sort of way," Nathan's mother said.

The driver announced that we would be making one last visit for his personal favorite display, known for its comic relief, and then take a spin across Duval Street and finally return to the high school.

"Only in Key West," the driver sang out as he navigated down a small one-way street near the cemetery. "Santa may be a little late this year," he announced, pointing to a blow-up Santa Claus splayed out on the front porch of a small home. Santa had an empty bottle of booze clutched in his right hand. "I saw mommy kissing Santa Claus" thrumming in the background completed the tacky picture.

We drove slowly past the display. "It's all good fun," I said, "but my favorite decorations are the most classic—the local palm trees with trunks wrapped in white lights and fronds strung with green lights.

"How do they decorate in your neighborhood?" I asked my mother-in-law, who at this point seemed a little stunned by the breadth of our island's holiday cheer.

"Fortunately, there are rules in our condominium complex," she said. "White lights only, green wreaths, preferably fake so they don't shed, and nothing too religious or flashy." She grinned, and I had no clue whether she was teasing or dead serious. I was beginning to suspect that Nathan had suggested this train ride rather than his mother requesting it.

We finished the swing across Duval Street, and as predicted, the drag queens, masquerading as Santa's elves, were in full form: dressed in very short red skirts and high heels and big hair topped with striped elf hats. The sidewalks were jammed with pre–New Year's revelers. It would be a bit of a relief to get back to the houseboat.

When the train had returned us to the high school and we loaded back into Miss Gloria's car, I asked Nathan's mother, "How did you like it? The only thing you didn't really get to experience was the boats dressed for the holiday on the Key West Bight. Maybe we can do that tomorrow. Snag a beer and some steamed shrimp for happy hour?"

I did a mental forehead thunk. Did she look like the kind of woman who'd want to *snag a beer*?

Before Mrs. Bransford could respond to that suggestion, Miss Gloria tapped me on the shoulder. "Would you mind terribly taking us down Olivia Street again? The house with the Santa drinking display. He drove too fast as we went by."

"Of course not," I said firing up the motor of the old Buick. Though it struck me as odd that she would select that home as the one set of decorations she wanted our guest to see again. And I was a little worried about my shrimp stew. But it wasn't far out of the way, and for now, I wasn't going to argue with any request from my passengers. No matter how peculiar.

"This is such a sweet neighborhood," Miss Gloria explained. "It's very close to the cemetery, so the neighbors aren't rowdy." She giggled. No matter how many times she told that joke, she always thought it was funny. "If Hayley and I didn't live on Houseboat Row, we'd probably choose something here instead. Maybe a sweet little two-family or a conch house with a guest cottage in back where an old lady could live out her golden years?"

"If that's what you want, you know Nathan and I will do it," I said, glancing at her grinning face in the rearview mirror. Though I was pretty sure she'd leave the houseboat only under the direst circumstances.

I parked the car in a residential spot a block from the Santa house, as Miss Gloria said she wanted to get out in order to see the details of the display up close this time. We made our way along the narrow sidewalk to the house in question. My foot slipped a little, and I noticed I'd stepped on a necklace made of blue beads. We were a little bead-crazy in this town, especially around Fantasy Fest and the holiday parades. I reached down to pick the necklace up so no one else would slide on the glass beads and stuffed it into my pocket.

As Mrs. Bransford approached the porch ahead of me, the tinny music pouring out of a boom box on the porch got louder. "I saw Mommy kissing Santa Claus"—over and over and over. The neighbors must be ready to wring someone's neck.

"There's a lot more drinking on this island than is good for anybody," Miss Gloria said. "Everyone makes jokes about it, and we have barhopping crawls where the object is to get stinking drunk, and too many establishments are open until four AM. I went on a ride-along with a police officer last year, and trust me, all the worst behavior happens after midnight. But it isn't healthy, and we know it. Hayley and I are careful about how much we drink, especially with a police officer living in our home."

I snickered.

She waved at the palmettos separating this property from its next-door neighbor. "While you admire the lights, I'm going to take a quick look around," she said as she veered into the brush.

Nathan's mother forged ahead of us, stopping only feet from the steps leading to the porch. She crouched down as though examining the display more clearly.

"This may seem strange to you," my mother-in-law said, pausing to look over her shoulder, "but I've got a bad sense that something is very wrong on that porch. And I've learned to pay attention when that little voice speaks."

I studied her profile with renewed interest. Finally something else we had in common aside from adoring Nathan: premonitions.

"I don't think that's a fake Santa," she said in a voice tight with tension and fear. "I think it's a body."

Chapter Six

Remember, it is never the knife's fault.

—Daniel Boulud

I moved a little closer and crouched next to her so I could see what she was seeing. The Santa wig on the figure had been pushed askew so that a few locks of blonde hair escaped. A woman, I thought. She had a bluish hue to her skin—the part that wasn't covered by the pelt of fake white hair and moustache and beard. I crept up the steps. I knew enough not to move her, but I held my palm above her mouth and nose, and could detect no sign of breath. Next I put my fingers on her wrist. No pulse. And her skin felt cool to the touch. Then I felt for a pulse in her neck, as sometimes the heartbeat was stronger there and easier to detect than in the wrist. Nothing. As I pulled my hand back, I noticed a faint line of bruises around her throat. I sank back onto my haunches, hands over my eyes, trying to control a wash of nausea.

"From the looks of it, I'm afraid she's dead." I stumbled back down the porch stairs and texted Nathan with an urgent request to meet us on Olivia Street, then dialed 911 for good measure. The dispatcher took my information and asked me to stay on the line.

While we waited for the police to arrive, Mrs. Bransford paced up and down the short sidewalk to the porch and then back to the street. She did not speak, but she looked distressed. In the distance, I heard the shrill moan of sirens careening toward an emergency. Miss Gloria had crawled into the bushes surrounding the house next door. Then, from a distance, I saw her drop to her knees, and I feared she would be sick. It was hard to chance across the horror of a dead body at any age, but maybe especially hers—on the back side of eighty.

"Miss G, are you okay?" I called out.

"I'm fine," she said, her voice muffled by the foliage, waving a hand behind her back.

The two blocks around us filled with police cars, blue and red lights flashing. The tall officer with the shaved head who had given me a traffic citation emerged from the first vehicle. His eyebrows peaked when he recognized me. No telling whether Nathan had spoken to him about giving me a ticket or what he might have heard about me through the blue grapevine.

"We had a call about a possible death?" he asked brusquely.

"Right over here," I said, gesturing that he should follow me to the porch. "I couldn't find a pulse, and then I noticed her neck . . . I'm Nathan Bransford's wife, Hayley Snow, and this is his mother, Mrs. Bransford." Which sounded ridiculous, but it was the only thing I had called her so far. "Miss Gloria is—" I spun around and saw her scramble on hands and knees through the greenery toward the crawlspace under the porch next door.

"Please stand back, all of you," the officer said. "Don't go any closer." He strode up to the porch and crouched down to look at the Santa exactly as we had done. An ambulance hurtled up the block, stopping directly in front of the house, followed by Nathan's SUV. The men tumbled out of the vehicles and made a beeline for us. Nathan came to me first, gaze lasering on my face even as he hugged me, then his mother. "Where's Miss Gloria?" he asked.

I pointed to her hindquarters sticking out of the bushes.

He clapped a hand to his forehead, as if he couldn't quite believe the scene. He sucked in a deep breath and muttered, "What in the name of god is going on here?"

I repeated the same few facts I'd told the first officer on the scene. Before I could explain anything more, the EMTs advanced up the sidewalk toward the officer guarding the perimeter of what appeared to be a crime scene now. "What's the situation?" one of them called back to Nathan. He summarized the little he knew: that the three of us had been on the Christmas Conch Train Tour and had returned to see this display up close, only to discover what appeared to be a body.

"We couldn't find a pulse, nor any sign of breathing," I added. "And the skin on her wrist felt very cool. And then her neck appeared bruised . . ." I rubbed my fingers together, wishing I hadn't touched her at all. "We didn't try CPR. Maybe I should have." My breath hitched; it would feel so awful to have had an opportunity to save someone's life and failed to even try. Though my Spidey sense told me that she had been dead for a while.

Nathan circled his arm around my shoulders and squeezed. It wasn't a new thing for me to feel hyper-responsible when something terrible happened. This was something he loved about me, but hated as well.

"Let it go, Hayley," he said. "It's our job now."

I nodded, and wiped away a tear that had leaked from my eye.

"Go around to the back of the property, knock on the door, and make sure there isn't anyone else at home," he told two of the officers.

I wished I had thought of checking inside the home earlier, as I could only imagine how awful it would feel to watch this unfolding from inside. Or perhaps they'd been watching TV and hadn't heard anything. Though the arrival of the cops had been noisy—but then so was the music on the porch. Or had the killer escaped inside before we arrived? How long had it been since this Christmas tableau had morphed into a murder scene?

"While they sort things out here, let's go back to the beginning," Nathan said, beckoning his mother and me off the sidewalk. "If you don't mind waiting, Mother, I'll talk to Hayley first?" She nodded, and we took a few steps away so he could question me privately. "What exactly led up to this? Are you all right? You're shivering."

I crossed my arms over my chest, knowing he needed to concentrate on what was happening here, not on his wife. "It's just the shock, you know? We went on the train ride to see the lights as planned," I said. "After a snack, of course." I couldn't resist leaning forward to whisper, "Though your mother doesn't eat much, does she?" From the look on his face, I could see he felt I was distracted from transmitting the important information he needed. Which tended to happen when I was upset. *Tell him the story, Hayley.*

"So then Miss Gloria asked if we could drive back around. So we came over to look at this set of decorations again." I gestured to his mother. "I'll let her tell you what she noticed."

He nodded curtly, and we moved closer to her so he could switch his attention to his mom. "Tell me what you saw, please, Mother."

"I'm not sure I would have noticed if Miss Gloria hadn't requested a second look, but once we got here, it was clear that this figure did not look like the blow-up dolls we've been seeing around town." Her nostrils flared a little, which I guessed meant she didn't care much for that style. "This Santa was lying very, very still. And kind of deflated. Maybe I noticed the blonde hair too? And maybe it was the way the hand was splayed open and draped off the step. It did not look like a stuffed figure, nor did it resemble the way a real live person would have been lying."

I couldn't help butting in. "And it doesn't really make sense that it would be a living person anyway, because how would they know who was coming by and when? It's not like the homes in New Town that get a ton of traffic and so they sit out on their lawns and drink cocktails and wave. This place is out of the way—I suspect none of the other Conch Train drivers made this detour." Could our driver have been involved somehow?" That seemed like a random and silly idea. "Anyway, would any person in her right mind lie on the porch acting drunk all night, just in case? Probably not. Though I suppose anything's possible in Key West."

They both turned to look at me as though I was losing my marbles. And I was a little, to be honest. This wasn't the first body I'd come across not long after a murder had been committed. And the pattern had quite naturally left me spooked. Maybe this time the body wouldn't turn out to be a crime-related death; maybe it was a simple case of too much fun. Or someone falling and hitting her head, which would mean the bruises on her neck were incidental. Even though those possibilities would feel awful too, it wouldn't be the same as someone's life getting snuffed out in a violent way.

In the background, I overheard the tall cop report that no one else was at home, and then the EMTs' estimation that the person on the porch was deceased.

Nathan sprang into action, directing the uniformed cops who'd first arrived on the scene. "We need to secure the perimeter. And take names and contact information of prospective witnesses." Nathan jutted his chin at the small crowd that had gathered on the sidewalk. "How long have they been here? Addresses? Connection with this resident and so on. And call the medical examiner and our photographer on duty. Meanwhile, let's get some photos with your phone," he told the bald cop. He bustled around the home, barking orders at the other cops and pushing the onlookers who'd gathered back onto the sidewalk. Finally he returned to us.

"Maybe she had a heart attack, end of story?" I asked hopefully. Though why in the world would this person be lying on the porch in a Santa suit if she was feeling peaked?

"Maybe." He beckoned me forward. "Hayley," Nathan said, "if you can handle looking again, could you say whether you recognize this person?"

My stomach lurched and I swallowed, trying to lubricate my very dry mouth and throat. "It's hard to tell; between the wig and the beard and the fake stomach, she looks like everyone and no one. Is it possible to move a little closer?"

Nathan nodded. "Be careful. No closer than the bottom step. Obviously we don't want to move or touch anything before the coroner gets a look." He squeezed my hand and then let it go, and I crept forward and stopped at the edge of the porch to study the woman's face. Maybe she looked familiar, but she wasn't someone I knew well enough to identify. I shook my head at Nathan and backed away. "I'm so sorry. I can't say for sure."

Nathan went over to talk to the neighbors gathered at the bottom of the sidewalk on the other side of the police tape. "Do any of you know who lives here?"

A gangly man in a red T-shirt answered. "I live across the street. Her name is Claudette Parker. She moved in back in October. She keeps odd hours, so we haven't gotten the chance to know her."

A woman piped up. "I think she owns the new bakery on Greene Street. Over by the bight? She makes a key lime pastry that's to die for. Really, it blows the rest of the bakeries in town out of the water."

I gulped. Even as we spoke, that same key lime napoleon from Au Citron Vert was sitting in my refrigerator with the other slices of key lime pie. It wasn't quite fair to compare puff pastry to a piece of pie, but since the owner of this new bakery refused to make a pie and yet had garnered an avalanche of reviews on the various foodie websites in town, I felt I couldn't ignore it.

Now I knew where I'd seen her face: only yesterday I'd seen her slam a wet pie into David Sloan's face when he dismissed her from his contest. If this person had been the author of that gorgeous flaky confection, she would never be making another. I was flooded with sadness. I glanced at Mrs. Bransford, noticing that the blood seemed to have drained from her face. "Are you okay?" I asked.

She shook off my concern, holding both hands up and taking a step away. "Fine."

Miss Gloria approached the sidewalk where I stood with Nathan's mother, watching Nathan interview the bystanders. She was carrying an orange tiger kitten with white paws, one of them half white, half orange like a frosted half-and-half cookie. Even though Miss Gloria crooned sweet kitty nothings to him, he seemed terrified, ready to bolt the instant she loosened her grip. He mouthed a silent meow.

"That's T-Bone," the chatty neighbor said. "I'm surprised you were able to lure him out of the shrubbery. He's a little skittish with strangers."

"Soft kitty, warm kitty . . ." sang Miss Gloria. He snuggled lower into her arms and I was pretty sure I heard him begin to purr, exactly like the kitten in the song.

"We've seen a lot more of him than we've seen of his owner lately," the neighbor woman said. "I live next door. I'm not sure she was feeding him regularly. He was over on my porch most mornings. I admit I gave him some snacks. He was probably lonely, too—he's so tiny. But I couldn't take him in; my big guy would tear him to bits."

She held her arms out for the kitten. "I volunteer for the Florida Keys SPCA, so I'll call someone to pick him up. I can check on him tomorrow during my shift."

Miss Gloria looked near tears, but we had about all the living things we could handle on our little houseboat. Adding a kitten would push us deep into the red zone of crazy pet people. She handed the tiger kitten over, and I circled my arm around her waist. "It'll be easy to find that guy a good home—he's wicked cute."

Miss Gloria whispered, "That's why I wanted to swing by this house again. I thought I saw a lost kitten in the bushes. Turns out I had."

"Wait," said Nathan, who had returned to our group. "You thought you saw a kitten, and it just happened to be next door to a dead person?"

She looked puzzled, seeming to absorb for the first time the reality of the macabre scene with the dead Santa. "Maybe I sensed something wrong here even though my mind was fixed on the little orange kitty . . . I feel so confused and upset." A tear had squeezed out of her eye and wandered down her cheek.

I hugged her shoulders and smiled at her and then Nathan's mother. "If we're finished here, let's head back to the houseboat. I think we all need a drink." I looked to Nathan for his okay. He nodded, and we started up the street to our car.

"I'll be there when I can," Nathan called after us. "Definitely don't wait on me for dinner. And I'm certain you'll be asked to talk to us again, especially about the question of what caused you to return to this house."

Chapter Seven

He was holding the cardboard cup in his fist and she thought the tension would make him squeeze it and spill the tea all over the table.
                                    —Ann Cleeves, *Wild Fire*

From the parking lot, I spotted my mother and Sam sitting on the deck of the houseboat, looking relaxed in the glow of the fairy lights glittering along the roof line and wound through our houseplants. A bottle of prosecco chilled in an ice bucket. As we drew closer, Nathan's dog, Ziggy Stardust, came hurtling up the dock, his shiny black fur glinting in the light of the dock's lamps, Evinrude and Sparky in hot pursuit. They knocked into Miss Gloria, circled around us, and bolted back toward our houseboat. Miss Gloria shrieked and grabbed a lamppost before almost falling into the choppy water.

"So sorry," I said to Mrs. Bransford, grasping Miss Gloria's elbow before she bobbled toward the water a second time. "Nathan's Ziggy is a love but a bit of a wild man, too. I'm afraid we passed the tipping point into chaos when he moved in. Come on down; we'll introduce you to the rest of the gang."

Ziggy had stretched out on my lounge chair, panting and grinning his doggy grin, as if he hadn't been the cause of the latest ruckus.

I introduced Nathan's mother to mine, and then to Sam, and listed the animals by name. And then I went inside to scrub my hands. I couldn't stop thinking about touching the dead woman.

"My gosh," my mother said when I returned. "That has to be the longest tour of the lights in Key West history! We never thought we'd beat you here."

"Unfortunately, we saw more than Christmas lights. Miss Gloria wanted to go back to the last display, and we found something very wrong."

"I thought I had seen a lost kitten—and I had, but it turns out there was also a dead body," Miss Gloria explained.

Sam poured drinks for all of us, and we reported the details of what we had seen. "Nathan said not to wait dinner for him because of course it will take some time to sort this out."

"Any idea what happened to her?" my mother asked.

"Not really. She didn't have a pulse when we came along, I know that much." I glanced at my hands. Had I soaped long enough? "To my eye, it looked like she had been dead for a while, would you say?" I asked the others.

"Her skin was very pale, almost bluish," Mrs. Bransford agreed. She still looked pale, and why wouldn't she, after finding a murdered woman?

"The neighbor identified her as the new pastry chef over on Greene Street—the one who makes those glorious napoleons," I said. "The one a lot of people expected to waltz away with Sloan's Key Lime Key to the City. And the exact same person he ejected from his contest and the one who slammed Sloan in the face with a pie yesterday. In public."

"Good gravy, that sounds like an ugly scene," my mother said. "And so tragic. Do they think Sloan killed her?"

"Nobody said anything like that," I said, "though Sloan was furious with her. But it's way too early to tell."

She turned to Nathan's mother. "The way your visit's started, you may want to stay on our back deck reading romance novels for the remainder of the week. It's very peaceful in our neighborhood."

While they chatted about other things to see and do on the island, I warmed up the sauce, dropped the shrimp into the bubbling tomato-paprika mixture, and heated up the rice in the microwave. After dressing the salad with a sharp mustard vinaigrette, Sam helped me ferry the food out to the deck where our table was set. The candles flickered in the breeze, our neighbor's wind chimes tinkled, and tunes from an old Simon & Garfunkel album drifted over from the next pier. The water of the bight slapped our hull in a rhythm from the sea, and I began to unwind a little. I was grateful to have my mother and Sam and Miss Gloria here to help entertain.

Dinner was delicious, or so said my family. Mrs. Bransford was less effusive. "There's a very strong flavor that I am not recognizing," she said. Which could have meant anything. Hated it? Loved it? Completely neutral?

I grinned and continued to chat, choosing to assume she liked what she was noticing. I was always happy to hold forth on a new flavor sensation. "It's a type of paprika from Spain. I saw it in a specialty bean catalog and could not resist it."

Sam patted his lips with a napkin and nudged me in the ribs. "Stand back when Hayley Snow or her mother gets on a foodie tear," he said. "Any kind of tear, in fact. They are two wonderfully dogged ladies. I bet you are, too," he added, to Nathan's mother. "It shines through in your son."

The ghost of a smile flitted across her lips. But she didn't say anything in return.

"When do you suppose he'll be home?" my mother asked. She glanced at her watch. "I hate for him to miss the welcome party. But we need to get going by nine."

I shrugged my shoulders. "It was a grim scene and lots of witnesses. But the kind of witnesses who didn't actually see anything but wanted to know everything about what was going on. I wouldn't be surprised if he's up half the night."

"What about dessert?" Sam asked hopefully. "Not that I need it." He patted his stomach.

I grinned. "No one ever needs dessert, not in a physical way. If you don't mind tasting, I have a roundup article due day after tomorrow on the best of the island's key lime pie. I have the first wave in the fridge."

My boss Palamina had been lobbying for this topic ever since she arrived in Key West. I'd explained many times that my introduction to key lime pie had been terrorizing to the point of producing posttraumatic stress. But she'd continued to nudge me until I had to give in, especially given that the conclusion of the big contest was happening at the end of the week. When my article published, our magazine would be ahead of the curve.

"How much room could one poisoned pie take up in a person's mind?" Palamina wanted to know.

A lot, it turned out. Nathan and I had first met when a woman died of poisoned key lime pie—and I was a suspect. The meeting had not been the least bit romantic—he played the fiercely suspicious detective and I played me, only more hysterical than usual. Not a good first impression for either of us.

I took pictures of the pie slices I'd collected earlier today, then arranged the slices on platters to bring out to the deck. "I wanted you to get a look at them before I cut them into pieces," I said. "Some of them are works of art, aren't they?"

My dinner guests exclaimed over the mile-high meringue from Blue Heaven, the lime zest flecks in the meringue from the Moondog Cafe, and the flowery piping of whipped cream from Old Town Bakery.

"This may be too sad to taste," I said, pointing to the sample I'd put on its own plate, a napoleon drizzled with a pale-green glaze. "It was prepared by the woman we found on the porch this evening. Or at least the recipe was designed by her."

My mother exchanged a glance with Miss Gloria.

"I vote we taste on," said Miss Gloria. "We'll be appreciating her legacy."

Mrs. Bransford had fallen quiet, barely nibbling each pie. She expressed a slight preference for the Moondog sample. "I'm not really a citrus pie kind of person," she said.

"Well, I sure am," said Miss Gloria. She tucked into each of her samples with gusto. "What's nice about all of them is that they tend to be a little tart, and that complements the crust so perfectly. I despise a sickly-sweet filling."

As I was making notes on the pie samples, Nathan called. I excused myself and hopped from the deck to the dock, then headed down to the parking lot to talk in private.

"I'm going to be quite late," he said. "It appears the victim was strangled. It's possible the woman was killed inside and then dragged out and arranged on the porch. Anyway, that's the working theory. We're going door to door in the neighborhood to see who was home and what they might have seen or heard." He cleared his throat. "I am sorry you had to deal with that. And I'm sorry to dump my mother on you this way the very first night."

"It couldn't be helped," I said. "You haven't been on call in a while, and I guess you had some excitement coming. Not a problem here. We're having a fine evening, considering how it started. But you're missing a key lime pie tasting."

"Save me a bite of the best one," he suggested. Probably only being nice—like his mother and unlike mine, he wasn't a sugar addict. "But don't worry about dinner; one of the guys went out for sandwiches. But definitely save me a space in your bunk."

"Always," I said. "Be careful. I love you."

"Love you too," he said.

I returned to Miss Gloria's place and reported what he'd told me. "He expects he'll be very late. Don't worry about cleaning up," I told my mother, who'd started to clear the dishes. "I know you guys have another big day on the calendar."

After hugs all around and assurances from me and Miss Gloria that we'd see our guest tomorrow, Sam and Mom guided Nathan's mother off the boat and disappeared up the dock toward the parking lot where my mother's vehicle waited. We collapsed on the lounge chairs, me and Evinrude on one, Sparky, Ziggy, and Miss Gloria on the other.

I listened for the sound of my mother's van starting up, a clattering noise followed by the catch and rev of an engine rather than the quiet whir of a perfectly tuned modern car or hybrid. Theirs was an old van with a lot of miles on it that Sam had helped Mom fit out for catering. The back of the vehicle had refrigeration, shelving from floor to ceiling, even a double sink with an enormous storage cabinet underneath. To my mind it had never completely lost the scent of the pool chemicals it had carried in its former life. Sam assured me that in fact the smell came from the bleach they used to keep the space clean. There was still no name painted on the side of the van, as my mother couldn't decide what to formally call her business.

"She's a perfectly nice lady," said Miss Gloria, after we'd heard the van drive away.

"I hate to say it, but it's a relief to have her staying somewhere else," I said. "Can you imagine if we'd decided to have her bunk on the couch?" I rolled my shoulders, which felt like blocks of concrete even without that disturbing vision.

"She runs a little cool, I'll give you that," said Miss Gloria, grinning. "Maybe she even shades toward cold fish. But let's give her the benefit of the doubt. She had a long travel day and then a big shock. And remember, Nathan didn't thaw instantly either when you first met. I bet she'll warm up to you in no time."

"Did she seem upset to you after she noticed the body?" I asked.

"Cool as a cucumber," Miss Gloria said.

"Maybe she shows distress quietly," I said. "She looked super-pale to me, but she didn't say a word. Maybe she keeps her feelings locked inside. I've heard that about southern ladies; it's not considered proper to let it all hang out."

"Maybe," Miss Gloria answered.

"But a death," I said. "A murder. Hard to imagine you wouldn't be rattled to discover such a scene."

"Completely. I was. It was so awful, I felt like my head was going to explode. Thank goodness the kitten distracted me." Her face fell, and she pushed her animals aside and stood up. "I'm pooped—going in to bed. This whole night turned into more excitement than I'd banked on."

I got up to give her a big hug. Sparky and Nathan's dog Ziggy followed her to her bedroom. Evinrude barely tolerated Nathan sharing our bunk; he'd made it clear that sleeping with a dog was more than he could take. And besides, Miss Gloria seemed to love the extra company.

I began to wash the dishes, letting my mind run over the day.

The question about how Mrs. Bransford was feeling following our grisly discovery made me realize I was in a bit of shock about the events of the evening, too. I'd been so busy worrying about entertaining my mother-in-law and getting dinner served and the pies tasted that I hadn't really thought about the facts.

Was it possible that part of Miss Gloria's mind had noticed the body from such a distance, in the dark? Why had the dead woman been arranged in such a grotesque way? Who in the world would strangle a woman and then dress her in a Santa suit and drag her out onto the porch? What kinds of secrets did Claudette carry?

That bit I could begin to answer by searching on the Internet to make a start on understanding her history. When the kitchen was spick-and-span, I went out to the deck with my computer, pulling an afghan around my shoulders and arranging Evinrude alongside me for comfort and warmth.

Claudette Parker had come from New Jersey—which I would not hold against her, as both my mother and I were Jersey natives. She was described as a talented pastry chef with a thriving business in her hometown of Glen Rock, which I remembered as a well-heeled suburb of New York City. She had studied at the Auguste Escoffier School of Culinary Arts and interned in Paris. By adding up her training and experience, I figured her to be ten or so years older than me, maybe mid to late thirties.

With such distinguished training and a thriving business, why had she moved to this island? There had to be a story behind that. I continued to read.

As her neighbor had told Nathan, Claudette was new to town, having opened her shop Au Citron Vert in October.

I remembered watching the empty storefront on Greene Street get transformed over the summer so that it now resembled a Parisian pâtisserie. Once the shop was open, her pastries had made a big splash, and from the press she was attracting, it had looked as though she might blow the other bakeries out of the water. The bakery and the pastry chef had scored a big feature on the front page of the *Florida Keys Weekly* right after Thanksgiving. I'd been home more than usual, tending to Nathan's injuries, and had the time to read all the local papers cover to cover. Had she made deadly enemies in Key West in the short time she'd been here? It sure seemed that way.

I closed my computer and went inside the houseboat to get ready for bed. I couldn't help wondering why my mother-in-law had come to visit in such a hurry without any notice. Maybe I could think of a way to ask Nathan about this so it wouldn't sound as though I was acting inhospitable. Or maybe it made no difference. I should welcome the fact that she might be ready to accept me as part of her family and put the past behind.

I lay awake for what seemed like hours, waiting for Nathan, my mind whirling with questions. I kept returning to one: had Miss Gloria spotted the body from the street when we first rode by, at least subconsciously? Could she possibly have known this woman? It didn't seem likely. The dead woman was from New Jersey, and Miss Gloria had lived in Key West forever. And Michigan before that. I remembered that as we got closer to the porch, Mrs. Bransford had experienced a premonition, or so she'd said. Could she have anticipated something like this? It almost seemed like she had expected something terrible to happen even before it did.

That seemed ridiculous. The frantic whirring of an over-busy mind. As usual. *Go to bed*, I told myself. *And start fresh tomorrow.*

Chapter Eight

But up front, next to the desk where the hosts have mastered the art of checking reservations without making eye contact, is a café/wine bar. A glass case there serves as a temporary prison for aging pastries and tragic snacks.
—Pete Wells, "What If Brexit Were a Restaurant?"
The New York Times, December 19, 2018

By the time I woke up the next morning to my tiger cat's incessant face patting, Nathan had come and gone. Last night, I'd finally drifted off to sleep after hours of rumination. I'd hoped to stay awake until Nathan arrived, but my eyelids had gotten heavier and heavier and I'd finally lain down on the bed with Evinrude to rest for a minute. I woke up with the sun shearing through the blinds, already late for my day.

I vaguely remembered Nathan climbing into bed and feeling the warmth of his body alongside me. Or had I dreamed that? He'd left a pot of coffee on the stove and a note on the kitchen counter.

I slept on the couch most of the night; you looked so cozy and I was restless. I didn't want to wake you. Besides, Evinrude was hogging my spot. I'm so sorry about the way this week is unfolding. If you can just keep an eye on my mother for one more day, I will owe you forever. Sorry not to see you awake. [Here he'd drawn a frowny face.] *Going in early and hoping they'll let me out this afternoon early. What's on the docket? Love you, Nathan.*

As if I had his mother's visit planned out like she was visiting royalty. Sigh. Dear, sweet Nathan—he was going to be an interesting husband.

Miss Gloria had left a note as well, explaining that she and Mrs. Dubisson, her best buddy from up the dock, had taken Ziggy Stardust on their early walk. Otherwise she was free for the day and prepared to help me entertain.

I pulled up the calendar on my laptop and looked over my obligations for the day. Personal training at seven thirty. Ugh. As much as I'd been eating over the holidays, this calorie outgo would be a drop in the bucket. And since I'd skipped a few sessions, all the work would feel that much harder. I thought of making oatmeal with blueberries and almonds to counterbalance the heavy load of key lime pie I'd shouldered last night, but instead I poured a second cup of coffee, dosed it liberally with milk and sugar, and scrambled two eggs in a big pat of butter and popped a piece of mango bread from Cole's Peace bakery into the toaster. I loaded up the cats' bowl with kibble and freshened their water. Nathan must've given them something at whatever hour he was up and out or they would have been hollering at six AM as usual.

I absolutely had to start working on my pieces due Friday, one of which was to focus on casual eats that would be both delicious and family friendly. I would not cover the usual tourist spots like the Waterfront Brewery, Turtle Kraals, and Pepe's, as visitors could find those without my guidance. Instead, Wally had suggested I seek out smaller venues, newer to the community, that served great food. The two I had in mind were Clemente's pizza, which had replaced the nude-dancing-girls establishment on Fleming Street, and Oasis on White Street, featuring casual Mediterranean food. I wondered if Nathan's mother would be willing to eat at either of those places—or enjoy them. She would have to . . .

Slowly, as my brain organized tasks for the day, I began to remember—and feel—the horror of yesterday's discovery. Nathan had not left any news about the murdered woman, but I would not have expected him to. He'd let out that one little snippet about how she might have died, but nothing more. Unless the case was wrapped up and the suspect on his way to jail, he would not feel free to share details from an active police department investigation. Even if I'd been part of the discovery. I took a quick shower, twisted my hair into a knot at the back of my neck, and dressed in clothing for the gym.

Replacing my wedding ring after moisturizing my hands, I noticed the beads I'd picked up last night on the dead woman's sidewalk. I'd dropped them into the little Japanese bowl on my bureau with the rest of the stuff from my jeans pocket.

I took them over to the window to see more clearly. Yesterday I'd assumed they were made of cheap glass, like Fantasy Fest beads. But in the light of day, I could see that these were gorgeous blue stones, some carved with tiny letters in a language I didn't recognize. Was this part of a necklace the dead woman had been wearing? Would it provide any clues to her life, or her death? Or had it been dropped by a random passerby?

I might find answers about the beads themselves at the gym. WeBeFit was a small space crammed with high-end workout equipment and bustling with personal trainers and their clients. Because of the small space, there was a continuous conversation that soared and sputtered and wove among the customers and the staff—politics both national and local, cats, the flooding of our Key West streets caused by global warming, food. It helped keep us from focusing on the pain of our sit-ups and weight-bearing repetitions, and kept the trainers from expiring of tedium.

One of the people who often worked out at the same time I did was a jeweler named Tony, an elegant older man with a mysterious past. I slipped the beautiful beads into my chest pocket and pulled the zipper tight. He knew everyone in this town, and he also knew everything there was to know about jewelry, including who might have given what to whom. I'd have him take a look and then hand everything over to Nathan when I saw him.

In the gym, a mix tape of Beatles songs was playing over the speakers. All the regular trainers were on duty along with their customers, who had probably overeaten during the holidays same as I had. I grabbed a stainless-steel water bottle from the fridge, picked my way carefully through the sweating clients, and stashed my backpack in the women's locker area. I was a little early for my appointment, so I had time to ask my jewelry questions. Tony was performing calf-strengthening exercises under the watchful eye of his trainer.

I waited until he finished his set. "If you don't mind, could you take a look at some beads I found on the sidewalk last night? They are so pretty and so unusual that I'd like to find the owner and return them. I realize this is a long shot, but maybe you will have seen them before?" I spread the necklace out on the desk inside the front door. Tony and his trainer and my trainer, Leigh, came over to look.

Tony studied the engraved beads without expression. "The necklace would have been valuable; you are right to want to find the owner. The stones are lapis lazuli, tiger's-eye, and a rare blue jade. Blue tiger's-eye is called hawk's eye, and crystal people believe it's helpful in reducing anxiety and fear."

"Huh. Any idea what the engraving on the other stones means?"

He looked at me, then back at the beads. "I believe they were part of a Hindu prayer bead necklace. Old. Probably one of a kind." He rubbed his fingers together as if he were counting the beads of a rosary.

"Have you seen something like this before?"

He shook his head. "The combination is unusual enough that I might have remembered, but I'll look through my records."

"He photographs everything he works on," Leigh explained.

I took a quick picture of the beads and texted it to Tony, then continued with my workout.

After finishing up, I rushed home, dropped the beads from the necklace in the bowl on my dresser, and dressed in street clothes (a notch above what I usually wore because of Nathan's mother). Then I drove my scooter down the island to the office.

Danielle was manning the front desk, which sat in a little bulge in the hallway that we called the reception area. Most of the work and living spaces and yards and gardens in our town were smaller than their counterparts would be on the mainland because of the space limitations that came with living on an island. And I'd grown to find that both cozy and endearing rather than claustrophobic.

"They're waiting for you," she said. "No one's out of sorts about anything in particular, as far as I can tell." She winked and made a face.

Both of my bosses, Wally and Palamina, tended toward moodiness in their own way. I counted on Danielle's people-reading expertise as a friendly barometer. I tapped on their door and went in. A faux-wicker folding chair had been set up next to Wally's desk for me.

"Good morning," Palamina said.

Wally only nodded. Okay, correction on Danielle's observations: Mr. Grumpy was in attendance.

"Sorry I'm late," I said, glancing at my watch. "Nathan's mother is visiting."

"We want to run over this week's issue, make sure the ducks are in a row," Wally said. "Remember we're going to send everything to the printer Friday afternoon."

Obviously there wasn't time for chitchat. I explained to my bosses that I had done most of the research for the key lime pie roundup and would have it finished by this afternoon. Tomorrow morning at the latest.

"And restaurants?" asked Wally, tapping a pencil to his lip.

"Since it's New Year's Eve week with lots of kids and families in town, I was planning to do Clemente's, the new pizza place on Fleming Street, and Oasis on White." I'd eaten once before at each and knew I could work up pithy reviews without a huge amount of effort.

As soon as the words were out, I started to wonder again whether either of these would be pleasing to Nathan's mother. Part of me felt that, since she hadn't given us any notice, she would have to go with the flow. On the other hand, she didn't exactly seem like a go-with-the-flow kind of person. But if she didn't like the sound of what I proposed, I'd tell Nathan he needed to take her out somewhere fancier. Maybe the Marquesa, which tended to emulate New York–style fine-dining food (and prices), if he could get a table. A little quality mother–son time couldn't hurt.

"Earth to Hayley," said Wally.

I smiled. "Sorry, there's a lot going on, as usual. Nathan's mom surprised us with an unexpected visit. And of course he's busy getting ready for the New Year's Eve onslaught. So I'm scrambling to entertain her. Yesterday turned into a crazy day."

"That's the worst," said Palamina. "I had a mother-in-law from hell myself for a little under a year. Can't imagine what it would be like for a lifetime."

I felt instantly guilty about dissing Nathan's mother when I'd barely spent any time with her. I should be grateful she'd deigned to visit instead of piling on the mother-in-law jokes. Best to change the subject back to work. "I have one question on the pastry article. The day wasn't crazy bad because of Nathan's mother; it was bad because we found a body."

Danielle got up from behind her desk in the hallway and came to the door to listen in. I explained about the brouhaha at the library, and then discovering Claudette Parker on the porch, and how the deceased was the author of the key lime napoleon. And also the deliverer of the pie to Sloan's face.

"Oh my gosh," Danielle said. "My boyfriend mentioned there was a body found in Old Town near the cemetery when he came in late last night. But I never imagined you were involved."

"Again," Wally muttered.

I shot him a scathing look. "Back to my question: should I include that napoleon and Claudette Parker in this piece? Should we postpone the whole thing until next week's issue? I sent you two versions, one including the library disaster and one without it. Maybe we should sit tight and see what unfolds with the murder?"

"We can't do that," said Wally sharply. "We have a huge backlog for the new year because of the holidays running together. And we pride ourselves on starting out fresh, as you know. No leftover gingerbread houses or recipes for fruitcake bread pudding or how to recycle candy canes so it doesn't look like you're regifting something stale from Christmas. So we've got to go with your roundup in this issue. And besides, since

David Sloan's closing key lime party is Friday, we planned to link those stories."

"Maybe leave that one confection out?" Palamina mused. "Or maybe better yet, if you have time, go over to the shop and see what's happening? Was she the owner of the place or the pastry chef? Or both? Any silent stakeholders? If the place is open and you see those napoleons in the case, we'll run with the pie piece as written. If it's not, reconsider. And maybe you can talk to the other staff while you're there and see if you can get any insider information about the death. It's hard to imagine the two events aren't linked—the pie-throwing followed in close proximity by Miss Parker's murder."

Wally's lips had hardened to a grim line while Palamina was talking. She waved away his protest. "Look," she said, "I'm not suggesting Hayley investigate the murder. But it's surely going to have a ripple effect on what she's writing, and we look like fools if we ignore that. Wasn't this whole contest predicated on the competition between key lime pastry chefs? It might mean something big that this woman is no longer part of that. And it wouldn't hurt a bit if we broke the story ahead of the other online rags."

I gathered my things and stood up, before Wally could voice his worries. Or worse yet, insist I start over, which I did not have time for. "I'll keep you posted about what I find." On the way out, I whispered to Danielle that she should let me know if she heard anything else from her beau.

My mother texted me as soon as I got to the bottom of the stairs.

We want to have you all to dinner tomorrow but busier than a one-armed paper-hanger today, as your grandmother used to say. See you at Oasis at seven. Meanwhile, call your mother-in-law. We're on our way out and she is pacing.

Yikes. I did as suggested. Only I took the chicken's way out and texted Nathan's mother instead of calling.

Good morning! Hope you had a restful sleep. Would you like suggestions for the day today? Visitors always enjoy the Hemingway house, for the cats if nothing else. Although they also offer a very cute Hemingway-focused tour. And the Harry Truman Little White House is full of charm and history. I have a few stops to make for work this morning but would love to take you to lunch later.

I sent that off to see if she'd bite. And then rustled through my notes about the pies we'd tasted last night to see what was missing.

If it's not too much trouble, would enjoy riding shotgun with you this morning, she texted back.

Yikes again. But what choice did I have? And how could it hurt to take her to the new bakery and maybe to a few others? I'd decided after looking over my notes that I hadn't sampled an adequate number of pies to fill up the allotted words.

Be there in 15, I texted back. *Depending on traffic. I'm on my scooter so dress accordingly.*

Maybe she'd bail out at the prospect of a scooter ride.

Chapter Nine

*"It's not about the chefs anymore," she said. "You can't
just come with a dollar and dream." Mainstays depart.
Now what?*
—Kim Severson, "As Mainstays Depart, Charleston
Asks Where Its Restaurant Scene Is Headed,"
The New York Times, May 7, 2019

O n the contrary, Mrs. Bransford was waiting on the back
porch of my mother's home. She wore jeans, sneakers,
and a gorgeous pale-pink cashmere sweater that made her
skin glow. The color matched my mother's pink helmet, which
dangled from her wrist.

"What's on the agenda?" she asked.

"I want to go by the shop owned by the murdered woman.
My major article for *Key Zest* this week is a roundup of key
lime pies, and my bosses are wondering whether it's appropri-
ate to include this woman's pastry." I paused to think this
over for a minute. "Not sure exactly what I'm expecting to
find that will make a difference, but if she was the architect of

the napoleon and she's the only real pastry chef, she won't be making it anymore. So there's no point in including it. It will only make readers feel bad because they can't get one. And we'll look tone-deaf in the worst way."

"And maybe," she said, swinging her leg over the scooter and sliding on behind me, "maybe someone will tell us more about what happened last night. And if they don't offer answers, we can ask some pointed questions."

I turned around to look at her in astonishment. "Your son would not be happy."

"And so?" she asked with a small grin. "This wouldn't be the first time, and it probably won't be the last. He's not my boss. I suspect he's not in charge of you either." She clipped the pink helmet over her perfectly coiffed hair and looked straight ahead—ready to go.

We drove out of the Truman Annex and across Whitehead to Greene Street, winding past groups of noisy tourists who spilled out from the bars along the way. Though it was well before noon, the party was in full swing. I parked in front of Old City Hall, a stunning brick building, dignified in the middle of the party chaos. We disembarked, and I pulled the scooter onto its stand.

"We can walk from here. It's hard to find parking closer to the harbor. And it occurs to me that we can visit the Key Lime Pie Company while we're this close. And Kermit's, too." A group of twentysomething women wearing glittery New Year's hats and short sundresses and carrying cups of beer jostled us off the sidewalk.

"By the way, if you take a tour of the city this week, don't let anyone tell you that Hemingway used to drink at Sloppy

Joe's," I told her, pointing back to the establishment at the corner of Duval that had swallowed up the sparkly tourist girls. "The original bar was located where Captain Tony's is now. Oh, and also," I added, "if you're interested in the writers of Key West, the literary seminar people give a wonderful walking tour. I can check later and see which days it might be running, depending on how long you're staying."

She didn't comment on either the tour suggestion or the length of her visit.

We found the new bakery in the next block. Last time I stopped in to check the place out, I'd been in a super hurry and it hadn't registered how close this was to both Kermit's Key West Key Lime Shoppe and to the Key Lime Pie Company. Very unwelcome competition, I suspected.

The bakery was not closed as I would have predicted. Either the dead woman had a business partner or she was not as important to the bakery as the previous press might have suggested. Or someone had made the decision that, death or no death, this was the busiest week of the season and the show must go on.

Ten or twelve people were already jammed into the small space, perusing the pastries behind the counter and chattering about what to choose. I listened for any word that the customers had heard about the death, but they seemed to be largely uninformed tourists.

The top shelf of the counter under the cash register was filled with key lime napoleons. I also noticed a glorious key lime pie with one piece removed. Odd, because I distinctly remembered Claudette announcing that key lime pie was passé. The filling was deeper than in many of the pies I'd seen so far, and not overwhelmed by meringue. The pastry appeared to be a flaky butter crust rather than the more traditional graham cracker. How could I not sample? When my turn came, I ordered a piece of the pie and a napoleon to go.

"I'm very sorry for the loss of your chef," I said to the man behind the counter. "What a terrible shock that must have been." He looked familiar, and I thought perhaps he'd been in the background of her photo in the paper when the shop first opened. Then it came to me—he was Paul Redford, who'd been introduced day before yesterday at the library as Claudette's assistant.

Paul rang me up, nodding in agreement. "In shock, that's what we are. We thought about closing up for the week at least, but we had all this stock and all these people clamoring for it. Plus all these people working in the kitchen who need their jobs. And I know the recipes cold. It made more sense to simply soldier forward."

Nathan's mother leaned closer to me and whispered, "Ask if he knows anything about what happened."

I wasn't going to argue. "Any word on who did this to her?" I asked.

Paul stiffened, staring at me and then at my mother-in-law. "Not that they've told me. If the cops ask my opinion, I will tell them she was killed by someone who resented her brilliance with pastries. She blew everyone on this island out of the water, and someone couldn't stand it. They couldn't tolerate that kind of competition. So-called key lime juice in a bottle was not going to cut the mustard any longer with sophisticated culinary tourists coming to the island. You know how it is here—transient chefs sink to the lowest common denominator when it comes to food."

This had not been my experience of Key West. Nor had I written anything like this—except in my poorly considered early article that David Sloan had rightly criticized. Yes, of course, chefs came and went. It was hard physical labor and turnover was part of the business. And some chefs had substance abuse issues and flailed around until they were fired for missing too many days of work or making mistakes with the menu. And some of them couldn't afford the cost of living in paradise—second-home owners and escapees from the northern winter tended to drive the prices of everything higher. And some of them couldn't handle the sheer physicality of the work.

But I didn't believe any of these problems was confined to Key West, nor did a majority of workers in our island foodie world have them. I took the bag of baked goods from Paul, along with a brochure from Key West's Finest about finding hidden gems off Duval Street that sat near the register.

As we left the pastry shop and started over to the Key Lime Pie Company, I began to muse out loud about where the dead woman fit into the key lime culture of the island. "Just about every restaurant on this island serves key lime pie—it's almost an obligation. With social media reporting on every new iteration of the basic recipe, owners must feel they have to serve something special." I glanced over at Nathan's mother, who did not appear fascinated.

"You think someone killed her because they were envious of her pastry like he said?" she asked. "It seems a stretch as far as motives for murder go."

"Maybe, maybe not," I said. "But she was new to the island and she was making a huge splash in our foodie world, and probably sucking business away from other shops." This happened sometimes with a brand-new restaurant. But my metaphor was a little off—her entrance had resembled fireworks more than splashing.

"Lots of other businesses have started out this way—she wasn't the first," I explained. "And many of them fizzled after that first burst of enthusiasm. 'Here I am, look at me, the best of the best,' and so on. The next thing you know, storefronts are shuttered and the owners and chefs limp off, headed back to the mainland for what they perceive to be an easier kind of life. Maybe after having squeezed several other local places out of business. Because we have limited real estate, obviously, there are only so many entrepreneurs who can be shoehorned onto the island. Same with contractors, same with health clubs—"

Nathan's mother cut me off. "I wish you'd pushed a little harder. Maybe asked some tougher questions, like who actually does the baking. Who made the decision to move here? And why? As you say, there're already plenty of key lime pies being made on this island. For better or worse." Mrs. Bransford frowned. "With all your foodie connections, you must know someone who would have some insider information on this."

I felt a bit like I'd been rapped on the knuckles. To cover my embarrassment, I glanced at the brochure I'd picked up in the shop—a catalog of off-Duval businesses collected by Amber Debevec from Key West's Finest. Amber was an entrepreneur with a huge social media following who specialized in telling tourists where to find the best of the best on our island. She pretty much knew everything. And in the past, she'd been quite willing to share her knowledge with me.

"I do know someone," I said. I texted Amber to ask if she might be free for coffee or lunch. She answered right away, and we arranged to meet up the next day at the Roof Top Café at noon.

"What's next?" asked Nathan's mom.

"I need to make a stop in the Key Lime Pie Company to grab a piece of pie for my tasting article."

The decor of this shop was an eye-popping key lime color, and it gave the place the impression of being a small company rather than a pastry shop, not nearly as homey as Claudette's place. That aside, this storefront was even busier than Au Citron Vert, crammed with tourists eating pie, eating ice cream, and buying key lime–flavored souvenirs. I tried to catch the cashier's attention for a quick word, but she was frantically ringing customers up, calling out orders, and refilling the refrigerated case with fresh pies. I recognized her as Sigrid, the short African American woman who'd presented the creamy pie that ended up in David Sloan's face. From the way she was directing and correcting other employees, she appeared to be either the owner or the manager. Someone who might well know something. I fell into the line.

Fifteen minutes later, my turn came. I ordered two pieces of pie to go. As Sigrid rang me up, I said, "You've had some wonderful local press recently. Congratulations on the Florida Weekly list. There is so much competition in this town, it must mean a lot."

She beamed. "It does mean a lot. We know we are the best, but it's good to have that recognized."

"Are you getting a run for your money from the new place up the block?" I asked. "What a horrible shock about their pastry chef."

"Yes, awful. Though I didn't know her, other than by sight and reputation," Sigrid said, glancing up at me with narrowed eyes. She handed my credit card back. "Still, it was a terrible thing to happen. People migrate down here to settle in paradise and bring their awful mainland problems with them."

Did that mean she knew something about Claudette's past, or was she making a harsh generalization about outsiders?

"How has the new shop affected your business?" asked Nathan's mother, who had pushed up next to me. "We imagine the people already established in this area could not have been pleased when Ms. Parker moved in."

Sigrid turned to look at Mrs. Bransford, a frown on her face. "No one was happy about another key lime pie shop on this street. For heaven's sake, it's already saturated." She waved her hand. "But I suppose she thought she'd get the best traffic from the cruise ships if she settled here. They often don't like to walk very far when they get off their boats, so Duval Street and Greene get a lot of their business." She called out some instructions to the girls behind her, who were slicing pies and pouring coffees. "And naming it *Au Citron Vert*? Really?

La-di-da. It would be one thing if she came directly from Paris, but she did not."

She turned to the next customer. We were dismissed. But Mrs. Bransford stopped her with a megawatt smile. "If you have one more second, we'd like to hear about the pie-baking lessons. We both need brushing up on our techniques." She gestured at the sign on the counter describing key lime pie classes.

I gulped. I'd not heard one peep about Nathan's mother's interest in either cooking or baking, and she'd barely tasted dessert last night. She was slender in the manner of a person who didn't even think about dessert, never mind actually baking it and eating too much of it.

Sigrid smiled back. "We hold classes on Thursdays and Fridays. They last an hour, and you may take your pie home at the end of the class."

To be honest, I doubted I would learn anything new at an hour-long class. I'd read so much and heard so much about key lime pies that I felt I could make one in my sleep. On the other hand, if Sigrid was teaching and the class was small enough, I'd have an hour's access to her. She knew something more about Claudette Parker; I saw it in her face. But in the work I'd done in the food community, I'd come to learn that casual chitchat while cooking always led to frank conversations.

Nathan's mother glanced at me, and I shrugged. "Tomorrow morning's clear. Sloan's contest is on Friday afternoon."

"We'll take two slots for the morning," she said. She held out her credit card.

"Make it three if you have them," I said. "Miss Gloria would enjoy this." Even if nothing else came of it, I could write a short piece for *Key Zest* on making the iconic pie.

"I didn't know you were interested in baking," I said, once we were back on the sidewalk.

Mrs. Bransford laughed. "Not at all. But I didn't believe for a moment that she did not know Claudette. Her shop is only one block from the French place. She admitted she knew the woman wasn't Parisian, and I suspect there was lots more she could say. I figured we'd hear more over an hour while keeping our hands busy in the class. She struck me as the kind of woman who was bursting to gossip if given the right opportunity."

I stared at her, impressed. That was exactly what I'd been thinking.

Chapter Ten

And so, bit by bit, on the backs of those traitorous breaths,
in snuck the fragrance of something baking in an oven.
—Erica Bauermeister, *The Scent Keeper*

After picking up more pie slices at Kermit's key lime shop near the harbor, known for its iconic owner/chef's costumed shenanigans and for a pucker-worthy taste, I stowed the pie in my scooter's storage bin and we drove to the last stop I had planned for the morning. A Facebook friend had insisted that Key West Cakes on White Street made the best key lime pie on the island. Other folks might dispute that, but I felt I had to test it for my roundup article to be fair.

And besides, I was getting hungry, yearning for one perfect piece to tide me over until lunch. We parked on White, a busy cross street that ran between Eaton Street and the Atlantic Ocean, and entered the shop. Just inside was a tall glassed-in case containing a gorgeous multi-tiered chocolate cake spackled in large flakes of chocolate, a baby shower cake, and a carpet of cupcakes. Large glass containers held piles of cookies. A hand-painted sign rested on a small pink chair. It read: *You are the Icing on my Cupcake.* I could imagine hanging that in Miss Gloria's kitchen, but I wasn't so sure about the kitchen in Nathan's and my houseboat. I feared Nathan would find it sappy. After snapping pictures of everything, I ordered two pieces of pie and a potpourri of sugar cookies at the counter from a serious man with deep blue eyes.

"Do you mind if we sit for a few minutes while I make some notes?" I asked my mother-in-law. "And maybe nibble on some pie?"

"Not at all," she said, pulling out her own phone. "But I'll pass on the pie."

I sank into a chair beside a café table in the window to sample and write. As I ate, I thought of the words I'd use to describe this pie: super-creamy with a crumbly, buttery crust and fleurettes of what had to be real whipped cream all around the edges. One delicious mouthful felt like it might contain the day's entire allotment of calories and cholesterol. The difficulty with this piece I was writing would be figuring out how to find words to differentiate the pies. I hadn't tasted a bad bite so far.

Nathan's mother had returned to the cash register before I even noticed. I stopped tapping into my phone to listen.

"You must have heard about the pastry chef who was murdered last night," she said to the young man piping frosting on starfish cookies. "So tragic."

He glanced up at her, his blue eyes narrowing. "I can't believe we got sucked into attending that ridiculous event at the library. Enough said."

"Ridiculous event?" she asked, her voice innocent as an ingenue.

"David Sloan, ridiculous. The more trouble he can stir up, the better he likes it."

"And he likes that because?"

"Conflict equals publicity, in his mind anyway," the man said.

"Do you think Ms. Parker was killed because of that event?"

"I'm not in the know, but anyone could see the rancor between the new shop and the rest of the bakers in town. She seemed so sure that her product was superior to any of ours." He sniffed, and turned the cookie to begin icing the other side.

As Mrs. Bransford returned to my table, I was scraping the little plastic container of its last creamy bite, feeling a little piggy in front of her. I couldn't help it—this was my job, and besides that, I loved food. And I was ravenous. Just then, Miss Gloria called.

"What's up?" I asked my roommate. "I'm just finishing the most lovely pie."

"Did you save some for me?" she asked.

"I've ordered you a slice," I assured her. Which I hadn't. But she could have the one I'd bought for my mother-in-law. Besides, we also had samples from two other shops.

"This afternoon, I was wondering, if it wasn't too much trouble, whether you would mind running me out to the SPCA?" Miss Gloria asked.

I glanced at Nathan's mother and then at the clock on my phone. I did not have time to run my guest back down the island, then return to the houseboat to pick up Miss Gloria and take her up to the next island where the shelter was located. And work on my article and get ready for dinner.

"I'm happy to ride along," Nathan's mother said.

Another mystery, because she didn't seem to be an animal lover. In other words, she hadn't dropped everything to chirp and cluck to get our cats' attention when they sashayed past her. Nor had Ziggy the wonder dog caught her interest. And he was adorable in a wacky doggish sort of way, and also the apple of Nathan's eye.

"We'll be home shortly," I said. "Then we can discuss." I brought the extra slice of pie for Miss Gloria and the cookies and tucked them all into the basket at the back of the scooter with the other assorted goodies. Nathan's mother hopped on, and we buzzed up to Houseboat Row.

Several construction vans were parked in the lot, and I could hear the happy sounds of nail guns and band saws— coming from my future home. A miracle! But as we walked up the finger of the dock, I saw the workers clustered on Mrs. Renhart's boat, not mine. Sigh.

Miss Gloria was waiting on the deck with the cats, who wound between her legs, meowing.

"Looks like everyone wants a piece of the action," I said, handing over her confections. "I didn't know cats loved key lime." I turned to Nathan's mother. "Can I get you a snack or coffee?"

"A glass of water?" she asked, perching on the rocking chair next to my roommate. "I've passed my pie quota for the year and caffeine quota for the day."

Miss Gloria hollered after me as I hit the kitchen. "And don't let those cats tell you they haven't eaten, because they scarfed down a whole can of cat food only twenty minutes ago."

I returned with three glasses of water, ice, and lemon slices. "Tell me about the SPCA. Are you thinking of volunteering?"

Miss Gloria had been working for a while now giving tours of notable gravestones and architecture in our local cemetery. Some people thought it was a little spooky for her to be working in the graveyard when she had crossed over into her eighties and might be joining the ranks of the buried sooner rather than later. But she paid no attention to their naysaying—she enjoyed bringing the dead people back to life by telling their stories and tales of old Key West. And she especially loved spreading the word that there was a lot more to Key West than drinking on Duval Street—the city was loaded with interesting characters and history.

"It's not that," she said. Several expressions flitted across her face in succession: mournful, embarrassed, hopeful.

She pointed to my houseboat-to-be, and then to the boat on the other side of us, where four strapping guys were nailing new siding onto the Renharts' home. "I got to thinking that pretty soon they will be making real progress on Nathan's place, and that drives home the truth—you will be moving out before I know it. And you'll be taking your husband and his dog and Evinrude with you. That's all I can think about, and it makes me feel so sad."

Her lips started to quiver and her eyes got a little teary. I leaned over to hug her, thinking I should reassure her that nothing would change. Which was exactly what I'd been trying to tell myself as well. Even though it would. We'd knock on each other's doors and ask politely if it was convenient to have coffee instead of stumbling out of bed and finding each other at the kitchen table or on the deck. And she'd worry that she was a drag on my new marriage if she accepted too many dinner invitations from me. And who knew what Evinrude would do—he might even refuse to make the move. He was a cat, after all, mercurial and unpredictable.

Why did any kind of change feel so hard?

Miss Gloria continued to talk. "Mrs. Dubisson knew I was feeling blue, so she called the shelter and found out that the orange tiger kitten I pulled out of the bushes last night is still there." She held up her hand to stop me from protesting. "I know we're one cat away from becoming crazy cat ladies, but all I can think of is you'll be leaving and taking Evinrude. The idea of having only one cat in the house feels pathetic and lonely."

"We'll be right next door, remember?" I said. "And Evinrude will not understand the concept of moving. He loves you so dearly. He and I will be over here all the time, I promise. You'll hardly notice a difference, except that you'll be able to get in the bathroom without queuing up."

I kept my voice cheerful and flashed a reassuring smile. But I was beginning to feel sad, too. We had developed something special and unexpectedly magical in our little home. She felt like my family in only the best way. No telling what would be left after the construction dust had settled.

"Maybe one of his owner's family members will show up to claim him. Wouldn't that be the best ending? They would keep a connection to Claudette by raising her cat. I know you would do that with Evinrude."

Miss Gloria's face fell. "I would, but I live with Evinrude. He *is* family. She hardly had time herself to get to know that kitten."

I sighed. This wasn't going anywhere. "I don't suppose it will hurt to look over the kitty."

She beamed and picked up her bag. "We better take the car, since there are three of us."

Chapter Eleven

At home, my mom was an indifferent cook . . . She would have been perfectly happy to take a pill that would allow her to forego eating altogether.

—Ivan Orkin, *Ramen*

On the way out to the SPCA, I described Stock Island points of interest to Nathan's mom—the botanical gardens, the golf course, the low spot where the old SPCA building stood, and the road leading to the overnight homeless shelter facility and the sheriff's department.

"Homeless folks are a problem in this town," Miss Gloria told her. "There are tons of them and they aren't going away anytime soon. Lots of residents and the visiting tourists don't want to face that ugly truth." She paused, nibbling a fingernail. "I can't get angry with these people, though. Wouldn't you want to come to a place like this too if you had no home?"

Mrs. Bransford shrugged. "I suppose. I hadn't given it much thought."

"It causes extra complications for the police department, too," I said. "They spend a lot of time answering calls from businesses about loitering, and taking drunken people to jail."

After we passed the decrepit building that had housed the previous iteration of the SPCA, I explained that the entire operation had moved up the road to a brand-new facility with lots more space. "And when the next hurricane comes, they can shelter right in place instead of evacuating all the traumatized animals up to the mainland. We'd like to think there won't be another storm like Irma, but with climate change and sea level rise, it seems inevitable."

We pulled into the parking lot of the SPCA, Miss Gloria vibrating with excitement and worry. "What if someone else snatched him before we got here?"

"If he's already taken, then maybe it wasn't meant to be," I said. "One thing for sure on this island, there's always another cat who needs a home."

Miss Gloria did not look convinced. She hurried ahead of us into the shelter's office and rushed to the counter to explain how she'd fallen for the orange kitten the day previous. The man behind the desk stood up and called for a volunteer to usher us into the cat quarters. "We'll see if he's still available."

"I'll wait for you here," said Nathan's mother. "I'm not really a cat person." She settled into the waiting area while Miss Gloria and I went back toward the cat rooms to look at the orange tiger kitten. When a volunteer came to meet us, wearing a roomy Florida Keys SPCA T-shirt, I wasn't surprised to recognize Cheryl, the murdered woman's next-door neighbor.

"Any news about what happened to Claudette?" she asked.

"Not that they've told us," Miss Gloria said. "And you?"

"Not a word," Cheryl said, and then introduced us to several cats in cages who were sick or so new that they were not able to mingle with the crowd.

"You can't imagine what a relief it is to be here in the new facility," she said. "Even the cats seem like they're breathing better. And sleeping better, too. And they've been flying out of here. I bet we've had a record number of adoptions. Now there's room enough for each little furry personality to shine."

We walked past a gray cat in a cage whom she called Saucy. "She's very sweet and wants a furever family badly, but she doesn't do well with other cats." She looked back at us, as if assessing our interest. "She'd make a perfect friend in a one-cat home."

We shrugged and smirked at each other, starting to crack up a little. "We already have two. And a dog. And three more shelter animals live only ten feet away on the next boat. So I don't think Saucy would thrive with us."

"We're especially interested in that orange tiger kitten you brought in last night," said Miss Gloria.

She turned to look at us. "You and half the island, apparently. His name is T-Bone, and he's got a lot of heat around him. That's cat-shelter speak for 'he's hot.' We can go visit him, but I'll have to check and see how many applications are ahead of yours."

Miss Gloria's shoulders drooped, and I put my arm around her and squeezed. I couldn't help thinking that it would be for the better if T-Bone had found a home elsewhere. We had an awful lot of chaos in our little quadrant of paradise already. And despite her early grieving over Nathan and me moving out, I'd seen enough construction glitches that I wouldn't count on that happening anytime soon.

Cheryl brought us into the kitten room, where T-Bone was busy wrestling with a gray tiger she identified as Ramp. "I'll leave you here to get acquainted while I go check on his status."

"I don't see how anyone comes in here without going home with a cat," I said, as we both settled onto the linoleum floor. "It's just too hard to see them all locked up."

"They're better off in here than out on the street most times," said Miss Gloria. She extracted toys from the bulging pockets of her sweat pants and brought a few more out of her bag, then began trailing a stuffed pink shrimp on a stick in front of the kittens. They took turns pouncing and rabbit-kicking the little felt toy. After a few minutes of play, Miss Gloria was able to coax the orange tiger onto her lap, where he settled into a ball of purring fluff.

Cheryl came back into the room. "I'm sorry to say he already has an application on him," she said. "And someone else in line in case that one falls through."

Miss Gloria looked as though she might burst into tears. "Could you put me in line after that?" she asked. "The thing is, since I found him in the bushes last night after his owner was killed . . . Well, it sounds silly, but we bonded. I have a feeling we are meant for each other."

"We could play with some of the other cats," I suggested. "That little Ramp is super-cute too."

But she shook her head. "I'm ready to go." She put the tiger kitten down and got back to her feet. In the office, she filled out the paperwork in case the other prospective owners should fall through.

Mrs. Bransford was waiting, scrolling through email on her iPhone. She looked up. "All set?"

"No," said Miss Gloria with a quivering lip. "Someone else got to him first."

The man at the desk said, "I'm sorry about that. After word got out that we had a new kitten who'd belonged to the murdered woman, he became something of a Facebook sensation. The phone hasn't stopped ringing."

We returned to the car, and Miss Gloria insisted on riding in the back seat. I couldn't think of a thing to say to cheer her up. She had had her heart set on that guy, end of story. I suspected it had something to do with death, perhaps a message from her unconscious about choosing life. Some of Miss Gloria's acquaintances were making the decision not to get another pet because the animal might outlive them, and who would take care of it after they were gone? Not my friend. She always expected people would rise to an occasion of need. And besides, she didn't believe her time on this earth was anywhere near its natural end. She would anticipate at least one cat's lifetime ahead of her, if not two.

Or maybe she couldn't help herself from helping the downtrodden and unloved; she'd been so welcoming to me when I was a stray. I glanced in the rearview mirror—she was fast asleep, her chin resting on her chest, a tiny bead of drool in the corner of her lips.

I glanced over at my mother-in-law and grinned. "She's a treasure, isn't she? I'll drop you off at my mother's place so you can freshen up and maybe even take a rest before dinner? You've been such a good sport."

Mrs. Bransford grimaced. "While you were looking at cats, I had the opportunity to talk with the dead woman's next-door neighbor who was coming on board for her shift. You know, the young woman who took the yellow kitten from Miss Gloria yesterday?"

"You mean Cheryl?"

She nodded.

I was so surprised that I nearly ran through the red light on Truman next to St. Mary's. All I needed was another traffic citation with Nathan's mother in the car. She must have waylaid Cheryl while Miss Gloria and I were playing with the kittens. I was beginning to seriously wonder why she was so interested in this case. And to be honest, I was completely astonished by her curiosity.

"I'd love to hear what you learned," I said.

She nodded. "You seem to be heading in the direction of believing Claudette Parker was killed because of a jealous baker. In other words, you assume this murder happened because of something in your small food world. But she had a whole other life, remember. And she'd only been in town a short while, isn't that so?"

"I believe that's right," I said. "Seems to me the first I'd heard of her was when I read a small article in the *Citizen* back in September about how they were working on the shop with plans to open in November. Everyone knows there's no

97

point in opening anything in September—still hurricane season. It's probably the emptiest month of the year on our island. And October is iffy too; you've got the ongoing threat of physical hurricanes, but also Fantasy Fest, a hurricane of a different sort."

And that thought sent me off on a different tangent altogether, which was to be grateful Nathan's mother wasn't visiting during that festival when our streets were chockablock with naked painted people. Many of them who might be better off wearing clothing, though that was a value judgment I knew I shouldn't make. Bodies of every shape and size were beautiful creations of the Universe—that's what Miss Gloria would have said.

"So is it reasonable to assume she made an enemy that deadly within the span of two months? Doesn't that seem unlikely?" Mrs. Bransford asked.

"I suppose," I said. "What did the neighbor tell you?"

"She didn't have a lot of time to chat," said Nathan's mother. "I asked her if she'd seen a lot of comings and goings from Claudette's house. She invited us over for coffee tomorrow, and I accepted the offer. I had the sense she would tell us everything if we were willing to drink her coffee and maybe nibble on stale pastry. Assuming we can fit that in and you can lower your standards. Though maybe I read her wrong on what she'll serve—my bad for assuming it won't be delicious."

I stared at her, my mouth agape, until the driver behind us leaned on his horn. "Of course, it's your visit. We're happy to do whatever you wish."

I saw Miss Gloria shake herself awake in the back seat. "Where are we? What's happening?"

"Dropping our guest off." I smiled in the mirror as I drove by the Southard Street guard shack at the entrance to the Truman Annex and stopped in front of my mother's house. "I think the plan is to meet at the restaurant at seven. Mom and Sam will bring you," I told my mother-in-law.

I watched her walk up the steps to the porch and disappear into the house. Perfectly straight posture and not a hair out of place, exactly as she'd looked this morning. I had to wonder if I'd ever feel as though I really knew her. Or she me.

Chapter Twelve

It seems to me that our three basic needs, for food and security and love, are so mixed and mingled and entwined that we cannot straightly think of one without the others. So it happens that when I write of hunger, I am really writing about love and the hunger for it, and warmth and the love of it and the hunger for it . . .
—M.F.K. Fisher, *Consider the Oyster*

B ack on the houseboat, I spent the remainder of the afternoon desperately working on my articles for *Key Zest*, intent on getting most of the work done before meeting the gang at Oasis at seven. But it wasn't that easy to pick apart so many good key lime pies. I couldn't get away with saying there are no bad pies on the island, because of course there were restaurants that imported desserts from distributors on the mainland. In those cases, you were going to get what you paid for—it probably wouldn't be fresh, and it certainly wouldn't be homemade.

And people had different threshold tests related to which pies they loved most—meringue versus whipped cream, for example. Butter-and-flour versus graham cracker versus chocolate wafer crusts. But was a towering pile of meringue better in an existential way than a fleurette of freshly whipped cream? As I wrote, I was forced to return several times to the refrigerator for a follow-up taste of one pie or another.

And all the while that I sorted through my notes and my photos, the comment Nathan's mother had made to me about the murder victim circled in my brain. *You assume this happened because of something going on in your small food world. But she had a whole other life, both personal and whatever came before Key West. It might not pay to think that small.*

I tried to concentrate on my work, but questions about the circumstances of the murder kept intruding. Did the killer have something against Christmas? Or Santa? Or had the murderer wanted the victim found in a certain way to send someone a message? Or had it been a spur-of-the-moment attack? Why, then, had she been dressed that way?

More questions rushed into my mind. How many Conch Trains had driven by that house on the night Mrs. Bransford noticed the dead woman? What time did it get dark? Early these days. So there had been time, at least a couple of hours, for the murder to occur before our train chugged by. I tried to remember exactly what our Conch Train driver had told us. That home on Olivia Street was his particular favorite. But it didn't strike me as the kind of display most people would enjoy or go out of their way to see. Except for a quick laugh or an Instagram post. In fact, it fell on the tacky end of the decoration continuum. And I remembered feeling a little surprised that the city allowed the Conch Trains to drive through a quiet residential neighborhood. Did our conductor have a particular connection to that area? Or to the residents of that home? It might be worth a call. Better yet, a visit.

I thought about what the woman at the SPCA had said about the kitten called T-Bone. *There's a lot of heat around that cat.*

This seemed to have been true for the dead woman as well. She'd blasted into town with a lot of heat and forced other chefs and restaurants to up their games. Her light and flaky key lime pastries did not live in the same universe as many desserts in town. Could it be that someone felt so annoyed or enraged that they felt they had to kill her? It seemed crazy, but crazy things happened. I began to reread the newspaper article that had come out about her earlier this fall.

Connie trudged up the dock from the parking lot, her baby on her back in a carrier. They both looked exhausted. She had started working again, managing the cleaning service she had launched years ago. She'd been kind enough to let me work for her back when my old beau Chad Lutz had kicked me out not long after I moved to Key West.

"Long day?" I asked. "You girls look pooped."

She smiled and patted the baby's hand. "We'll be better when we get a little dinner into us." She held up a fragrant package. "Since you're busy this week and not turning out fabulous feasts and sending the spillover to needy neighbors, I turned to takeout at Fausto's. How's it going with your mother-in-law?"

"She's not really what I expected. I'd say she's very strong-willed and up for anything. And she has strong opinions about everything except food and doesn't hold them back." I told her about finding the body, and about ripping around town talking to pastry shop people, and then about the trip to the SPCA. "We're packing a lot in, and that's an understatement. And we're not visiting the usual tourist destinations, that's for sure."

I realized Connie would be curious to meet her, and that it might be rude not to have a party to introduce her to our neighbors and friends. But the idea of organizing and cooking for a gathering felt a bit overwhelming. And I had the rest of Sloan's key lime pie event to attend and write up. Besides that, the truth was, I had no idea how long she was staying. In fact, I had mentioned that issue in an exploratory way several times with no response. It would be really rude to keep on pushing. Especially since she wasn't staying at our home. And especially since Nathan had barely visited with his own mother.

"I'd love to have you meet her, but we're playing it by ear. It's too bad she chose to come during what could be the busiest season in Nathan's career."

"Not to worry," said Connie. "Let's see what works out. You'll see when you have a baby that there isn't a lot of planning that goes on anyway." She laughed. "Have a good night."

I returned to reading, remembering that Claudette had gone to the same culinary institute my friend Jennifer Cornell had attended. Was it possible the two had overlapped? Like the pastry chef/owner of Old Town Bakery, Claudette had spent a few years training in France. I wondered now whether she had even changed her name to sound more French.

Miss Gloria wandered out onto the deck where I was sitting with the animals. She was wearing a pink sweat suit with *Why the hell not?* written on it in rhinestone-studded script. "Aren't you chilly?" she asked. "Are you going to change for dinner?"

I glanced at the clock on my phone. I hadn't realized how much time had passed. Our fairy lights were shimmering in the gloaming, and I imagined I could hear the happy sounds of supper being started in the boats nearest us—pans clashing on burners, soup spoons stirring, vegetables sizzling as they hit hot oil. My favorite time of day.

I saved my work and stood up, shaking Evinrude loose from the wrap I'd draped over my legs. "I do need to put on something warmer. On another subject," I said to Miss Gloria, pausing at the door to our houseboat, "what was up with the Santa suit on the dead woman? Was she already wearing it when she was killed? From what our train driver said, it seemed as though that decoration was on the porch every night. Surely someone wasn't lying there pretending to be a drunk Santa each of those nights. There had to be a blow-up doll or some kind of other figurine in the house that she used other nights. And when you think of it, from what little I know about Claudette, I wouldn't have pegged her as a tacky-Christmas-display kind of person."

"You think of things no one else would ever come up with," said Miss Gloria with a snicker.

Mrs. Renhart, our next-door neighbor, hopped off her boat onto the dock carrying her elderly Schnauzer, Schnootie. We called out hello.

She settled the elderly dog on the decking, where he shook himself, almost falling over. "Did you notice that the lamp by our place is out again? It's been winking on and off for days." She pointed at the streetlight, which was dark. "I suppose I should call the office tomorrow. At least tonight I'll be able to sleep without that blasted thing blinking through my blinds."

Miss Gloria waited until she'd passed by and then whispered, "Mark this day on your calendar. She actually saw the bright side of something."

Chapter Thirteen

Some food isn't pretty and does not need to be.
—Kat Kinsman, "In Praise of Ugly Food,"
SeriousEats.com, December 1, 2015

At six forty-five, Miss Gloria and I trotted out to the parking lot and buzzed over to Oasis on my scooter. The food at this place was yummy, with a far-ranging menu focused on homey Mediterranean food. On the other hand, the ambience was not the least bit fancy. Most of the seating was outdoors under umbrellas with Astroturf underfoot. No white tablecloths, no obsequious waiters saying chef suggests this or that—but from what I'd seen of my mother-in-law so far, she simply didn't care enough about eating to be bothered by those details.

I had stopped here yesterday to request a table at the back, a distance from the traffic noise on White Street and the busy takeout business at the bar. A heat lamp was positioned near the table to knock off the chill. My mother, Sam, and Nathan's mother were already seated. Nathan was missing in action as usual.

"Hope we're not late. I was getting a lot of work done and lost track of the time." I kissed my mother on the cheek and waved across the table at the others. "How was your event? I bet you're exhausted."

"It was a wedding luncheon at the Little White House, so we know the ropes," said Sam.

My mother's company had been hired to cater the biggest event of the year last winter—a Havana/Key West conference that took place at the Harry Truman Little White House. Sadly, the event had been derailed by a series of disasters, including a murder. Still, everyone insisted that my mother had handled everything thrown at her with aplomb—and the food had been to die for. Not literally, of course.

"The bride was sweet, the family was lovely, and everyone seemed to appreciate what your mother made. As they should," Sam said, hugging her shoulders, "because every bit of it was delicious."

"I was nervous about this," my mother explained to Nathan's mom, "because a lot of wealthy Key West people were in attendance. And that's how I get my business, word of mouth. Not that the people who aren't wealthy don't deserve delicious food, but you know what I mean. These people have the money to pay for other parties." She looked pained as though she'd suddenly realized she'd stepped in some kind of glop and didn't have a way to shake it off.

I recognized that she was flustered by Nathan's mother, too; it wasn't only me.

Nathan came hurrying in and took his seat next to me. "Sorry," he said with a tight smile and no further explanation.

"Have we ordered? Unfortunately, I have to go back for a couple of hours after we eat to finish up."

"Oh no," I said, pushing a stray lock of hair off his forehead. Nathan only nodded.

Sam waved over the waiter, and we ordered a variety of dishes to share for appetizers. "When you get back," he said to the tall man taking our order, "we'll be ready with the rest of it."

"I love this place," said Miss Gloria, "the problem being there are so many things that I enjoy that it's hard to choose just one. And I do want to save room for dessert."

"Dessert?" Mrs. Bransford asked. Her voice vibrated with disbelief, maybe even horror.

I assumed she was picturing the pie I'd eaten before lunch and the other pieces Miss Gloria and I had tested this afternoon. "Anything but key lime pie," I said with a grin. "They make killer baklava. And I did go to the gym this morning, so I can absorb the extra calories."

"And I am an old lady," said Miss Gloria with an even bigger smile. "Not expected to live forever. So my theory is seize the moment, seize the sugar, seize the love, seize the carbs, seize the cats." She plucked at her sweat shirt with its *Why the hell not?* maxim.

The food came out quickly and we ate falafel, and stuffed grape leaves, and spicy sautéed eggplant, and cold beet soup, and Greek salad, and something resembling spanakopita. I took notes and photos and jotted down snippets of sentences I thought I might use.

"And what did you ladies do today?" Nathan asked.

I deferred to his mother, interested to hear how she would describe our day.

"We met some cats," she said. "Apparently Gloria does not have enough pets in her life."

Miss Gloria laughed. "I'll explain it all to you later," she said, patting my husband's arm.

"Anyway, we also went on a kamikaze tour of Key West bakeries." Mrs. Bransford widened her eyes. "Your wife has an article due soon, so we were obligated to taste key lime pies until we were green in the face."

More laughter.

"Those two went to the shop where the owner was killed," said Miss Gloria. "But I didn't get to hear what anyone said about her. Not that you can trust what people say after someone has been murdered. They're not going to say she got what she deserved. Not in public, anyway."

But I could see Nathan's expression hardening. He looked directly at me. "I hope you weren't investigating. I really hope you weren't."

Ulp. "Claudette Parker and her shop are an important part of the bakery/pastry scene in town right now. Or they were, anyway." I heaved a sigh as that awful porch scene flashed into my mind unbidden. "I couldn't very well skip that stop entirely. My sense was that she was pushing baking to a new level, like throwing a big rock into our small bakery pond." I was babbling, but I really did not want to have a fight with Nathan here at this dinner table. In fact, I despised fighting with him any time at all, but especially in public.

"What's happening in town?" Sam asked Nathan. "With all our catering events this week, it feels like our heads are buried in fish dip and deviled eggs and crudités. Though why everyone insists on crudités when they are always left over—" He shook his head mournfully. "We hate to waste good vegetables. And the conundrum is that guests don't eat many of them, but hosts want to offer them."

"Crazy, as you'd expect," Nathan said. "I am in charge of scheduling security this week," he explained to his mother. "We expect seventy thousand additional people on the island for New Year's Eve, most of them jammed onto Duval Street. I had every hole in our lineup plugged last week with imported talent from Miami. Yesterday, cancellations started pouring in, so I'm reduced to begging our local guys to take double shifts and to negotiating with the sheriff's department, too. You can imagine how well that's going."

"Tell us the truth," said my mother to Nathan's, "did you always know that Nathan would become a police officer? With my Hayley, she was always interested in what was happening in the kitchen. When her grandmother baked, she stood on a stool beside the counter and stirred the batter or decorated cakes. And she used to write little books with recipes and stories in them. Even before she knew how to write, she was pretending she did and drawing pictures of dinner. So her becoming a food critic doesn't surprise me in the least."

"Honestly, I was hoping he'd grow out of it," said Nathan's mother with a rueful smile. "When he was three or four, he insisted on having a uniform. His favorite babysitter sewed it for him. And he would hardly take it off to sleep or bathe. We had to have another one made so we could wash one. He had a little sheriff's star and a belt with a plastic gun in the holster."

By now, instead of looking fondly at her offspring as my mother had when she described me as a child, Mrs. Bransford had a grim set to her mouth.

"His father and grandfather were in the police business, so I suppose it was inevitable. Even though we gave him every kind of lesson you can imagine—art, music, and many sports that of course he excelled at. I kept hoping he'd find another passion. But here we are. Policing in paradise." She added a smile that I imagined was supposed to soften the hard edges of her remarks.

Nathan rolled his eyes. "Can we please move on to another subject?"

"Isn't it funny how our babies become their own little people very early on?" my mother asked.

"Whether we like it or not, I suppose," said Nathan's mother.

Miss Gloria and my mother began coaxing Mrs. Bransford for more stories about Nathan as a boy. "He won't share anything like that, and he claims he doesn't have pictures of himself as a baby," said my mom.

"He was cute," Mrs. Bransford said. "Curly hair, and always those green eyes. And I admit, when he had that little police uniform on, I wanted to eat him up."

I felt the same way about him these days, but I suppressed the impulse to overshare. He'd never forgive me. But I couldn't stop grinning and gave his thigh a little squeeze.

"His father gave him a toy walkie-talkie, and wherever we went, he'd make calls to an imaginary dispatcher describing the problem and stating what kind of backup he needed."

"Nothing has changed at all!" Miss Gloria crowed.

Nathan had flushed red with embarrassment, but I could sense him lightening up and enjoying the teasing too. "It's been such fun being the butt of your jokes, but I have to go back to work." He stood up and leaned over to give me a kiss. "Hopefully, I won't be too late. Mother, I'll see you tomorrow. I'm hoping to have more time to spend with my favorite girls."

Chapter Fourteen

The soup course was a clear lemony broth dotted with parsley and scrolls of spring onion. It filled the air with a sunny fragrance, and I thought the cook was a genius to make such a dish on so dark a day.

—Barbara O'Neal, *The Art of Inheriting Secrets*

As soon as we got out of the car and started down the finger of the dock, I could see that something was wrong at our houseboat. The fairy lights were no longer strung in loops from the rafters—they were hanging down willy-nilly, almost as if a storm had blown through. But the night was clear and Oasis was only a half mile away, so that hadn't happened. One of the large pots of tropical plants on our front deck had been tipped onto its side. There was something smeared on the windows, though we were too far away to tell what it was. My mind skipped to the pets, and I felt a literal body blow as I absorbed the invasion into our space, terrified and furious all at once.

Miss Gloria started to run toward the boat. I ran after her, grabbed her arm, and yelped, "Wait! Don't go down there.

We don't know what's happening in that houseboat. Whoever did this might still be inside."

We returned to the parking lot, holding hands as we passed our boat next door, which was dark, of course, because the electric work was not yet completed. Huddled in the light of the laundry building, I dialed the police. Then I texted Nathan for good measure.

Stay put, he texted back. *Will be there shortly. Do not get on the boat. Get in Miss Gloria's car and lock all the doors.*

We did as he'd told us, pressed close together on the front seat. "Can you text Mrs. Dubisson?" my roommate asked. "I forgot to bring my phone. See if she noticed anyone she didn't know on our dock? But tell her to stay home and lock up until we give the all clear."

"Good idea," I said, and quickly shot her and my friend Connie and our next-door neighbors a message, warning them to stay safely put.

Two police cars with sirens blaring and lights flashing arrived minutes later. We rolled down the windows of the car to introduce ourselves and explain what had happened.

"Wait here while we go take a look," one of the police officers said. They set off down the dock's finger, guns drawn, their flashlights aimed into every dark nook where a bad guy might be waiting.

"I hate that this happened," I said, tapping my fingers furiously on the steering wheel. "There are too many damn people on this island. It's like rats in a cage and people turn mean."

"Maybe it was only kids, party people looking for fun, and things got out of hand," Miss Gloria said. "They probably had one too many beers and didn't mean to cause this damage."

"Maybe," I said, marveling at how she could be gracious and optimistic even under these circumstances. Especially considering that twice since I'd known her, she'd been attacked on this very dock. And seriously hurt. I shook my head, not wanting to think about what might have happened if we'd been at home. On the other hand, maybe the lights and the flickering TV screen and the smell of supper cooking would have deterred them.

Maybe, I thought, it was homeless types, looking for cash or expensive jewelry. Though why they would expect to find such a thing on a modest houseboat was beyond me. More likely it was druggies who had become angry and destructive after finding nothing worth selling. I sure hoped it wasn't something more personal.

I strained to see what was happening—whether I might spot the cats hunkered down safely outside. A faint woof emerged from the boat.

"Ziggy!" Miss Gloria exclaimed. "I hope all the guys are all right."

I grabbed her hand and squeezed. Another police vehicle careened into the parking lot, this time Nathan's SUV. He rapped on our window, holding a hand up as he went running past our car. "Stay where you are," he hollered, drawing his gun as he ran.

We heard a shout from one of the first cops. "All clear!"

I opened the car door and hopped out. Several of the neighbors had begun to gather on the dock just off our boat. Miss Gloria and I joined them.

"What in the world is going on?" asked Connie's husband, Ray.

"You can come in now," Nathan said, emerging from the living room onto our deck. "We'd like you to look around to see if anything is missing. But don't touch."

"We know that much," Miss Gloria said, managing an impish grin.

He turned back to the neighbors. "We'll have some officers checking to be sure there's no one left on this dock who doesn't belong. So remain here for a few minutes? We'll also be touching base to ask a few questions about what you might have seen or heard."

We went into the cabin, stepping carefully over a smattering of broken glass and what looked like ketchup on the kitchen floor. I paused to peer at the junk smeared on the front windows—goopy and creamy and pale yellow.

It resembled the piece of key lime pie I had selected for Miss Gloria from Key West Cakes earlier today. The whipped cream and the key lime filling ran down the glass and pooled on the floor; the plastic container had been cast on the heart-shaped rag rug in the kitchen.

"Maybe you could get a fingerprint from that," I said to Nathan, trying to be brave. "At least I'd already tasted that one."

Nobody laughed.

A little farther into the house, a drawer of silverware and linens outside my bedroom door had been yanked out and dumped on the floor. Clothing had been pulled out of my closet and the bedclothes were rumpled. But as far as I could see, nothing was missing. Even my computer still sat on the small desk in my room. And my grandmother's pearls were there too, tucked into the lingerie drawer.

Miss Gloria yelped and I dashed into her room, Nathan right behind me, and following him two uniformed cops. She was kneeling in front of her closet, where Ziggy quivered in a small brown heap. He leaped out and flung himself into Nathan's arms and began licking his chin, wriggling with the joy of the reunion. Miss Gloria giggled, the policemen laughed, and even Nathan had to smile. Hearing a pair of outraged meows, she hurried down the short hallway to the back deck, where both of the cats were crouched, peering through the screen door. She swung open the door, clucking to them in reassurance. They crept inside.

When we returned to the front deck, Nathan looked at each of us in turn. "Any idea what this is about? Did you see anyone lurking in the parking lot earlier before you left for the restaurant?"

"No and no," I said. "We saw Mrs. Renhart walking Schnootie on our way to the car."

"She noticed the streetlight was out," said Miss Gloria, pointing to the lamppost. "And then she went on down to the parking lot with the dog, and we drove to the restaurant."

"No cars you didn't recognize? People who didn't seem to belong?"

"We weren't paying attention to anything but the time," I said, perching on the edge of a lounge chair. "It was such a busy day." I always felt like I was letting him down when I didn't notice details. I was trying to get better at this, because

I knew it helped with both of our jobs. But busy lives led to busy minds that didn't leave a lot of space to spare for cataloging observations. Especially if you were running late and not expecting trouble.

"I'll be back shortly," he said. "I want to do some checking around. Go ahead and straighten things up as soon as the officer is finished taking photos."

When the young cop left, we began to tackle the mess, replacing the silver and linens in the drawer, straightening the bed, and rehanging my clothing.

"This is such a bummer," Miss Gloria said. "We had everything cleaned up around here. It's never looked so good, right? Ever since Nathan sprung the news that his mother was coming, you've been on a tear."

"True enough." I tried to keep the tremble out of my voice so she wouldn't worry about how rattled I felt. When things were in reasonable order, we took a break and stood out on the deck, watching the cops go door to door. Our little haven, our safety zone, had been breached. I took a seat in the rocking chair, thinking the motion might soothe me.

When Nathan finally returned, his jaw was clenched tight. He looked worried and angry. "Nobody saw anything. Mrs. Renhart thinks maybe someone broke the streetlight on purpose, and the glass around the filament is smashed, so that makes some sense. If someone was planning to break in later, darkness would help." He paused, green eyes boring into me. "This is exactly why I didn't want to marry you."

"Wow." I leaned back in my rocker, feeling as though I'd been socked in the jaw. If I hadn't been so tired and so frightened by the break-in and worn out by pretending I wasn't feeling any of that, I could have made his comment into a joke. Lightened things up. Saved the moment. But I *was* feeling all of that, and I lashed back before I could stop myself.

"So someone trashes our home, and now it's my fault?"

Miss Gloria started. "I bet he didn't mean it that way . . ."

"That's not what I meant at all." Nathan took a big gulp of air and let it out slowly. "When something happens to you and Miss Gloria, I have to consider the possibility that somebody's coming after me, but choosing to get at me through you."

He choked up a little and tapped on his chest with his fist. "You know how much I love you, right? Both of you. And so that thought makes me heartsick." He sank onto a lounge chair, dropping his head in his hands. Then he looked up at me. "I'm sorry, sweetheart. Don't worry, we'll get to the bottom of this. We've got the best minds in the department figuring out what happened. I'm probably overreacting and it was some crazy kids."

But he didn't believe that, I was sure. Nor did they have enough staff to focus on one break-in where nothing was taken. Right in the middle of the New Year's insanity.

Finally the other cops cleared out, leaving a familiar stillness in the air. I collapsed into bed right after Miss Gloria, done in by the busy day and the stress of the night.

"I'll be in soon," Nathan said. "I'm going to take a shower and catch up on some email."

He woke me a little later, jostling to make room between Evinrude and me. I snuggled up against him, glad for his warmth, preparing to drift off. But beside me, his body felt stiff as a board, every muscle knotted.

"You're not going to be able to sleep, are you?" I asked softly, rubbing my hand over his chest.

"Probably not."

"Can I help? Want to talk about it?"

He turned to face me, his lips only inches from mine. "Tell me everywhere you went today. Everyone you talked to. Everything you said."

I sighed a big sigh, but I could see I owed him this. And if it solved the problem of our break-in, it would be well worth an hour of sleep. So I went through each of the pastry stops, detailing as much as I could remember of whom we'd spoken with and what questions we'd asked. And finally I described the trip to the SPCA to check on the orange kitten.

As I talked, I could see nothing that might be tied directly to the destruction on our houseboat.

"Do you know any of those people?" I asked. "Do any of the chefs have a criminal history?"

Nathan shook his head. "Not that I'm aware. I'll have to get the names from you tomorrow and run them through our system—maybe I issued a citation or slapped someone in the Stock Island jail for a drug bust. You never know who's going to react badly to what when the police are involved. And grudges can last a long time."

"Yeah," I said. "Like your officer who scared me to death the other day and slammed me with a ticket. I won't forget that anytime soon. Though I wouldn't trash his house and scare his wife, no matter how upset I was."

"Thank goodness for that," he said, and kissed me on the nose.

He drifted off to sleep finally, and I tried to follow, but the names of the people we'd visited kept circling through my head. Nothing really made sense—we hadn't figured a damn thing out about the murder. On the other hand, apparently we'd stirred up a lot of potential hornets' nests.

Chapter Fifteen

My mother's interest in food was strictly academic.
       —Ruth Reichl, *Save Me the Plums*

When I woke the next morning, feeling a bit logy from the cream and sugar overload of yesterday's pie tastings and sick about the break-in, Nathan had already left for work. And Miss Gloria was off on her morning walk with Ziggy. I zipped through my email and social media postings, and found that Nathan's mother had already sent me a text message. She was up and ready for the day. Waiting for me to let her know when we'd be picking her up. Sigh. I could not figure her out. She didn't seem wild about me, but on the other hand, she wanted to tag along on every stop I made.

My mother had texted too. *Try not to freak out about your mother-in-law,* she'd said. *She knows we're all in the middle of our busy lives, and either she will go along with you on your errands or maybe she will want to sit out on your deck and enjoy the peace and quirkiness of your neighborhood. It's too darn boring for her to stay here in the Truman Annex.*

If they only knew how un-peaceful our houseboat neighborhood truly was.

I took a quick shower, downed a cup of coffee, and drove down the island to my mother's house. The traffic was even worse than yesterday—the closer we got to New Year's Eve, the greater the number of partying guests who wedged themselves onto the island. After nearly flattening a family who had stopped in the middle of Southard Street on their bicycles, helmetless, to take photos of a panicked black hen and her six cheeping chicks, I felt I needed more coffee—hot and high-test this time.

I pulled off the street next to the vegetarian café and dashed across the short alley leading to the Cuban Coffee Queen. I lurched to a halt when I saw the length of the line, starting at the counter and snaking through the picnic tables out to the sidewalk. Most of the people in the line were studying the enormous menus posted outside the open-air seating section and above the counter. Probably first-time holiday visitors. Their turn to order would arrive and they would have a million questions and no idea what they wanted. What are plantains? And what flavor is mojo? What's the difference between café con leche and café cortadito? This would take forever. But my barista friend Eric, who waited on me most days and loved to talk politics, both national and local, spotted me and waved me to the pickup counter on the side near the empanada case.

"I've got you covered," he said.

"You're a lifesaver," I said, blowing him a kiss and dropping five dollars into their tip jar. Within minutes, he handed me a large café con leche. "Thanks a million. If I had to face my mother-in-law without espresso, there's no telling what might happen. Good luck with your day." I tipped my head at the tourists and grinned.

Back on the street, I tucked the coffee into my scooter's cup holder and drove the short distance to my mother's home. Mrs. Bransford was pacing on the back deck, a white mug of coffee in hand, coffee cake and a bowl of cut-up fruit waiting on the table.

"Good morning," she said. "Your mother and Sam have gone to their industrial kitchen to do some prep work for an event tomorrow. But he insisted on making breakfast—they said you can't resist this cake." She gestured at the food, and the second place set beside her. We both sat.

I noticed she had a plate in front of her—she must have already eaten.

"They know me well." I snickered. "This is my great-aunt Alvina's famous recipe. One of my mother's ancestors, of course. All the foodie stuff got passed down from that side of the family. We had to do some tweaking to bring it up to modern standards so today's cooks could understand the directions. As written, it listed things like 'Add milk until the dough runs off the spoon' and 'Bake in a hot oven.' Who the heck knows what those really mean? But it's basically flour, two kinds of sugar, a little cinnamon, a little baking powder, eggs, milk, and a ton of butter." I stopped nattering and grinned.

She didn't appear very interested, maybe already glazing over from too much food information. *Eat, Hayley*, I told myself. *At least you won't say something idiotic while you're chewing.*

Though I'd sworn off fats and sugar this morning, I cut a small piece and loaded the rest of my plate with healthy fruit. I hated for her to think I was a glutton. But after I'd finished the fruit, I was still hungry. She was quiet, watching me eat, and that made me more nervous. What in the world was she thinking? And the moist cake topped with cinnamon-butter-sugar crumbles was irresistible. I cut myself a second piece, this one bigger, and proceeded to chow down.

"How did you sleep?" she finally asked.

I suspected I looked exactly as bleary-eyed as I felt. "Not that well. We had a little problem on the pier after you left us last night." I described the mess made in the houseboat, how frightened we'd been (although I played this down), and Nathan's distress. She didn't say anything, but I could see her jaw tensing as I talked.

"Have they caught the perpetrator?"

I shook my head. "Bottom line, Nathan's worried about the possibility of the break-in being connected to him. His old cases are always popping up in one way or another, or so he says."

"Did he think this was related to the body we found the other night?"

I shook my head. "He didn't say that. But he wants to keep us all safe, so he insisted I stay away from questioning anyone who could in any way be involved with that woman's death. He was very clear about that. And I think he's right to be worried."

"I think he is, too," she said, "but there are some things you don't understand." She uncrossed and recrossed her legs and took a sip of the coffee in front of her. "First of all, please call me Helen."

I felt my face flood with heat, and I began to stammer. "Of course, I'm so sorry, I'm an idiot. I know we should have straightened that out when we first met. I've never had a mother-in-law and I didn't know quite how to handle that."

As my face reddened, I realized I was terrified of this woman. Terrified of not being found good enough for Nathan, and terrified of being frozen out of her family—because that would have an effect on him, wouldn't it? What if Mrs. Bransford—Helen—never cared for me? My own mother had certainly warmed up to Nathan, though to be honest, perhaps she wouldn't have chosen him as my soul mate. She didn't like the police business any more than Nathan's mother did. Too dangerous, too risky, too many terrible things that could happen while he was protecting our little island paradise.

"Please don't worry about it. This all takes a little getting used to, doesn't it?" She pointed to herself and then to me.

I nodded, relieved that we had moved that awkwardness out from the dark recesses and onto the table. Though I still didn't have the nerve to ask how she felt about Nathan's first wife. Or to bring up the fact that she hadn't attended our wedding.

"One thing I've been thinking," Helen said, "we shouldn't get distracted by the Santa costume. One person did this, one person with either a lot of rage in his heart, or nothing in his heart at all."

She rubbed her chin and pushed a piece of pineapple around her dish with her fork. I registered too late that the only thing on her plate aside from the one piece of fruit was the shell of a lone hard-boiled egg. There were no telltale crumbs anywhere. She hadn't eaten any of the coffee cake. I had eaten enough for both of us.

"If we are to have a chance of solving this case," she said, "we should split the possible suspects up. You and Miss Gloria take some and I'll take the others."

"Nathan would kill me. And with good reason. No disrespect," I said, "but he specifically told me to butt out." I sighed. "I don't know if he shared this with you, but Miss Gloria is over eighty. She's lived through two attacks in the past few years. If you could have seen her face last night when we realized someone had broken into the houseboat. Again. She was devastated. And terrified. She acts brave, but it's so frightening to have someone push into your private space. And I couldn't bear it if I thought I had done something to bring this hostility on."

She said nothing, but got up and paced to the edge of the porch.

I glanced around at my mother's deck, the large potted plants, containers bursting with rosemary and basil and mint, the inviting deck chairs with thick striped cushions. Through the foliage shading the house from the Truman Waterfront Park, I could see a sliver of a view of the harbor and the hulking gray metal *USCGC Ingham*, a former Coast Guard ship now a maritime museum. It was a warm day, a little breezy, so the palm trees rustled and sighed. A normal visitor would've happily settled here on a lounge chair with a novel. Apparently not Nathan's mother.

"I don't think you understand," she said, spinning around to face me. "I know what it's like to be married to the law. How badly things can go when a good guy puts bad guys away. Sometimes the good guy is punished for doing the right thing. And that isn't fair to him or especially to his family."

She twisted her hands in front of her. "My son's first wife, Trudy, already suffered by being married to Nathan. I can feel"—she put her hand on her heart—"that you understand my Nathan, how dedicated he is to doing what's right. It's really hard to love someone in this profession." Her eyes were glistening with a few tears. "But would you want it any other way?"

The truth was, I wouldn't. But that didn't mean I thought we should dash around town investigating. Besides, the day was completely packed. Mostly with interviewing people who might have been involved in the murder. Could we do a little of each? But Nathan had made me promise. That promise had to come first.

"The day is booked, and I hate the idea of splitting up. If you want to go along with me and Miss Gloria, we'd love to have you. But I don't wish to try to investigate anything."

She shook her head, ran her fingers over the perfect gray waves of her hair, and sat down again.

"I mentioned last night that Nathan's father and grandfather were both in law enforcement," she said. "So I know more about crimes and criminals than any normal person would want to. I did not want my son to go into this business." She sat up straight and rested both hands on the table. "But he is driven to help the world in this way, and there was simply no diverting him from it. Believe me, I tried."

"He's stubborn," I said, smiling. Boy was he ever.

She nodded. "Even though Nathan's father no longer lives in my home, I still have access to the law enforcement databases he used." Her eyebrows lifted. "There's a good reason the computer experts advise you to change passwords often."

My eyes widened. She was wily in a way I hadn't expected.

"And so I follow Nathan's cases. I am able to track who he puts away, how long their sentences are, and so on. And several of the people he was instrumental in catching and jailing have been released. Bad people. Angry people."

I could feel the coffee cake settle leaden in my gut, freezing me with terror. This was my worst nightmare, loving and marrying Nathan, and then worrying about losing him to an old grudge or vendetta.

"Then we have to talk to him, convince him to take a vacation. Because of his injuries, we never did manage to get a honeymoon," I said, feeling a tiny blossom of hope.

"What are the chances that he would listen to me, or even you, about leaving the island for a while until the danger passes?"

I didn't even have to think about this. This was one of the busiest weeks on the Key West calendar, with tens of thousands of extra visitors jamming the streets and filling bars. He was in charge of a lot. And the break-in felt very personal to him, so he'd be worrying the case like a starving dog with a bone. And he certainly wouldn't go off with me somewhere and leave Miss Gloria behind. Alone. And the idea of taking her along on a honeymoon made me giggle. Preposterous.

"Slim to none," I said, and she gave me a glimmer of a smile. I stood up, pushed my chair in, and gathered up the remnants of our breakfast.

"We won't do anything that might put us in danger, we will simply follow up on the conversations we had yesterday. And then if we learn something new, we will pass it along." She followed me into the kitchen and watched me rinse the plates and stack them in the dishwasher.

"Do you have any theories? Someone specific you're concerned about?" I asked, as I covered the coffee cake with one of my mother's reusable food wraps. "Maybe just let Nathan know—"

She crossed her arms over her chest. "I'm afraid I've already worried you more than I should have."

Had this been my own mother, I would have said, *Really? It's a little too late to be acting coy.* But it wasn't my mother, so I kept quiet.

"I think we should do something besides pinging haplessly around the island asking questions," Mrs. Bransford said.

I must have looked dismayed, because she made a clucking noise with her tongue and waved her fingers.

"It's not that I'm trying to be critical; it's that you wouldn't approach your own work this way." She paused, looking at me. "How would you plan out the research for an article on key lime pie, for example?"

"Well, I'm always listening for recommendations, whether it's restaurants in general or particular dishes or pastries. And when someone says they love something—or hate it, for that matter—I make a note of that. And then when I have enough notes, the theme for an article takes shape."

She was still listening, so I kept talking.

"Sometimes the subjects I pitch to my bosses are merely coincidence or convenience. For example, the other piece I'm writing this week is about casual food. When we heard you were coming unexpectedly, I knew it was going to be hard to make reservations and also that my mother and Sam were extremely busy and so was Nathan, and so am I, for that matter. Since we couldn't plan on cooking elaborate meals, checking out these places made perfect sense."

She looked concerned, and I realized I had stumbled into yet one more idiot remark, this one making her feel unwelcome and burdensome. I ignored my hot face and staggered forward to finish my explanation.

"I also know that lots of families and groups visit our town who might not have the kind of budget for thirty- to fifty-dollar entrées. One of my important mantras in this job is to remember that not everyone has the money to eat out at an expensive restaurant. Or not very often, anyway. So when they go somewhere based on my reviews, I want them to find good food, reliably good food. If the dishes in a restaurant taste great, I report that in our magazine. And if the food isn't very good, I tell that truth, too."

She wasn't fidgeting, so I couldn't help adding a little more about my philosophy of reviewing. "I refuse to be one of those food writers who gets a free meal in exchange for saying everything is terrific when it isn't. Sam Sifton or Pete Wells or Frank Bruni or Ruth Reichl would never say food was delicious if they didn't mean it. And they would certainly never accept free food." I stopped to catch my breath. "Sorry, rant over. In any case, I chose a couple of places for us to eat that I've discovered recently to have reliably good food without costing a bloody fortune. Last night's dinner was one of those."

"That makes sense," Helen said.

"Oh, and one more thing, sometimes my bosses point me in a direction they feel would be popular in the magazine or that people have asked them to cover or that would be controversial in a good way. And the pastry chef was one of those subjects even before she was murdered, and obviously more so now."

Helen watched me wipe down the counters and put the leftover fruit in the fridge, looking thoughtful. "You say she was controversial even before the murder. What would be your theory about her death? This is what my ex-husband always used to wonder aloud." She flashed a wry smile. "He wasn't much good at being married and monogamous, but he was very smart about his work." She glanced over at me, and I wondered for an instant whether she was going to confide in me about what had gone sour in their marriage.

She didn't.

"Who wanted this person dead badly enough to take the chance of committing murder?" she asked. "It's a very, very extreme step with enormous consequences. Would someone have strangled this person because she sold more pie then they did? Pastries, if you want to get technical."

"Well no," I said. "When you put it that way, it sounds ridiculous. But I did get the sense at the opening event yesterday that she was a menace to other businesses. The financial pressure can be enormous if you are producing only one product and half the businesses in Key West are making exactly the same thing. All these shops are vying for tourists' attention, vying for reviews on Yelp and TripAdvisor, vying to be on all the lists."

"What kind of lists?" Helen asked.

"The best dessert in the Florida Keys, best key lime pie in Key West, Hemingway's favorite pie, and so on. As if Hemingway ate pie." I laughed. "If the stories are to be believed, he drank his sugar and calories in alcohol, thank you very much. This all might sound silly, but it's pretty simple: publicity drives sales."

"And Claudette Parker was garnering a lot of attention."

I nodded. "Competition is tough in this town, and to make it harder, businesses have to earn most of their money in the high season. Which starts about now and runs through March. Then the locals can breathe a little sigh of relief, though it definitely means a drop in revenue."

"So it's not inconceivable to think that if Claudette was functioning at the top of the pastry food chain, she could have been a target."

"Maybe. If someone was a little off-balance to begin with."

"And on the other hand," she continued, "maybe she'd been flying under the radar, but this new venture brought her a lot of publicity. And perhaps garnered the attention of someone she'd rather not have tangled with."

I glanced at my watch and shrugged. "Maybe. We don't know enough about her to figure that out. We better get moving if we're going to pick up Miss Gloria and make it to the pie class on time."

Chapter Sixteen

I also ask for a hot chocolate with whipped cream, because
whipped cream can remind you why it's good to be alive.
—Deb Caletti, *The Fortunes of Indigo Skye*

We zipped up to Houseboat Row, where Miss Gloria was waiting in the driver's seat of her big Buick with the engine running. She had the windows open and some kind of rock music pumping out from the radio.

"Want me to drive?" I asked.

"No thanks," she said cheerfully. "I don't want to get rusty. And we don't have far to go, so how much damage can I do?" She cackled as we got in, then craned around to grin at Helen in the back seat, gunned the engine, and lurched out onto Palm Avenue. I gripped the door handle and gritted my teeth, waiting for the sound of blaring horns and the crash of metal. Mercifully, none of that came.

"We've got a lot on the schedule today, don't we?" Miss Gloria asked. "I figure we'll park in the garage on Caroline Street and then walk to the Pie Company, right?"

"Right," I said. "And Helen and I have agreed, we aren't investigating. On the other hand, if some tidbit related to Claudette falls in our laps, we'll gather it up and pass it on to Nathan."

"Remember to think about the person behind the crime," Helen aka my mother-in-law said, leaning forward and grabbing the driver's side headrest. "We're not only collecting recipes, we're understanding a murderer. And his victim."

"Oh, Hayley is unbelievable at that," said Miss Gloria, glancing in the rearview mirror. "She has more friends than anyone I know—and that's because she knows what makes people tick. And even if she doesn't care for somebody, she works at understanding why they're crabby. And the next thing you know, they're friends. I'm certain Nathan's told you how she solved a couple of crimes. Not that he appreciates that one bit."

She chuckled, and I squeezed her arm to thank her for sticking up for me, but then let go fast so she would concentrate on swinging around the curve that led into Eaton Street without taking out cars in the oncoming traffic. She found an open space in the Caroline Street garage, avoided nicking anyone's paint job, and we wended our way through a mob of visitors to the shop on Greene Street.

"Please," I whispered to Miss Gloria, "let me ask the questions?" I didn't dare say the same to Helen, but I hoped I'd made my point clear.

We signed in at the cash register, and Sigrid led us to the back room of the shop with three other students—Lori, Judy, and Louise, friends visiting from New Jersey to celebrate the New Year and escape a week of bitter-cold temperatures. Sigrid gestured for us to stop next to two large sinks.

"No one starts the class without washing up and dressing in our chef's costume," she said, grinning. She described how we should scrub our hands and then don plastic gloves and aprons and finally a hairnet.

"All you ladies look so cute," said Miss Gloria. "You are rocking those hairnets. We need pictures of this."

"Give me your phones," Sigrid said, "and I'll take some pix."

I hardly wanted this outfit broadcast on social media. The net flattened our hair against our heads, and the clear plastic on our hands and torso made us resemble packaged meat. Not a good look for any of us. On the other hand, Palamina would love it if I posted these photos on Instagram and Facebook. Pictures of pie after pie after pie could be broken up with some comic relief. And it might relax the instructor if we behaved like normal students rather than murder inquisitionists. I took off one of the gloves, dug in my back pocket, and handed over my phone.

Miss Gloria clapped her plastic-covered hands together. "I feel like we're Lucy and Ethel in the chocolate shop— remember that episode in *I Love Lucy*? I watch it once a week, along with the video about the cat who sings 'Twinkle, Twinkle, Little Star' with his owner. With the world such a mess, it pays to find things that make you laugh. I'll find it for you when we finish the class," she told the ladies from New Jersey.

Mrs. Bransford looked a little googly-eyed. My roommate could have that effect on people until they got used to her chirpy nature.

We were taken on a brief tour of the rest of the kitchen. In my current frame of mind, I couldn't help noticing that the cooler and the freezer were each large enough to stash a dozen bodies. Sigrid explained the story of how the shop's founder had fallen into some financial difficulties and had the idea of reaching out to the guru of the TV show *The Profit*, Marcus Lemonis. "After profits improved, Lemonis ended up purchasing the company from the original owners," Sigrid said. "Now he insists that we stick to the original recipe—no shortcuts allowed."

Once the tour was completed, we followed her out to the cooking stations, which were separated from the tourists eating ice cream and pie in the seating area by a glass wall.

"I've done some of the mixing ahead of time," Sigrid said. "So we can focus on the fun parts. The graham cracker crust in these pies is not made of actual crackers but rather the ingredients that would make them up, that is, flour, sugar, butter, and honey."

We each dumped a scoop of crumbs into a mini aluminum pie plate and pressed them out evenly with a second pie plate.

"No one wants to see a fingerprint in their pie," Sigrid explained, smiling broadly. "Another secret to our award-winning recipe is whipping cream added to the filling."

She gestured at an enormous mixer that rotated, then helped Miss Gloria pour in evaporated milk and heavy cream and, finally, lime juice. When the filling had thickened, we ladled the mixture into our miniature crusts. Watching my mother-in-law, I suspected she had little experience with even the basics of cooking. Sigrid had made it as easy as possible for our class of students, preparing large quantities of batter and the miniature crusts ahead of time. But even pouring the liquid into a graham cracker crust seemed difficult for Helen. Sigrid came over to help.

"Wasn't that awful about the pastry shop up the street?" Helen asked, once her pie shell was filled. "Did you know Miss Parker well?"

Now I wondered if she'd pretended to be inept so she could query our host. I decided I should never, ever underestimate her.

Sigrid grimaced. "Hardly at all, though I hated to hear that news. She was so young and so talented."

"Have you heard anything about what might have happened? Who might have wished her ill?"

"Nothing like that. But between my shifts here and my son at home, I'm not out and about much either." She crossed over to the far counter and prepared us each a plastic bag with a metal tip, then filled the bags with whipped cream. "Feel free to decorate your pies as you wish," Sigrid said. She grinned, watching Miss Gloria make a smiley face on the pie's surface with her cream.

After we completed our pies, Sigrid took multiple pictures with each person's phone. "You are invited to take your pie with you. Or if you prefer, we can keep it here in the freezer and you can pick it up later."

"If you can spare a fork, I'd like to eat mine now," said Miss Gloria, almost dancing with anticipation.

"Remember we're due for lunch at noon," I said. "Sure you don't want to save it for dessert tonight?" Although who was I to be giving advice about holding back on sweets, especially to an eighty-something woman? She was the one who'd taught me that holding back on anything was a mistake. Because who knew when we might be snatched from this earthly adventure and sent on to the next?

"Or maybe we leave two of them here and taste yours?" I suggested.

"Perfect. The best of both worlds—the appearance of abstinence, followed by gluttony." She folded up her plastic apron and laid the gloves on top, then carried her smiling pie to a table in the shop. She handed us each a plastic fork. I took a bite and closed my eyes to savor the flavors and think of how to describe them. Super-creamy, with a hint of tartness underneath, and finally a welcome crunch of graham. Helen only dipped her fork in the pie and licked the filling off.

"Delicious," she said to Miss Gloria. "Good job." She lowered her voice so the people around us wouldn't listen in. "What was your sense of Sigrid as a possible suspect?"

I paused, looking at Sigrid behind the glass wall, cleaning up after the class. She was chatting and laughing with another worker. The tables around us were filled with tourists drinking coffee and eating slices of pie like ours. This place was very successful, and it felt as if Sigrid was part of that.

"She seems to really love her job," I said. "I don't think the enthusiasm about this company's history was faked. I also didn't get any inkling that this shop was threatened by Claudette Parker."

"I'm guessing not," said Helen. "We certainly didn't get much out of her on the subject of Claudette. As in, nothing. But she isn't the owner of this place. So she probably isn't invested financially. Other than as an employee. And she appears to be performing her duties well. Didn't it sound as though she was fully committed to the Pie Company and excited about its story?"

"Yes," I said. "And if you consider how busy this place is, it's hard to think they have been affected by the new pastry shop. If you compare the pie we made to Claudette's key lime napoleon, they are really not the same product. They wouldn't seem to be in direct competition, because I could imagine different audiences for each of them. These pies are probably purchased for folks who yearn for the magic of Key West, while the other pastry is a gourmet experience, bigger than our island."

"And besides," said Miss Gloria, "she said they shipped those things all over the country. I can't see that happening with the fancy flaky pastry."

I nodded my agreement. "It wouldn't hold up. It would arrive as a soggy mess."

"But this makes me think," said my roommate. "Didn't the pie on our picture window look a lot like this?" She pointed to the dish we were eating. "Why in the world would someone like Sigrid break into our place and smash her own pie?"

I glanced over at the commercial kitchen again, watching Sigrid work and trying to imagine her creeping down our dock in the dark, ransacking our houseboat, and smashing her own brand of pie on the window. "That doesn't make a lot of sense."

Helen nodded her agreement.

"And I couldn't swear it was this exact pie. All I remember for sure is that it wasn't topped with meringue."

Miss Gloria and I finished eating half the pie, and then we wrapped the remainder up to finish after lunch and went outside. Greene Street was even busier than it had been an hour ago, and the sun had broken out fiercely, steaming last night's spilled beer and who knew what else out of the sidewalks. We walked around a tangle of rental bikes that had fallen into a heap of spokes and down two blocks to Fitzpatrick Street and over to the Roof Top Café. As we passed Sloppy Joe's, I heard a bass guitar pumping out of the open doors and noticed all the tables were full.

"You probably won't want to get any closer to that bar than we are right now," Miss Gloria advised. "I took my son there once. It's a young person's game."

Chapter Seventeen

Bake it, share it, and love it. Add the extra eggs, build stiff peaks in her honor, let your pie send sweet music into the world like Anne did, and every time you serve the pie, tell the story of Anne Parker Otto.
— David Sloan, "Robert the Doll's Killer Key Lime Pie," *Keys Weekly*, April 26, 2019

We met Amber upstairs in the Roof Top Café, a beautiful restaurant featuring tall ceilings painted in rustic white, set off by bamboo dividers and hanging plants and ceiling fans over the white-clothed tables. Amber was a young woman with long dark hair and bangs, black liner circling her eyes, and a vivid personality. This served her well for the business she had developed as a "concierge" to all things Key West. From the looks of our primo location in the upstairs dining room—near the porch but not outside in the sun—she had already made friends with the hostess. She greeted my mother-in-law effusively and began to make lunch recommendations. The waitress stood by to take our orders.

Amber set her phone on the table. "Since you are just visiting and probably aren't here that long"—she winked at me, as if perhaps I'd been complaining about my mother-in-law's visit—"I always recommend the taste of Key West. That includes half a Cuban sandwich, two conch fritters, a cup of black bean soup, and everyone's favorite, key lime tart."

Helen groaned. "Please, no key lime desserts. Remember we're going for tea and cookies right after this. And nothing fried. Maybe a salad?" She glanced at her menu. "I'm not really hungry. I'd like the Sunset salad, dressing on the side, and an unsweetened iced tea." She switched her focus from the waitress to the rest of us. "Have you noticed that in a lot of restaurants, even if you ask them to dress a salad lightly, they seem incapable of complying?"

"That's never a problem for me," said Miss Gloria with a laugh. "I will have the Caesar salad with grilled chicken, load on the dressing. And I'll take whatever extra you don't put on hers." She winked at the waitress and pointed to Helen, who laughed. She was beginning to appreciate the conundrum that was Miss Gloria.

After Amber and I placed our orders, the waitress click-clacked across the wooden floor and Amber began to grill my mother-in-law. Where had she come from? Had she ever visited Key West before? What was on her bucket list? Did she need any suggestions?

Helen admitted she'd never been to the island but then turned the questioning back to Amber. "Tell me about your business," she said.

"My newest brainstorm is a brochure featuring establishments that are located just off Duval Street. Lots of people roll off their cruise ships and never get any further than the bars and T-shirt shops on Duval. Which is a terrible shame, since we have so much to offer, don't you think?"

"Amber has a Facebook following you wouldn't believe," explained Miss Gloria. "And every day she has multiple posts about real estate, bars, restaurants, music. Her top fans comment all the time."

"They do," said Amber, grinning broadly. "Miss Gloria could be a top fan if she ever retires. The people who comment the most get a special badge identifying them as such."

"In fact, I bet if you posted a question on your Facebook page about the key lime killing, you would get all kinds of insider information and theories," said Miss Gloria.

"No," I said sharply, almost a bark. "Absolutely not. Please don't do that. Nathan would kill me." All three stared at me as the waitress delivered our drinks.

"That doesn't mean you can't tell *us* what you might have heard," said Helen to Amber. She squeezed a lemon wedge into her tea and stirred the drink with a tall spoon.

Amber swiveled around to look at me. "You were at the library event, weren't you? What a mess. I assume the police will be talking at length to David Sloan. He seemed to have had it in for Miss Parker, don't you think?"

"Well, she didn't follow the rules," I said. "She obviously didn't believe they applied to her."

"Even so, her pastry was exquisite—so gorgeous, and it tasted divine as well. Why be such a beast about the details?

145

Sloan was getting extra attention because she was there, so wouldn't that be to his advantage?" She sipped her Diet Coke. "It doesn't add up to me. There must've been some other conflict between them; that's all I can think of. You might be able to get Paul Redford, her assistant, to talk about it if you bought him a couple of beers."

"How in the world would we set that up?" I asked. "We can't very well plow into his bakery brandishing a six-pack."

"Easy enough," Amber said, flashing a big smile. "Drop by the Green Parrot most evenings and he'll be right there at the bar, unwinding from the day."

"Anyone else that you think we—or the police—should talk to?" Helen asked. "Hayley promised our Nathan that we'd pass on anything we heard. We've just come from our pie lesson at the Key Lime Pie Company, but we couldn't imagine that our teacher would be involved."

"Oh, Sigrid," Amber said. "She wouldn't hurt a fly. She loves her job, and they pay her well, and she has a son, so she needs the work. She wouldn't do anything to endanger her position. I'm sure the cops are already talking with David Sloan, though you wouldn't think a pie in the face would be a good motive for murder. A guy like that has to be able to take a joke. But on the other hand, why was Claudette that angry with him? Makes you think there's more to that story."

She took a bite of the salad the waitress delivered and declared it fantastic. She took a photo and sent it off to her Facebook feed.

"Oh, one more idea—the pastry chef at Blue Heaven. Her name is Barbara Thistle, but she goes by Bee. She's probably been in town the longest of any of the local chefs, and so perhaps she had the most to lose with a new fierce competitor. Imagine, you've been famous for your pie with the towering meringue all these years, and suddenly all these other bakers sweep into town and want to knock you off your mountaintop. I think you could feel resentful," she said, looking thoughtful.

Which honestly I found curious, because it wasn't as if Amber herself had been born and raised here and had generations of conch relations in her history. And yet she had a business that was built on providing insider Key West information. That was the way of the world down here: It was as if each new person who fell in love with the island felt as though they had discovered the whole thing. And knew it more intimately than the rest of the infiltrators. And deserved to revel in its pleasures more, too. Had she experienced the kind of resentment she was hypothesizing as a murder motive?

We spent the remainder of our lunchtime discussing Amber's business and the articles I was supposed to be writing and the frantically busy state of our island. Amber scraped the last bit of lunch off her plate, ate it, and set her fork on her plate. "I hope you don't mind, but I have to rush off," she said. "Especially since no one's having dessert." She winked, put some money on the table, and headed toward the exit.

"That girl has a lot of energy," Miss Gloria said, watching her take the stairs two at a time.

"I'll say," said Helen, as we gathered our belongings and went to pay at the desk. "We should be careful about assuming the death was all about pie—pastry, if you will."

"But what else would it be about?" asked Miss Gloria.

I wasn't going to be the one to tell her what my mother-in-law had explained to me this morning about the law enforcement databases and Nathan being in danger. That was her news if she chose to share it. So I waited.

"I'm thinking about old grudges," Helen said as we started down the stairs to the street.

Miss Gloria nodded slowly. "People do hold on to old slights sometimes, and it can poison them. Somebody feels betrayed and life goes downhill a bit, and they start to blame the other person. It can turn into a death spiral. They could pull themselves out of it, but they're not seeing the way." She scratched her head. "I think you're thinking we shouldn't be afraid to go deeper. We shouldn't skate on the surface of this pie contest."

"Do I hear an echo?" I muttered, hopefully low enough so neither heard.

"So what do you think, jilted lover? Unattainable boyfriend? Embezzled business? Impossible loans come due?" asked Miss Gloria.

"We should listen for the subtext in what people are saying," Helen said, as we walked back to the parking garage. "Not impose preconceived notions on their present words. That Bee person, she deserves a closer look. And certainly David Sloan."

Nathan texted before I could respond to her.

Sorry to miss you this morning. Hope you are having a good day. Any problems at the pier call me instantly.

All is well, made pie and had lunch with Gloria and your mom, I texted back.

He texted right back again. *You are a trooper for entertaining her. I feel like a heel.*

You didn't know she was coming, couldn't be helped. She gets that it's the busiest season of the year.

Going to be super late again tonight. Probably won't be home for dinner until after the New Year. He pasted in a frowning emoji. *I will creep in like a wraith and try not to wake you up.*

A sexy wraith? Go ahead and wake me, I miss you.

I signed off with two hearts and tucked the phone into my jeans pocket. I could feel myself blushing. "That was Nathan. He says hi to everyone and sends his apologies about his absence."

"I wouldn't think that making key lime pie and lunching with ladies would be his thing anyway," his mother said.

With her energy beginning to flag a bit, Miss Gloria allowed me to drive to Olivia Street. I parked a few blocks from the home of the murdered woman, and we strolled along the edge of the cemetery.

"There's really not a lot of room for newcomers in this place," Miss Gloria explained, gesturing at the nearest multi-unit cement crypts. "Some of the family vaults bury people on top of people. Or you can buy a small slot in these condominium crypts. Oh, I could you tell you so many stories."

"She's a guide here; did Nathan tell you that?" I asked Helen. "She is very popular."

"We've had some adventures here, too," said Miss Gloria, "like the time we found a fresh body in an old crypt."

Helen looked horrified.

"That was truly freaky," Miss Gloria continued. "But it was your daughter-in-law who noticed the smell and a little bit of hair that had escaped through cracks in the cement. That was the time we saved Lorenzo."

"Lorenzo?" Helen asked. "Another one of your Key West character friends?"

"Oh, you must meet him and get one of his tarot readings," Miss Gloria said, even though I was madly trying to goggle my eyes and shake my head behind my mother-in-law's back.

Lorenzo read cards every night for tourists on Mallory Square. He was perhaps the most unusual friend I'd ever had, and the most tuned in to the Universe around him, able to notice and read ebbs and flows of energy that most people ignored. He was warm and empathetic. My mother-in-law was tough and pragmatic and probably not a fan of psychics, like her son, my husband. I simply couldn't imagine Helen and Lorenzo together.

When we reached the home of Claudette Parker's neighbor, we paused on the sidewalk. I shivered, and had to assume the others were having flashbacks, as I was, about what we'd seen the other night.

"How did you ever notice that it was a body on the porch and not a blow-up doll?" asked Miss Gloria. "I never did understand that. Though my eyes are not as good as they once were. And I was buried deep in the bushes looking for the kitten."

"Sometimes I get a feeling when things are off," Helen said. "It's hard to describe, but all my sensors were buzzing.

Kind of like if you had a table full of silenced cell phones and they all started vibrating at the same time. That's what it feels like in my brain sometimes."

I paused, staring at her and feeling astonished. Maybe she and Lorenzo were not as far apart as I'd predicted.

At that moment, the neighbor Cheryl came out her screened door onto the porch, with its welcoming wooden rocking chairs. "Hi, ladies."

Helen took the lead. "Good afternoon! Thanks for the invitation to tea. Hopefully you don't mind that I brought the others? We were all here the other night and thought it could help to talk with you."

"Of course not," said Cheryl, holding the door open. "Go straight on through to the back. This way there will be enough laps for all the cats."

And it did seem like a wave of cats met us at the door and followed us down the hallway, winding between our legs.

"Be careful," I said to Miss Gloria. "This is how old people fall and break their hips."

"They trip on cats?" asked Miss Gloria with a snicker. "Last week you told me it was throw rugs."

I had to laugh along with her. "I hope I'm not turning into a nag."

Cheryl brought us out to her back porch and settled us in wicker chairs overlooking her garden. In addition to tropical flowers, the yard contained a little pond with a waterfall, surrounded by beautiful palms. A big tortoiseshell cat sat on the edge, batting at any goldfish that swam too close. Cheryl went back inside and came out with a tray of iced tea and a plate of cookies, a combination of what looked like key lime bars and snickerdoodles. I did not look at my two companions, afraid we'd break into hysterical laughter.

I grabbed a snickerdoodle and nibbled, hoping that Miss Gloria might sacrifice herself and go for the key lime bar. I couldn't count on my mother-in-law, that much was sure. "Oh, my. This is delicious. It has a different flavor in it that I'm not placing."

Cheryl smiled broadly. Every cook and baker loves a compliment. "Chai spice. I worried a little that you would all be on post-Christmas diets and refuse cookies, but the upside of that is more cookies for me. This is the combination I always make to welcome new neighbors—the key lime for island flavor and the snickerdoodle for comfort. Don't you think everyone feels a little lonely and uprooted when they move into a new place?"

"I know Hayley sure did," said Miss Gloria. "But she'd been thrown out—" She caught my horrified look and stopped before blurting out the sordid story of my first Key West boyfriend in front of Helen.

"Of course, I had no idea Claudette was a pastry chef when she moved in and I trotted over with baked goods trying to be a good neighbor. She must have thought I'd lost my marbles—bringing coals to Newcastle." Cheryl patted her lap, and a gray cat with a white tummy and paws jumped up and nudged her hand until she stroked him. With a key lime bar in one hand, Miss Gloria dropped down to the ground to play with the tortoiseshell.

"You know what, though, I bet she really appreciated the gesture," I said, dangling my fingers in front of a third cat, this one an enormous gray tiger with a ragged ear and a missing eye. A warrior. He sat about a foot away, watching me and switching his tail. "Most chefs are so busy cooking for everyone else, and no one thinks to make something for them. You were being friendly."

"Sadly, it seems as though I'll have another new neighbor soon. Have you heard anything more about Claudette's killer?" Cheryl asked. "No one knows much out at the shelter."

"Nothing new," said Helen. "And Key West seems like the kind of community where word travels fast." She chatted a little more about how in Atlanta, no one told anyone anything, probably to put Cheryl at ease.

Cheryl laughed. "Everything you need to know about the insider's Key West is on the Key West locals Facebook page. I've seen lots of theories, but not much in the way of facts."

I made a mental note to scan that page when I finally got home. Although it was a time sink and I tried not to visit often, the page was a good place to get local recommendations and opinions. Unbridled opinions. And notices like what was up if the power went out, and how long we might be in the dark, and who was really evacuating from an impending storm. What we needed from Cheryl was insider information on Claudette the person. Something only a neighbor might know.

"Did you ever learn anything about Claudette's background?" I asked. "Did she have a husband or a boyfriend?"

Cheryl shrugged. "She pretty much worked all the time, trying to get that shop off the ground in time for the high season, though a lot of good that did her.

"I didn't get much of a personal insight into her because of all the late hours. She moved down here from New Jersey, where she worked in a very successful shop. But like so many of us, she got in mind the Key West dream, and she said she saved until she was able to swing it. I don't think the competition fazed her in the least. She was so talented, she just didn't even bother to look around her because she didn't believe anyone could catch up."

Driven, single-minded, talented, a loner. That's what I was hearing so far.

"That's why I was surprised she took on the kitten," Cheryl added. "I didn't think a new kitten was a good match for someone working twenty hours a day. That's why he ended up over at my house half the time." She chirped at the one-eyed tiger. "Even though this guy hated him."

"You will keep me in mind if the other applications fall through, right?" asked Miss Gloria, a sad look on her face.

"Of course. I'll call you the minute I hear."

"Have any relatives come down to take care of her home and her shop, clear out her stuff?" asked Helen.

"Not that I know of," said Cheryl. "And I've been watching, because I brought those cookies over to her on a Gien plate and I sure would like that back." She shook her head. "What was I thinking? After I'd already baked the cookies and figured out who she was, I guess I got caught up in her being a French chef and thought I'd better be fancy in my presentation."

My baloney barometer spiked. Hadn't she just finished telling us that she didn't know Claudette was a baker?

"I wonder if she had a partner in the shop and whether it will keep operating?" Helen put it like a question.

Cheryl didn't answer. Because she didn't know or wouldn't say?

"She poured a lot of money into setting the business up," I said.

"For sure. Not a detail was missed." Cheryl stroked the tuxedo cat, and he began to rumble with a satisfied purr. "All the equipment in the shop is top-of-the-line. And there wasn't any faux–Jimmy Buffett–style wicker furniture in her store, either. I sat in one of those maroon leather club chairs to have a cup of tea. Nicer than anything I own, for sure," she said.

"On the day that Claudette was found on her porch, what time did you get home?" Helen asked.

"I finished my shift at the shelter by five or so and came right here. I am lucky to have off-street parking on the other side of my home." She pointed to the small space between her house and the neighbor on the other side, now filled with a beige sedan. "So I often don't even notice what's happening on that side." Now she pointed to Claudette's little house, which looked abandoned and bereft without any lights to cheer it up, the yard already starting to look spiky and over-grown. "It was dark by six, and maybe I remembered a light in her kitchen? But I couldn't swear to it."

"What about the Christmas display on her porch? Did that surprise you?" I asked.

"We talked about it one time early in December when I saw her putting up the lights. She said she wasn't a fan of

Christmas—too many expectations for happy times with family that were never going to come true. Made me wonder what went wrong with her family. Was her father a drunk who ruined every holiday? Anyway, I wasn't going to ask questions that personal." She chose a key lime bar from the plate of goodies and nibbled around the edges. "This is one of Martha Stewart's recipes, by the way." She brandished the cookie, spraying crumbs on the cat in her lap. "She's another one who definitely knows her desserts. Anyway, Claudette certainly had classy ideas about her shop, so I suppose this choice of decorations didn't match with that."

Which was exactly what I'd been thinking. The Santa thing was downright weird. Now I was super-curious about Claudette's sad family. But Cheryl was beginning to look restless, probably tired of our questions. That didn't stop my mother-in-law.

"So were the Christmas lights on that evening when you got home? Do you remember the real Santa lying on the porch?" she asked.

"Most of my neighbors have their lights on a timer, including her, so I would have to say the lights were on. I came out back to feed my fish." She gestured at the pond. "And so I think I would've noticed if they weren't."

"You know that we spotted her body when we came by on the Conch Tour Train," I said. "I'm kind of surprised that the train brought us down this street. Aren't these tours usually banned from residential areas?"

She laughed. "It's Christmas in Key West. All bets are off. The drivers go anywhere the best lights are displayed. They realize that if they give the tourists a better show, the tips flow."

"I assume you would have mentioned this, but did you see anyone coming or going from Claudette's home that evening?" Helen asked.

I noticed that Miss Gloria had abandoned the cat she was playing with near the pond and was crab-walking over to the crawlspace where she'd found T-Bone the night we'd discovered the body. Not another kitten, I hoped. But even more than that, I hoped she wasn't starting to lose her marbles.

"Come over here a minute," she called to us in a voice tight with excitement. "Cheryl, do you have a flashlight?"

I shrugged and got up to join her, followed by the others. I aimed the flashlight app from my phone under the house, and Cheryl shined a big black flashlight into the back recesses of her crawlspace.

"I should have said something about this the other night," said Miss Gloria, "but I was so focused on luring the kitty out. Maybe I saw this out of the corner of my eye, but I kind of forgot about it." In the beam of the flashlight, something red and white and plastic took shape. "I think it could be the blow-up Santa from Claudette's porch," Miss Gloria added.

"I suppose we'd better leave it there and call the cops," said Cheryl, looking resigned.

Within ten minutes, two police officers arrived, and Miss Gloria explained what she'd seen and why she thought she'd missed it earlier. After patrolling the area around Cheryl's house again, the cops wriggled into the crawlspace, took photos, and retrieved the deflated Santa.

Once we were cleared to go, we thanked Cheryl for the tea and cookies, patted the cats again, and headed to the street. As we reached the sidewalk and started toward Miss Gloria's car, I asked the others the question that had pushed into my head. "Could she possibly have hidden that Santa under her own house?"

"Why would she do such a thing?" Helen asked.

"She killed Claudette and then panicked?" It didn't make a lot of sense.

"Someone who rescues cats and works at the SPCA is not going to be a killer," said Miss Gloria.

My mother-in-law raised her eyebrows. "Even good people who do good things in their lives can be pushed to cliffs of desperation that they never imagined." She bit her lower lip. "But she didn't seem anxious as we talked to her, or even upset about anything much other than having to adjust to another new neighbor, and getting her cookie plate back. If she was really the killer, she wouldn't be that cool. She wasn't anxious about your Santa doll discovery, did you think?"

Miss Gloria shook her head. "Maybe a little annoyed. Whereas I would think she'd be nervous about a killer on the loose in her neighborhood," she said. "I sure would be."

Honestly, I didn't think we'd gleaned anything new, other than adding to our backlog of calories and unanswerable questions. And discovering the blow-up Santa, which was police business now. We loaded into the Buick, and I took the next right and headed back down Truman Avenue toward the

Truman Annex and my mother's home. I pulled up beside the curb and turned to Helen.

"We're meeting for pizza at Clemente's on Fleming Street at six thirty," I said. "Nathan won't be able to make it, but my mom and Sam will bring you."

"Pizza?" she asked, looking a little stunned. "After everything we've had today—pie, cookies, lunch, coffee cake—I don't know how the rest of you don't weigh a million pounds." She wasn't looking directly at me, but she surely meant the question for me.

"We keep moving, and so we need our fuel," said Miss Gloria, pretending to march in place. "Hayley's like a hummingbird, and you wouldn't believe the amount of sugar they consume to keep going." I could always count on her for backup.

Once Helen was out of the car, we motored up the island toward our houseboat. On the short drive home, Miss Gloria's head dropped against the seat, her eyes fluttering. "Time for a cat nap," she said as she got out of the Buick.

She turned to look at me as we approached our deck. "One piece of advice I'd give you is, don't cross your mother-in-law."

"I wouldn't dream of it," I said, laughing.

"And don't try to hide something from her either—she's dogged." She disappeared into her room with Sparky on her heels.

I took Ziggy for a quick walk, freshened up his water, and shook out a few kibbles into his bowl, then stretched out on my bunk for a brief rest. I couldn't stop thinking about all the people we'd spoken with over the long day. In some ways, it seemed ridiculous to imagine killing someone over a pie.

On the other hand, it wasn't only a pie. The financial stakes were high. But who might also have had an emotional stake in getting rid of Claudette Parker? I remembered something Mrs. Bransford—Helen—it was hard to get used to calling her by her first name—had gotten me thinking after we'd visited Au Citron Vert. *Didn't Claudette Parker have a pie she could have entered in David Sloan's contest instead of the napoleon pastry? If so, why didn't she submit it?*

I opened my laptop and rechecked the Facebook page about Sloan's contest. The rules were clear: the contest was not for pastry, it was for pies. The best key lime pie on the island. Period. And Claudette had a pie in her shop that was simply to die for. I walked out to the kitchen, Evinrude following closely behind, remembering that we had stashed one piece of that pie in the fridge only yesterday. It wouldn't hurt to taste it again to confirm my first impression.

Although I had enjoyed and even adored most of the pies I'd tasted over the last few days, this one was killer good. The crust was flaky and light, almost replicating Claudette's napoleon layers. The filling was light and citrusy. And in the whipped cream, still tasting so fresh it might have come from a cow that morning, I identified two flavors—almond and vanilla, my two favorites.

I scrolled over to the Key West locals Facebook page and searched for comments about Claudette's shop. The majority complimented her pastries, but others critiqued her decision to crowd the shops already on Greene Street.

"And where is she getting the dough to fund this place?" a disgruntled local asked. "And why does she have to ruin businesses that have been here for years?"

And that led to a series of remarks about how the world would be better off if people kept their effing opinions to themselves.

If she did have a financial partner in Au Citron Vert, I wondered whether it had been she or the partner who'd insisted on stocking the pie along with her pastry. Had she resisted and insisted on entering the pastry in the contest instead of the pie? A logical person to ask would be Paul Redford. Maybe I could fit a stop at the Green Parrot into my already busy night.

Then my mind wandered back to David Sloan and the pie-throwing incident. Was the anger I witnessed between the two of them confined to the contest? Or had he done something or said something to damage her shop that might explain the pie in the face? Could he possibly be an investor? No, that was a reach—it made no sense. Because why would he ban Claudette's pastry from his contest if it was going to improve the bottom line of the business he had invested in? It would be as if Marcus Lemonis torpedoed the Key Lime Pie Company by refusing to carry their pie in the company's distribution warehouse. A smart businessman just wouldn't do it. And although David Sloan might be a showman and a wild card, he was also very good at business. And all that aside, why would she want him involved in her business?

I went back to bed, Evinrude purring beside me, hoping to drift into my own cat nap. But sleep wouldn't come. Instead

I found myself thinking of Miss Gloria's question: why hadn't Cheryl seemed worried about the possibility of a criminal in their neighborhood? Because I was worried sick about the latest incident at Houseboat Row.

And Nathan. Could what my mother-in-law told me this morning about Nathan, the possibility that someone had him in their sights, relate to the break-in? And could that someone have been in this very room, pulling things out of my drawers, flinging pie on the windows? Had they been looking for something they didn't find? Sending a message? Would I ever feel safe here again? How in the world had Miss Gloria bounced back and moved on from the vicious attacks she'd suffered?

We could fool around all we wanted pretending to solve this horrendous murder, but the truth was, Nathan could be in serious danger. And there was very little I could do about that.

Chapter Eighteen

Baking is for the rule bound, the people who sat up front in cooking class and paid attention, who wrote things down, rather than relying on the feel of a recipe.
—Meredith Mileti, *Aftertaste: A Novel in Five Courses*

M iss Gloria and I found a residential parking space on Simonton Street and threaded through crowds of tourists a few blocks to Clemente's Trolley Pizzeria on Fleming. This was a fairly new restaurant that had operated out of a trolley food truck a few years previous, then moved to the real estate that had been occupied by an establishment boasting nude dancing girls. Limousines used to idle along the block alongside the establishment, and girls in skimpy outfits often loitered on a bench outside the door.

The neighbors had been thrilled when the property turned over and a pizza joint moved in. Inside this tiny space, the owners had built a bar, an enormous pizza oven, and a small seating area with a painted backdrop of an old-time trolley by local artist Rick Worth. We were lucky to grab the last two unoccupied tables and push them together. Shortly after we sat down, my mother, Sam, and Helen bustled through the door. My mother looked a bit bedraggled, and I felt bad that I wasn't able to give them a hand with their jobs this week.

"Where's Captain Wonderful?" Sam asked. We all laughed.

"Nathan texted," I explained, "and he won't be home until late. I told him we'd pack up the leftovers so he'd have something to snack on besides key lime pie when he gets in."

"We certainly won't be up late tonight," my mother said, "but I'm so glad you thought of this place. The idea of eating New Haven–style pizza instead of leftover canapés could not be more appealing. And I certainly wasn't going to cook!"

Sam chuckled and rubbed her back. "Nor would we ask you to."

"That's exactly what I was telling Helen earlier—cooks and chefs love to eat other people's food," I said.

We ordered beer and wine and negotiated our way through the menu, eventually choosing three pizzas, a mushroom-and-pepperoni, the chicken Parmesan special pie, and a vegetarian loaded with things that would be mostly good for us. At least above the crust and underneath the cheese. We also ordered two salads, one arugula and beet, the other Baby's special with garbanzos, blue cheese, and homemade Italian dressing. Unbelievably enough, my mouth watered at the prospect, and even my stomach growled in anticipation.

"Tell us about your day," Sam said to Helen, while we were waiting for the food.

"We learned the secret to a creamy key lime pie; we had lunch with Amber, the doyenne of Key West's Finest; and we had cookies with Claudette Parker's next-door neighbor. And Miss Gloria found the blow-up Santa doll that belonged on Claudette's porch under the neighbor's porch. But don't tell that to Nathan," Helen said.

I swiveled my head quickly to look at her.

She patted my hand briefly. "Don't worry, I know you feel you have to tell him everything. But I don't. He'll hear that soon enough through official channels."

"Did you get any leads on the murder?" my mother asked.

"It's a puzzle," said Miss Gloria. "Claudette dressed in that Santa costume is frankly throwing us for a loop. Maybe it had nothing to do with her death. Maybe she was on her way to a costume party? Or a special Christmas event? And got waylaid by a random intruder?"

"Except that we're past Christmas now and almost to New Year's, and from the way her neighbor described her, she didn't have time for socializing," I said. "But it does make me wonder. Did someone kill her and then dress her up? Or was she dressed up and then got killed? None of it makes a lot of sense."

Sam looked around the little restaurant. "Speaking of costumes, where did the girls go who used to perform here? Do you suppose they're working somewhere else?" He tapped his chin, thinking. "Was Claudette wearing that kind of costume, a sexy Santa?"

I met Miss Gloria's eyes, and we both shook our heads. "I wouldn't say so. Not attractive at all. More like what you'd see at a low-end department store, what a low-budget Santa would wear getting his picture taken with random kids at the mall."

The food arrived and we tucked into dinner. As I ate, I paused to make notes on the pizza toppings and tried to figure out the secret to the Italian dressing. Parmesan cheese definitely, with garlic, onion, and basil. I'd have to experiment with this if life ever slowed down. Once we'd finished dinner and boxed up the remaining pieces of pizza to take home to Nathan, I could see Miss Gloria was drooping, sliding lower in her chair as the evening went on. We hadn't had time for a decent nap, and we'd consumed a week's worth of carbohydrates and sugar and careened around the island like a pool ball that kept missing its pocket.

But I was feeling restless. Though the day had been very busy, snatches of the conversations we'd had kept bursting into my mind like mini-fireworks. The niggling worry that had begun when my mother-in-law told me this morning that someone might be after Nathan was gathering like a thundercloud of dread.

After turning down offers of both chocolate chip and key lime cannolis, then paying the bill, I said, "I feel like I've gotten a second wind. Anyone up for walking over to Mallory Square to see if Lorenzo is still there?"

"I hate to miss Lorenzo, but truthfully," said Miss Gloria with a smile of chagrin, "I am bushed."

"How about if we drop you ladies off?" my mother suggested to my roommate and mother-in-law. "And Hayley can take Gloria's car?"

"I'd like to walk over with you, if you don't mind," said Helen to me.

"Of course, I'd love your company. And you should see Mallory Square in the evening, though it's a little late to experience the madding crowd at this point."

"I've seen plenty of crowds already today," she said. "And more to come, from what you've been telling me."

Once on the sidewalk, I noticed that the Key West Island Bookstore across the street was still open, with a sandwich board outside that read *Bookapalooza—New Year, New Book! Start the new year right with a book by local author David Sloan!* People were spilling out onto the sidewalk holding beers and some kind of green drink, pale and frothy. Many wore New Year's Eve hats and T-shirts, or sparkly headbands with *2020* written in fancy script.

I could see through the open door that the owner, Suzanne, was at the register chatting with a customer. Further in, Sloan sat at a card table with a pile of books and a line of eager customers.

"Isn't that the fellow who's running the pie contest?" Helen asked. "He's the Energizer Bunny. We should stop in," she added, at the same time that I said, "Do you mind if we stop?"

We grinned at each other. "Great minds," I said. "And besides, the owner knows David Sloan and the whole key lime pie scene well, so maybe she's heard something more about Claudette's death."

"How about you chat with him," Helen suggested, "and I'll watch his body language. I'm pretty good at telling when people are lying."

"Sure," I said, widening my eyes. She was full of surprises.

The store was crammed with jolly people drinking and talking loudly. Helen disappeared down the first aisle to observe David Sloan's interactions while pretending to peruse the bookshelves. I waited in line until I reached Sloan, who appeared to be selling books like proverbial hot cakes. I stepped forward to greet him.

"I own all of your books already, but I'd love to buy a copy of the bucket list for my mother-in-law. She's visiting this week and probably hasn't done a single thing that you suggest."

"Of course," he said, pulling a book toward him and scribbling his name on the title page. "Do you want it personalized?"

"Sign it to Helen, please. And maybe say something about how Key West will grow on her?" I lowered my voice to a whisper. "So far, she's not the biggest fan." I suspected Helen would leave her autographed copy behind at my mother's house, but that was okay. I needed a minute to chat with him while he signed.

"Is the contest going on as scheduled tomorrow?" I asked. "How devastating to have one of your contestants murdered."

His face grew serious, his dark eyebrows drawing together. "It's proceeding as planned in spite of that sad ending. You were there, I think, at the library?"

I nodded.

"She was not going to make the cut anyway," he said. "She imagined herself to be so brilliant, and yet you saw how impulsive she was. Real bakers don't run off the rails like that; they follow rules and recipes exactly so the product is always the same. Even though they say any publicity is good publicity, I don't think that goes in this case."

"Were you acquainted with Claudette before the contest? I admit I'm terribly curious about the pie-throwing bit. Why in the world . . . ?" I let my words trail off, hoping he'd fill in the blanks.

He shook his head with disgust, rubbed his goatee with the heel of his palm. "Yeah, that was crazy. I can't say I knew her well. She contacted me eight or ten months ago to talk about the possibility of opening a pastry shop in town. She'd heard that I knew everyone who mattered on the island."

"Which of course, you do."

He smirked. "I told her that her plan was crazy, we are so full of key lime pie in Key West. And it's rising like a king tide—we are up to the lips of our hip waders in lime-scented custard. But she seemed determined. So I chatted with her about what shops were already in town, those specializing in pastry and baked goods. And I also reminded her how every restaurant with a local flair and even some without included key lime pie on the menu. And I told her we had several store-fronts devoted entirely to key lime pie and its spin-offs, so she'd be truly insane to plan something like that. And for her to be looking at a property on Greene Street? Certifiable insanity."

He shook his head solemnly. "This was my direct quote: Even if you think you have your own genius marketing plan, Greene Street is particularly saturated. With the Key Lime Pie Company and Kermit's on the same street . . ." He shook his head again as though wondering how anyone could even think about a venture that dumb. "Obviously she thought I was full of crap."

"So she didn't take any of your advice?" I asked.

"I don't think she actually wanted advice. I think she wanted investors. And I am a lone-wolf kind of guy." He grinned, showing a mouthful of white teeth, and took a sip of his beer. "I also took a stab at reminding her that we already have serious bakers in town. At least two—at Old Town Bakery and Key West Cakes—and the chef at Moondog is pretty spectacular, too. And Cole's Peace does a good job with bread and cookies. I told her she had to have something different to give her an edge. Or else she'd go the way of the sand the city adds to Smathers Beach after a storm—she'd wash out quickly like so many chefs before her."

He pushed the signed book across the table. "I never imagined she'd try to force her way into the contest with that hideous and pretentious mille-feuille."

"You knew nothing about her entry before the event?"

"Nope. Everyone had their pie covered up so they could surprise and wow the audience. I was frankly shocked." He looked over my shoulder at the tourists queuing up behind me. "Don't forget to buy a raffle ticket for the pie drop. And try the key lime martini. They are fabulous." He pointed to a bartender handing out plastic cups of something frothy and pale green. I wasn't surprised to recognize him as Michael Nelson's library assistant. The cost of living was high on this island and shooting higher. Lots of ordinary people worked two or more jobs to survive.

I went to the desk to pay for the book. The bookshop owner, Suzanne, looked slightly frazzled but delighted with the turnout. "He's good for business, isn't he?" I asked with a smile.

"Absolutely. And he's a hoot too. Make sure you try one of David's martinis. Christopher's a wonderful bartender—executes a recipe perfectly." She slid a bookstore bookmark into the book and handed it to me along with the receipt. "David borrows him for events when he's not working a shift at the library. Beware, they do pack a punch. Don't drink these if you're driving your detective somewhere, or likely to get pulled over."

We both laughed, and I wondered briefly if she'd heard about my stop sign incident. I hated to think that story was already making the rounds. I walked over to the man tending the table at the end of the fiction bookshelves. I remembered that he'd been trying to contain the pie-throwing damage after the incident in the library auditorium, along with Michael, the administrator.

He raised his eyebrows and smiled. "Martini?"

"Why not?" I said, thinking this could be another roundup article for *Key Zest* during the high season: key lime–flavored drinks were as hot as key lime pies, it seemed. He mixed Stoli Vanil, Licor 43, and heavy cream in a shaker with ice, shook it, and then poured it into a plastic martini glass rimmed with graham cracker crumbs. I took a sip.

"Wow," I said, as the heat of the booze blazed a path down my throat. "She wasn't kidding—that packs a wallop. It's nice that you can moonlight sometimes. My mother has a catering company, and she's always looking for extra bartending help. Do you have a card?"

As he shook his head, one diamond stud sparkled in his left earlobe. "I'm pretty well booked up even without advertising, so I can't promise availability. The library aside, David has so many events planned for this season that I'll be hopping."

"You were close to the action on Monday at the library." I lowered my voice and glanced over at Sloan, who was charming a pair of tourist women who'd been sunburned to lobster red. "Did you see that pie-throwing business coming? We feel so terrible about what happened to Claudette. She had so much talent. It sounded as though your boss might have felt a little threatened by her."

He threw his head back and laughed. "David's not threatened by anyone. He's a flat-out marketing genius. And not a bad cook, either, and definitely a pie whisperer. There would be no reason for him to feel threatened by her—they operated in different worlds. Refill?"

"Better not," I said. "I'd have to crawl home."

He winked. "You wouldn't be the first."

Chapter Nineteen

A lot of people don't know that the true secret to piecrusts
is that the baker cannot talk to others while making it.
— Maddie Dawson, *Matchmaking for Beginners*

I collected Nathan's mother, and we left the bookstore and walked the half block to Duval. Several police officers were posted at the corner, directing traffic. As New Year's Eve drew closer, the crowds were continuing to mushroom. I wondered again how many revelers this island could absorb.

"We'll cross here to avoid the worst of the chaos and go over on Whitehead to Mallory Square. Stick with me," I told my mother-in-law. I was tempted to take her arm and keep her close as we forded the sea of people. Afraid she might think that was patronizing, however, I didn't.

"Did you learn anything from Sloan?" she asked, when we'd emerged to a less crowded part of the block.

"He really did not like Claudette. He claims he offered her a lot of advice and she appeared to take none of it. Maybe he saw her as competition? Or he felt dismissed?"

"Did he not like her enough to kill her?" she prompted.

I rolled that over in my mind. "Hard to say. He claims she wanted him to invest in her shop. But how much sense does it make to ask your competition to put money into your venture?" I shook my head. "The bookshop owner loves him, though. It's not only that he brings traffic to her store; she seems to genuinely enjoy him."

"Murderers have friends and relatives, too, same as us normal people," said Helen. "Usually these people come equipped with whopping blind spots. You hear them all the time on television after their neighbor or relative commits some horrendous crime. *He was such a quiet boy, so devoted to his mother . . .* and so on."

"In this case, the bartender described Sloan as a marketing genius and a pie whisperer," I said. "While you were watching, did you get the sense he was lying? I'm super-curious about what you'd look for."

Helen shook her head. "I didn't spot anything obvious. He could have been lying, but if so, he hid it well. I watch for things like sweating, blushing, dry mouth, tiny shakes of the head that go the opposite direction to what the person is saying . . . There are a lot of possibilities."

"Uh-huh," I said, wondering how she'd come upon this expertise she was describing. Maybe simply living with cops would be enough to sensitize you. Maybe I'd end up as a lie super-sensor too.

"Another thing has been bothering me. I can't imagine any of these key lime baker people having any connection with a criminal who is after Nathan," I said. "Wouldn't it have to be someone who's recently arrived in Key West, who maybe isn't known to the locals? The only real newcomer to town is Claudette, and she's dead."

"Sometimes people delegate the worst jobs to their hatchet men," said Helen, looking grim.

I wished I hadn't brought the subject back up, because it made me sick to my stomach to worry that deeply about my husband. I forced my mind over to another worry—smaller but more immediate: whether my mother-in-law and Lorenzo would hit it off. Not that it mattered in the long run, but I hoped she wouldn't say something rude about his work, or communicate nonverbally that she thought him a crock.

Every evening, street performers and buskers and bartenders and sellers of Key West T-shirts and jewelry and painted coconuts and other memorabilia set up to welcome tourists for the Sunset Celebration. The schedule of this event followed the path of the sun—so it began earlier in the winter months and started later as the days grew longer. Tonight, the sun had already dropped below the horizon, meaning that most of the celebratory crowd had left the square in search of more drinks and hopefully, for their sakes, dinner. The sky was still tinged with pink and orange, and the streetlights had come on, throwing enough light so we could see that some of the performers were in midshow. We stopped to watch Tobin and his partner, Dave, finish their acrobatics. Both wore distinctive red pants and black slippers. Tobin now stood on his partner's shoulders, juggling fiery wands and keeping up a patter of conversation with the audience.

"He's a terrific athlete," I told Helen. "He often plays tennis in the morning with the gang at Bayview Park."

In the far corner of the square, a collection of homeless types and teenagers had gathered to drink and talk. A whiff of marijuana floated in our direction and one girl's hand-lettered brown cardboard sign told passersby that leftovers were gratefully accepted. I was glad I had given the boxed pizza leftovers to Miss Gloria to carry home, or I would have felt guilty about holding them back.

We found Lorenzo set up near the water, his table covered by a deep-blue cloth and illuminated by a tall golden lamp. He was chatting with Dominique the cat man. His face lit up when he saw me, and he came over to give me a hug. I introduced them both to Nathan's mother.

"This is her first visit to Key West, so I told her she'd want to meet you," I added, winking at Dominique.

Helen was staring at them, taking in first Lorenzo's white shirt, tie, and high-waisted black trousers, then the cat man's yellow-and-black cat knee socks, his baggy knickers, his long curly gray hair.

"He trains his cats to do amazing things, including jumping through fiery hoops," I told her. "We tried working with Evinrude and Sparky, but it's harder than it looks."

"Ees she purrfectly een harmony with the Universe?" Dominique asked in his exaggerated French accent, cackling with laughter and twirling on his tippy-toes. He loved tweaking the edges of a straightlaced customer with his antics. "I'm off to my kitties," he called without waiting for an answer, skipping over the bridge toward his caged cats and their equipment, set up in front of the Margaritaville resort.

"And Lorenzo, of course, is a brilliant reader of tarot cards."

Helen took a half step back from the table.

"Sometimes Lorenzo does a three-card reading for me—if you're not up for the whole thing," I told her. "If you're interested."

She shrugged. I felt a little bad about pushing her into this, but our joint anxiety about Nathan propelled me forward. I could have requested a reading for me, but somehow at this moment I felt like it was her unconscious knowledge and her feelings that he needed to channel. Finally she nodded, and we took the two seats in front of the table.

After he had closed his eyes to meditate for a moment, Lorenzo explained that he would start by asking her to shuffle the deck. When she handed the deck back to him, he divided it into three piles and asked her to choose one. She tapped the pile on her left. He dealt out the top three cards: the three of swords, the moon, and the nine of swords.

He studied the table, then looked at her face. "The three of swords can mean heartache, sadness, and pain—these can be old hurts, hard to heal. And sometimes there is a sense of guilt and remorse. Perhaps you have some regrets. Perhaps someone in your life was missing?"

I glanced at the card again—a heart pierced by three swords.

Helen's face gave nothing away, neither confirmation nor denial.

The second card showed a bright-yellow moon with a grim face staring down at two barking dogs and a lobster crawling from the water. "Sometimes people say this is the classic card representing fear. Because the moon is unknown. And we humans don't know how to interpret shadows in our night—we don't see them that clearly. Things may not seem as they appear. When the moon is out, it's important that you allow your dreams and feelings to guide you."

Again, nothing from Helen. Although none of this so far conflicted with what I knew about her state of worry about my husband, it didn't exactly make things clear, either.

Lorenzo tapped the third card, the nine of swords. On this card, a figure sat up in bed with his hands in his face. Clearly distraught about something.

"You may be having some sleepless nights," Lorenzo said. "Again, it's important to pay attention to your hunches and feelings. But also, get some perspective from outside sources."

Helen pursed her lips together but remained silent.

Lorenzo reached across the table and touched her hand. "Follow your hunches. Sometimes we feel helpless, but when we look back, there were signs pointing to a path that we should have taken, or that might have illuminated the right direction, if only we had chosen to see them."

Finally she said, "I don't believe in cards telling the future. But I do believe in receiving information by tuning in to my intuition."

Lorenzo nodded, his gaze focused deeply on my mother-in-law's face. "In bygone days, women had an evolutionary advantage by sensing danger," he said. "We've moved away from needing to worry about tigers and lions, but that doesn't mean danger isn't lurking. Remember, Hayley?" He switched his attention to me. "When Nathan was in trouble? You knew something terrible was wrong and you didn't ignore it."

"Did you ever read *The Gift of Fear*?" Helen asked suddenly. "The author says when you are in danger, you're filled with a powerful sense of knowing. And if you pay attention, it directs you."

Lorenzo was nodding again. I wasn't sure they were talking about the same thing at all. But there was some overlap, and I was glad they'd found a way to connect. Nathan and Lorenzo had yet to find that kind of comfort together. As we gathered our belongings and left the table, I promised Lorenzo I'd call him for lunch when life slowed down a bit.

I didn't have the guts to ask her how she felt about Lorenzo's words, but with all the talk about danger, figuring out who'd killed Claudette Parker was beginning to feel urgent. "We can swing by the Green Parrot and see if Paul's there, if you have another stop in you?"

Helen nodded her agreement.

"Then you'll be a quick three blocks from Mom and Sam's place. We'll pick up Miss Gloria's car, and I'll run you right over."

We walked along the pier, pausing for a moment to watch Dominique as he packed away his cats and their performance gear. A cluster of tourists stopped to buy his T-shirts, and he greeted them with moves I recognized from a childhood ballet class, a pirouette and grand jeté. Past his display, the harbor in front of the Margaritaville resort was in big-time party mode, the slips full of expensive-looking yachts. Some had parties or dinners raging on their decks in full view of the gawking passersby.

"This scene is light-years from Houseboat Row," I said with a laugh. "That suits us better—funkier and down-to-earth with real people as neighbors. People may envy us because they yearn to live in Key West on the water, but I don't feel as though I'm rubbing my good fortune in their faces the way I would if we lived on a yacht."

"Your tastes are modest," she said, "and I can see how that must appeal to Nathan. Trudy was on the opposite end of the spectrum, expensive and expansive. You should have seen her wedding extravaganza."

I didn't know how I felt about this—hearing about my new husband's marriage to the woman who had taken her place by his side before me. But I tried to remember that she was old news and I was fresh. Nathan barely talked about her, and I'd probably be better off leaving that alone. But on the other hand, I'd only seen Trudy once up close in Nathan's office and once from a distance. She'd struck me as beautiful—stunning, really—and vivacious. And I was still intensely curious about why Nathan had chosen her and then why their marriage had ended.

"What was the wedding like?" I asked, since she'd left an opening I could not resist.

"Eleven bridesmaids in pink ruffles. And a ring bearer and two flower girls. If you can picture all that. She came from a Cuban family in Miami, with many cousins and childhood friends who couldn't be left out without triggering World

War III, or so she told him. So poor Nathan was left to rustle up eleven matching groomsmen."

"He must've been dying," I said. Nathan was not the kind of man to have a group of close men friends. He loved his buddies at the police force, and he had workout friends, but he seemed happy enough to leave all of them behind when he came home.

"There were three bridal showers, and a bachelorette party where all those girls trooped off to Mexico. Trudy could not understand why Nathan didn't want to go to Las Vegas or even some exotic surfing locale with her brothers and his coworkers. He finally folded and hosted a dinner for the male attendants, but only if they promised there wouldn't be any strippers."

I couldn't help a snort of laughter. This sounded so Nathan.

"I suppose that when you're in the police business, people's thoughtless shenanigans seem less funny and entertaining than they might to another man," said Helen. "But he's always been a serious fellow. I should've warned you."

"I figured that out pretty quickly." I felt my lips quirk into a smile. "It's both aggravating and endearing." I paused, then took the plunge. "But you loved Trudy dearly, that's what Nathan suggested."

She smiled, looking a little sad. "We couldn't have been more different. She is effusive and outgoing, and I am reserved and stiff." She held her hand up. "No need to protest; I understand that much about myself. But we grew to love each other underneath all that."

At this point we had arrived at the Green Parrot Bar at the corner of Whitehead and Southard Streets. And the truth was, I was starting to feel a little queasy, happy to get away from Trudy as a topic of conversation. Even though it wasn't a surprise to hear that Helen had loved her former daughter-in-law, and even though I was the one married to Nathan now, not her, I felt insecure enough that the confirmation stung.

Although the Parrot, as the locals called it, loomed large in many tourists' and residents' minds, the bar was anything but fancy. Large wooden shutters opened to the outside, so the sidewalks became part of the party. A U-shaped bar surrounded by barstools took up one half of the interior, and further along there was a stage with rustic seating. A colorful parachute hung from the ceiling. Tonight most of the seats were taken and a bluegrass band played on the stage.

I shouted over the din. "They host a regular parade of great musicians, and on quiet nights they hold bingo games or ukulele concerts. On New Year's Eve, the party will probably stretch all the way across the street." I pointed to the people sitting on a red bench in front of the Courthouse Deli on the other side of Whitehead. "That's probably the only bench in America that has its own Facebook page."

We stood at the edge of the bar watching the scene and looking for Paul. As Amber had predicted, he was sitting at the bar with a bottle of beer in front of him. Though he was wearing a T-shirt with an enormous pink cupcake on it, he looked decidedly glum.

Before I could even decide how to approach him, my mother-in-law was headed his way. I scrambled after her. She tapped him on the shoulder, introduced us, and reminded him that we were big fans of Au Citron Vert and devastated about the loss of Claudette.

"Have you heard any more about who killed her?" Helen asked. "Have they made an arrest?"

He seemed stunned by her straightforward assault, but answered anyway. "Nothing. Most likely the cops are so over-whelmed by the holiday crowds right now that nothing much will be accomplished."

"I attended the library event the other day," I said. "What in the world happened between Claudette and David Sloan? It looked as though that was a shock to you, too."

"Pardon my French, but that man is truly an ass. There was no good reason he couldn't have included her in that competition except for the fact that she would have trounced the old guard. Our pastries are on a higher plane than any-thing else served in Key West. Maybe someone was paying him off to diss her. More likely he was pissed because she had more talent in her pinkie finger than he could hope for in a lifetime." He drained the last of his beer, and Nathan's mother signaled the bartender to bring him another.

"And Claudette had a temper. She was not one to be pushed around. But even I was a little astonished when the pie hit his face." He began to snicker, but then he seemed to remember his boss was dead and his expression returned to somber.

"Is it possible that she had some kind of personal thing going on that had nothing to do with her shop? An angry boyfriend or ex-husband maybe, or girlfriend for that matter, who might have wanted to kill her? Did she seem upset lately?" I asked.

"Wired. She seemed wired. But it's not like I've known her forever. This could be her personality baseline, for all I know. And it's a lot of pressure to get a business up and running, hire all the staff, and train people to do exactly what you want. She was a stickler for details. Over the last two months, she'd already fired five people."

And that brought to mind the recent news stories about disgruntled employees returning to their previous places of employment to express their rage with guns. "Would any one of those people have come after her to retaliate?"

"Really, I have no idea," he said. "I'm sorry, but she was extremely private. I wasn't in her closest confidence."

"What do you think will happen to the shop now? And the people working there?" Helen asked.

"Oh, we've all worked in a million restaurants around this town. We'll land on our feet if the place goes belly-up," he said, waving his hand in air.

"Who owns the shop at this point?" I asked. "We've heard rumors that Claudette had a silent partner in her business."

"I suppose that will be a question for the estate," Paul said, frowning and worrying the label on his beer bottle. "Right now, they're not telling us much of anything. So we'll keep working until we're told otherwise. I've unofficially taken charge of the back of the house, so we're still producing the products."

"By the way," I said, "I bought a piece of the classic key lime pie in your place yesterday. It was so good. Really head and shoulders above a lot of the other pies we've tried this week."

"And we've tried a lot of them," said Helen.

Paul's face lit up. "Thank you."

"Your recipe?" I asked. "And if so, will you share the secret?"

"We can say that I made a major contribution," he said, his smile wide. "But you know how it is, a chef has to keep some things close to his chest in order to get a leg up on the competition. So not sharing right now."

"I understand." I smiled back and high-fived him. Keeping secrets was definitely a chef's prerogative. Especially with this key lime pie contest yet to be completed. With great honor and kudos to be awarded to the winner. And even more important, Paul could very well be unemployed once the dust settled on his boss's murder. He would want to take any special recipe with him.

"Will you be participating in the contest tomorrow?" I asked.

"I think so—not with her pastry, though. I wrote Sloan an email saying we'd love to be allowed to compete with our classic pie. Hard to say whether he'll dismiss me because of my connection to her." He turned away from us, so I tugged on Helen's sleeve. Time to go—he was clearly tired of our questions.

"What did you think of him?" asked Helen as we made our way back up Southard Street to find the car.

"He's intense," I said, glancing at her face to see if she was testing me or whether she really wanted my opinion. "He cares very deeply about what he's doing, and also about his pie and his work. He's testy, but maybe not a murderer?"

"Maybe," she said. "But on the other hand, her death seems to have benefited him greatly. He's the head honcho now. He's in a position where he can spotlight his own recipes. Personally, I wouldn't rule him out. And he seemed uncomfortable talking with us, which would make sense if he had something to hide."

"I see your point," I said, feeling as though my observation skills had been found lacking.

"So what did you decide to write for your piece? Where's the best lime pie in town?" she asked.

I dodged a group of kids gathered in front of Charlie Mac's and sighed. "It's like the Wizard of Oz. It doesn't exist."

"You've spent all week eating and visiting pastry shops; you surely can't get away with saying that in your article," she said.

"But it's true. There is no best. It all depends on what your taste is. If you like a super-creamy pie, you're going to like what we made at the Key Lime Pie Company. As you saw, they add extra whipping cream to their toppings. If you like meringue with a twist, try Moondog. I think that was your favorite, right? If you like flashy meringue, then you want to eat Bee's pie at Blue Heaven. And so on. A true pastry chef's pie might be found at Key West Cakes or Old Town Bakery.

"That's why this question is really a big publicity stunt. Newspapers and magazines and websites like it because we need something to write about, and if there isn't something real, we might have to make it up."

"Who would do this kind of job?" she asked, stepping off the curb into the street to avoid what appeared to be a bachelor party in full party mode. The men wore T-shirts with tuxedoes silk-screened onto them and carried tall beers. "Pastry chef, I mean."

"People who need money, of course," I said with a smirk. "To be serious, though, I see it as a calling."

"But you're basically making something that is bad for the people who buy it. Heart attacks. Diabetes. Obesity. Dental problems. It all comes down to fat and sugar, and both of those are a huge problem in this country," she said.

This didn't feel right to me—in fact, it was antithetical to everything I believed. It would be hard to argue her point, but I couldn't pretend I agreed. "I don't see it that way. Of course, I realize that Americans are too fat and couch-bound; I read that everywhere. But I believe obesity has more to do with fast food and sugary soda pop than pastry chefs. I see baking things as a gift for the people who are going to eat them. Especially if they're made at home, especially from scratch—like Cheryl's cookies. Those were a gift of love." I grinned. "Even the key lime squares, despite the fact that key lime anything was the last thing we wanted."

We arrived at the car, and I drove the few blocks to drop her off at my mother's house. "I need to work in the morning, but Nathan or I will be in touch to make plans." I tried to look friendly and warm, but my smile felt a little tight.

I drove home, feeling uncomfortable, as though I'd been exposed as beneath Mrs. Bransford's standards. I wondered what her first daughter-in-law had done for a living. What was she passionate about, aside from Nathan? I could tell from dating and now living with Nathan that he was not a big food person, not like me and my mother. He ate to live, whereas we lived to eat. Miss Gloria fell somewhere in the middle, although secretly I felt this had to do with her lack of skills in the kitchen. The few times she had insisted on cooking for me, the results had been dreadful. She had told me her husband had done most of the cooking over the course of their long and happy marriage, and I believed that was from a sense of self-preservation.

It would be hard to worm my way into the graces and heart of a mother-in-law who didn't care what she ate. And eschewed sugar. She was tall and willowy and clearly didn't consume one ounce more than what her body called for. Ectomorph to my endo.

Waiting at the traffic light by St. Mary's, I thought more about Nathan and his relationship with food. Our first date several years ago had been for a meal at Michael's restaurant. He stood me up because there had been a terrible incident with a hanging at the harbor. None of that was his fault or really representative of his feelings about eating, but all the same . . . was it a premonition of things to come?

I pulled into the parking lot by our pier, got out, and locked the doors. Then I crept up the finger in the dark, watching for unfamiliar shadows and listening for noises that weren't familiar either. A muffled *woof* came from Mrs. Renhart's boat, with an answering *woof, woof* from ours that had to be Nathan's little dog. I wondered if Miss Gloria had thought to take him out before she hit the hay. She probably had, knowing her, but if he was left loose in the living area, I'd take him again anyway.

Our fairy lights still hung willy-nilly from the rafters. I would straighten them in the morning before I went to work. Maybe if our place looked normal, that would help us all feel less anxious. Was there anything worse than feeling frightened about going into your own home? I didn't think so.

All three animals were waiting for me on the living room couch, so I hugged and kissed each of them in turn and distributed treats. "I missed you guys," I told them. I grabbed Ziggy's leash from the hook beside the door, and he began to circle around with excitement.

"Just a quick one," I told him.

Coming home was reminding me that all my regular activities were out of whack. I was barely cooking, I had only been to the gym once this week, and Ziggy and I had not gone to the dog park to exercise with Eric and his dogs.

"Next week, buddy, I promise things will be back to normal."

But thinking of Eric reminded me that I was committed to helping him with the Cooking With Love event at the Metropolitan Community Church on Saturday. If Nathan's mother was still in town—I couldn't keep a small sigh from escaping— I'd recruit her to go with me. Not that I thought she'd be a big help in the kitchen, but at least we'd be spending some time together. And Eric, being a psychologist and a generally gentle and easy soul, would surely make a connection with her. It wasn't that I didn't like her, but the constant sense that I was dog-paddling to win her approval was exhausting.

On the way into my room, I noticed that Miss Gloria had left a note on the counter: *We forgot to pick up our homemade pies from Sigrid. Could you possibly do that tomorrow? I have a walk scheduled with the old ladies (ha, more like a death march!) and then a shift at the cemetery.* Signed with lots of *x*'s and *o*'s.

Lying in bed, my head spinning even though my body was weak with exhaustion, I couldn't help thinking about the people we'd met over the day from the pastry world. I needed to make notes and send them to Nathan. But not tonight. The sound of a swish announced a text arriving on my phone. A long one. From my mother-in-law.

One more thing I meant to say. Your mother told me about how your premonition saved Nathan from almost sure death. I thank you for that. It's so, so important to pay attention to those messages. I've honed mine over the years. I came down because they are tingling like crazy.

Wow, who would have guessed that this tough, straight-laced woman would end up having that much in common with Lorenzo? I was glad I'd taken her over to meet him. I didn't dare tell Nathan what his mother had revealed—that she was worried about an enemy coming after him. Telling her secret was not my job.

And yet keeping a secret felt just as wrong.

I wondered if I'd ever sleep.

Chapter Twenty

I never wrote a negative review without worrying about closed restaurants, lost jobs, and fired chefs; there was no joy in thinking about the harm my words could cause.
—Ruth Reichl, *Save Me the Plums*

It barely registered when Nathan slid into bed with me and the cat. The clock on my side read one AM. And he was gone again before six. I forced myself up shortly after I heard him leave, played with the cats, and made a quick breakfast, enough for Miss Gloria to eat too when she returned from her walk. Considering the sweets we'd been gobbling and the influx of pizza last night, I concentrated on protein—hard-boiled eggs with a side of crispy bacon—and a bowl of fruit. I dressed in jeans and my favorite red sneakers and a cheerful pink swing blouse, then headed to the office on my scooter.

For two hours, I worked without interruption on the articles that were due by noon. I had decided to use my conversation with Nathan's mom as the lede in my key lime pie story: Where and how does one find the best slice of pie in Key

West? It depended, of course, on individual taste and preference, but asking the very question could lead a visitor on a wonderful tour of the island.

When that piece was polished, I started to work on the short sidebar article about quick bites that would provide delicious food for all ages without breaking the bank. I'd already made notes on our dinners at Oasis and Clemente's, so it was not hard to put this together. Finished earlier than I'd expected, I decided to make a brief visit to the library to talk with Michael, followed by a stop at Blue Heaven restaurant. With any luck, I could catch their pastry chef, Bee, and ask her a few questions for my article's context. And while I was there, nose around about what she might have heard about Claudette.

I crossed over on Bahama Street to Fleming, and then up a block to the pink stucco library. I climbed the steps, passing several weathered men smoking and subtly asking for change. Christopher, the fellow who'd made martinis last night at Sloan's book event, was manning the front desk, sorting through a pile of returned books and movies.

"You're a busy guy," I said. "From martinis to the Dewey Decimal System in less than twelve hours."

"A man of all seasons," he agreed, matching my smile. "Can I help you?"

"Is Michael Nelson in? I'm following up on a few questions about the pie event held here the other day."

"Let me see if he's available." He disappeared into the back room and returned with the librarian, who had his short dark hair gelled into an impish peak and wore a set of Bluetooth earphones around his neck. He gestured for me to come around to the side of the front desk in order not to block the trickle of patrons who'd followed me in.

"Good morning," I said. "I'm finishing up my article about Sloan's pie contest this afternoon—still trying to figure out the incident with David Sloan and Claudette Parker. I hoped you might have gleaned some insight into what happened between those characters, since you were the host."

"*Characters* is the right word," he said, making a face. "I might have suspected that Sloan set the whole thing up as a publicity stunt had it not been for Ms. Parker's death. That makes the memory of the day so much more ominous."

I nodded my agreement. When I pictured Sloan's face covered in pie, what came to mind was his shock and fury. From that angry reaction, I would never have guessed he'd *planned* to be covered in whipped cream, no matter how many Facebook posts ensued.

"How well did you know the other contenders? Or did you delegate those kinds of details to your staff?"

Michael looked puzzled, probably wondering—and with good reason—what this had to do with a food critic's assessment of pie. "We're a little short-staffed because of holidays and vacation, so I made the contacts myself. And Christopher's been pitching in when he can." He tipped his head at the man helping patrons check out books. "What exactly are you looking for?"

"Personalities, backgrounds of the chefs, something to help me and the readers understand the undercurrents of the pastry scene in town. There must be something dark underneath the surface, right? Or the day wouldn't have ended the way it did."

He adjusted his earphones and squinted. "Not one of the chefs behaved like a diva. They all seemed pleased to participate, if a little stressed by the holiday week timing. Claudette was clearly the most high-strung, as though maybe she felt she had the most riding on the outcome."

"Which being new to the island, she probably did," I said.

Michael straightened the stack of papers on the desk while he thought this over. "And she was the only one who had her assistant hovering around while she barked orders. The rest of them came solo. But I would have said that was her wanting to make a perfect presentation rather than lord something over her staff."

"What about Sloan himself?"

"He's harmless enough," said Michael, "in spite of the big mess he made. Although ultimately I hold him responsible for what happened at the event. A less contentious, flamboyant person might have been able to calm Claudette down, but Sloan fanned the flames. At least he was apologetic and offered to stay and help clean up, even though he was obviously steaming. And he can write well enough, actually very well, when he bothers. I would say he has a personality the opposite of Claudette Parker's. She was absolutely detail oriented and meticulous and fastidious. Sloan? Fast and furious."

I lowered my voice. "Do you think it's possible he killed her?"

He cocked his head and made a face, as if to say, *Really?* I waited him out.

"Possible, maybe. Probable, maybe not. He was pissed about the pie, but at some level, I think he might have appreciated the emotional intensity of her gesture. Even if it made him very angry. He appreciates a big show."

I murmured, hoping to encourage him to keep talking.

"From my perspective," he said, "it would make more sense if she had killed David Sloan. She despised the clownish nature of the contest, from what I saw. She thought he had no class. You know the publicity stunt he did several years back for national television?"

I nodded, remembering that the weather person from one of the major networks had visited the island several years earlier. Sloan was chosen as one of the local celebrities to meet her—and he presented the biggest key lime pie in the world on air. Who knew if that *biggest in the world* claim was true, but it was said to feed a thousand visitors.

"He performs the same stunt every summer for the Key Lime Festival, and I think he even made a supersized pie in Boston. Anyway, Claudette and I were chatting before the event. She seemed a bit perplexed about Sloan's background, so I described a few of his antics, including the oversized pie. She made it very clear that she thought a pie that big was grotesque, and quite possibly dangerous to anyone who ate it. Because where was a refrigerator large enough to keep it cool?" He twirled his headphone wire around one finger. "She was going along with the events he set up because she wanted the publicity for her shop, but she didn't consider him a professional."

I nodded vigorously. "They weren't exactly competing on the same field. He loves flashy stunts and events, and she,

I think, was focused on her elegant products." I tried pressing him again to give an opinion about the murder. "Do you think her disdain hit its mark with him—could it have bothered him enough that he wished her harm?" I wondered.

Michael had begun to fidget. "I didn't know either of them well enough to weigh in on that."

I attempted one last query. "Think about it, killing someone in a public way and leaving her splayed in a Santa costume was not a subtle way of getting rid of her."

"David Sloan is not a subtle person," he said. "And that's all I can say on that matter."

I tried to thank him for his time, but he vanished before I could get the words out. Christopher came over to the side counter, his face serious. "Michael won't say it in public or for the record, but we all think Sloan killed her. Probably not intentionally, but you were there—we all saw the rage on his face." He shrugged. "Personally, I like the guy. And I certainly like what he pays me on the side. But he's a loose cannon and might well have done something in the moment that he regretted later. She could have invited him to her home and then made him so angry . . ." He mimed a strangling motion with two hands on his own throat.

"Angry about what?"

A new patron approached the desk, asking for assistance in finding Florida writers from Hemingway's days. "His lack of professionalism? His ridiculous contest? His cookbook? Too many possibilities to even list." He tipped his head at the patron. "Sorry not to be more helpful."

"You were helpful, thanks." And yikes, I thought.

I waved to Christopher and headed outside into the creeping humidity and warmth of the day. If Sloan was the killer, he had ice in his veins. I simply couldn't imagine strangling someone to death and then proceeding with a martini-laced book signing and other key lime events as if none of that had happened.

Chapter
Twenty-One

Blackberry jam: tart, dense, and passive aggressive, something you might spread on toast like gelatinous fury early in the morning while tears pour down your face as you imagine all the seedy things he's done.
—Jennifer Gold, *The Ingredients of Us*

Traffic was beginning to pick up on Fleming Street, probably visitors who'd overslept after a late night and were now looking for the libation-laced lunch that would relieve their hangovers. I collected my scooter, determined to squeeze in one more stop before picking up the pies from Sigrid as Miss Gloria had requested. This time I'd nip into Blue Heaven to see if I could chat with their pastry chef, Bee. She'd been around town a long time and might have some insights about David Sloan different from those I'd heard at the library. Or maybe her impressions would confirm them.

Blue Heaven was located at the edge of the neighborhood referred to as Bahama Village, where natives of Bahamian heritage clustered. The restaurant had a lot of history, including claims of being a former brothel, not to mention the home to boxing matches refereed by Ernest Hemingway. Most of the dining room was set up in an enclosed plaza, with a fresh-air bar, a stage to host live music, and chickens famously pecking at diners' feet. I'd never seen the restaurant without a crowd of visitors waiting to be seated—whether for breakfast, lunch, or dinner.

I was in luck—Bee was taking a break outside the kitchen door, enjoying a splash of sunlight, smoking a cigarette, and watching her bit of the world go by. She was dressed in a colorful patchwork skirt that fell almost to the floor, a sleeveless orange T-shirt that showed her pastry-kneading muscles, and a white apron spattered with evidence of her morning's work. She wore a handful of beaded necklaces around her neck and had her hair tied back with a faded blue bandanna. She jerked up when I spoke her name and blew out a ring of smoke, her eyebrows raised. "Yes?"

As she didn't seem to recognize me—and why would she?—I introduced myself again. "I'm working on a big feature for *Key Zest* magazine about the key lime event this week. And I'm also writing a piece about the individual pies that I've been tasting. Yours, by the way, is delicious."

She nodded her thanks.

"Do you have any idea about what went on behind the scenes between David Sloan and Claudette Parker? I'd love to understand the psychology behind that pie-in-the-face moment."

I realized as soon as the words were out of my mouth and saw the blood draining from her face that they did not follow from what I claimed I was working on. She'd have to think I was a nosy parker, or maybe worse, an undercover police officer. Neither of which would encourage her to talk freely. "Whatever undercurrents existed between them can't help but be part of my story," I hurried to explain. "The smashed pie is on everyone's mind. I've seen it all over Facebook and Instagram."

She squinted, then shook her head. "I was as shocked as anyone else when she hit that bozo in the kisser with the pie." She snickered, tapped the ash off with her pointer finger, and then dropped the butt and ground the remains into the sidewalk. "I have to admit, I was glad she didn't choose mine. I suppose Sigrid's pie made more of a mess, if Claudette was thinking that far ahead. That extra creaminess, you know?" She snickered.

"Had you met her before the event last week?"

"Only by reputation. I kept meaning to go over and buy a few of her pastries and see what all the fuss was about. But we are so busy here this time of year. And honestly, once you've made a thousand key lime pies in a day—for years—the idea of eating someone else's version is not that appealing."

"Claudette arrived brand-new on the island this past fall, right? Do you have any idea how she recruited her workers?"

Bee fingered the packet of cigarettes in her apron pocket, finally extracting another and lighting it up. "She poached a few, of course. One of my assistants gave notice unexpectedly, and I'm pretty sure that's where she went. But that's okay. People move around to different restaurants all the time, hoping to move up the ladder. Or maybe they just need a new experience. Or some new energy. The kitchen can be an intense place with big personalities jammed into a small, hot space. People get on each other's nerves."

She sighed as if she was finished explaining, but I waited her out, hoping she'd say a bit more.

"This is hard work, and we're taught from the beginning that cooking and baking aren't meant to be about how we feel. How our customers will feel as they eat must always come first. But sometimes the stress and frustration of the job gathers bigger and bigger. And that's when you might see a person blow up"—she threw out her arms—"and stalk out." She shrugged. "Time for a new job." She inhaled deeply and then blew out a cloud of smoke.

"What about her number-two guy, Paul? Where did he work before she hired him?"

She squinted and scuffed the sidewalk with one worn clog. "I think he's worked just about everywhere on the island—everywhere where they have pastry on the dessert menu. He's very talented, but also super-ambitious. So he has little patience when he feels he isn't being appreciated."

This was getting interesting. Because by all appearances, Claudette Parker had not completely appreciated him. At least not enough to feature his key lime pie in her bakery case. But good gravy, would you kill someone just because they weren't gaga over your pie? He'd been working for her only a few months, and it seemed to me he ought to have given the process some time.

I smiled at Bee. "You'll be at the finale of the key lime event this afternoon at the lighthouse?"

"Wouldn't miss it."

"I guess the owner of your restaurant must be on board for the contest? It would be hard to compete and give up work hours during such a busy time if you didn't have support from above."

"He's all for it."

Her sentences were getting short and snippy, but I had a few more questions. The more restless she appeared, the more I wanted to know. I kept thinking about my mother-in-law's revelation about how she could tell if someone was lying. Bee seemed so uncomfortable, as if she'd much rather not be talking to me at all. About what? was the question. Murder?

"Were you the original architect of the mile-high meringue?"

"Who remembers back that far? For all I know, it might've been Hemingway himself who made the first pie with mile-high meringue." She dropped her cigarette, ground it out, and then picked up both of the butts and slid them into her apron pocket.

"And you're happy with staying on here?"

She narrowed her eyes, looking me over as though I might be a spy. "Very happy."

But there was no joy in her voice.

"I'll see you this afternoon," I said. "Wishing you and your pie all the best in the contest."

She thanked me and disappeared into the kitchen.

Was she bored with baking the same things over and over? I wondered. At least in my job, there were no repeats, no reruns—at least not yet. If I stayed in the same job for years, I'd probably run out of new restaurants to review. But at least

I wasn't making an actual physical object for each customer at *Key Zest*. Somehow my work felt a bit less personal.

Or was fidgeting a sign of something more ominous, such as a very guilty conscience?

As I returned to the rack for my bike, Miss Gloria texted. *Don't forget to pick up the pie. And Helen is here. She wants to ride shotgun for the afternoon if that's acceptable.*

Sheesh. My mother-in-law had turned into the original eager beaver. I texted back a double thumbs-up and buzzed across the town to Greene Street again. Thank goodness I didn't have a car to park, because there was not a space open anywhere. The din of partying visitors had gotten louder since yesterday. And music blared out of most of the doors I passed.

As it had been yesterday, the Key Lime Pie Company was jammed with visitors. I waited in line to pick up the pies we'd made the day before, wishing I hadn't made this promise to Miss Gloria. Finally I reached the counter, where Sigrid recognized me immediately. She went to the huge freezer and returned with the two little pies.

"Any news on Claudette Parker's murder?"

"Sadly, no," I said.

"I was thinking about this after the lesson yesterday," she said slowly. "Remember what I told you about Marcus Lemonis investing in this place?"

I nodded.

"There were a lot of rumors circulating when Claudette was renovating and opening her place. You've visited the shop, right?"

I nodded again. "It's gorgeous. All top-of-the-line."

"A couple of weeks ago, I stopped over when it wasn't so crazy busy in this town. I was going to welcome her to Greene Street." She grinned. "Of course, I took her one of our pies. She'd stepped out to the bank, but her assistant Paul showed me around the kitchen. From a few of the things he said, I got the impression that he'd invested some money, maybe before she hired him."

"Did he have complaints about how her kitchen was outfitted?"

"From the way he talked, I gathered that there was stress between the two of them. Maybe he thought she was spending too much at the outset? He mumbled something about how at least we listened to our investors. He's apparently an excellent baker himself, but there was only room for one name on that marquee. Hers."

She pushed the pies across the counter. "Anyway, after I thought it over, I figured you should know."

Chapter
Twenty-Two

*His voice, as one fan wrote in a YouTube comment,
sounds like what melted chocolate tastes like.*
—Maureen Dowd, "Tom Ford, Fragrant Vegan
Vampire," *The New York Times*, April 20, 2019

With the pies safely bundled into my basket, I zipped
across the back roads to Houseboat Row. Miss Gloria
and Helen and our three animals were waiting for me on the
porch. I went inside, tucked the pies into a tiny space in the
refrigerator, and returned to the deck.

"Everybody ready? I guess we better take the car." It
wouldn't be easy to find parking near the lighthouse where
the pie finale was to be held, but I could probably find something closer to Bahama Village.

"I'm waiting for a call from Cheryl," said Miss Gloria.
"The first applicant on the list for the orange kitty backed
out, and now they're making home visits in order to choose
the best situation." She thrummed her fingers anxiously on
the small table beside her lounger. "I've scooped the litter

box and washed the cat bowls and put out that fluffy bed and the scratching tower and the toys that our guys ignore. I'm trying to make it look like a fun and happy place for a new kitten. There's not much else I can do to make it look appealing." She looked as though she was near tears. "I feel like that kitty is destined for me, but it's out of my hands. Anyway, you two go ahead on the scooter. If she gets here in the next hour or so, I'll take an Uber to the lighthouse."

I couldn't think of a darn thing to say to ease her nerves or give her comfort. We already had a lot of animals living in a small space, and there wasn't anything to be done about that. Other than explain to the people making the decision that Nathan and I would be moving soon, taking two of the furry guys with us. We hoped. I couldn't imagine there would be a pet lover anywhere on the keys who would dote more on this kitten, or provide more fun, than Miss Gloria. But she was right, it was out of our hands.

"She'll see when she gets here that you would provide an amazing home," I said. Then, to distract her, I described what I had learned from talking with the library staff, the Blue Heaven pastry chef, and Sigrid at the key lime pie factory. "Bottom line? We need to keep a close eye on both Paul Redford and David Sloan. And Bee Thistle, too. Those are the names that keep coming up."

"Got it," said Helen, fastening her bike helmet into place over her perfect hair. "Ready for action."

* * *

Key West lore has it that Hemingway used the lighthouse to find his way home on nights when he'd had too much to drink at Sloppy Joe's. Whether the story was true or not, the lighthouse was located directly across Whitehead Street from the home Hemingway had shared with his second wife, Pauline. And it was the highest place on the island, with a gorgeous view for those willing to make the climb to the top.

The perfect place from which to drop pies, I supposed.

A mob of people circulated on the grounds around the lighthouse keepers' home, a cute little museum that honored the history of the tenders of the light. I recognized pie tasters, pie bakers, interested onlookers, and a smattering of press.

"How is this supposed to work?" asked Helen, once we were inside the gates on the lawn.

"Sloan's billing the event as a fund raiser for the soup kitchens in town—Cooking With Love run by Metropolitan Community Church and the one operating out of St. Mary's. The first fifty people to pony up fifty bucks get to taste all the pies and vote on their favorites, and most of that money goes to charity. As a professional food critic, I am not eligible to vote. Besides, I'd hate to have to describe something by eating one bite. However, I bought Miss Gloria a ticket . . ." I blushed and started to stammer. "I didn't get one for you based on what you said last night about sugar and all."

"That's perfectly correct," she said. "There is no way I'd be interested in tasting all those pies. Especially since we tried most of them over the last two days. Sometimes if I hear too much about a certain food, I lose a taste for it altogether.

I know that isn't true for everyone. You foodies, for example, never seem to tire of talking about what you're eating and what you ate yesterday and what's on the menu tomorrow." She tucked a strand of silver hair behind her ear. "I'm glad you didn't waste fifty bucks on me."

In one way, I thought she was trying to make me feel better about not buying her the ticket. But in another, she was letting me know—again, even if unintentionally—how very different we were. The more she talked, the more self-conscious I felt. So I just grinned stupidly and began to walk around the display tables to take photos of the pies. Everything was there, from the creamy pies made by the Key Lime Pie Company, to the tall peaks of brown meringue produced by Blue Heaven, to the understated creaminess of the pie from Key West Cakes, to Kermit's strawberry–key lime bars dipped in dark chocolate. Everything I had been sampling and writing about and more, only in miniature form.

Wearing a white chef's coat with his name in lime-colored cursive on the chest pocket, David Sloan bounded up the steps to the stage and took the microphone. "Welcome to Key West's premier key lime event! We hope you will enjoy every minute, and we sincerely and fiercely hope you will patronize all the shops and bakers who have participated. And if you will indulge one small reminder, my books, including the *Key West Key Lime Cookbook*, are for sale at the table on your way out. Even if you did not purchase a tasting ticket, please make your donations to our soup kitchens generous. And we are thrilled to have local celebrities Mayor Teri Johnson, Judy Blume, and Suzanne Orchard in attendance."

The crowd clapped and cheered. "Now, before we begin the events of the day, I would like to introduce our new police chief, Sean Brandenburg, who has a few words to share."

Chief Brandenburg, a tall, good-looking man with a shaved head, wearing sunglasses and the trademark blue police uniform, climbed the stairs and shook hands with David Sloan, over whom he towered. Our previous chief had been a small man with a large presence. Brandenburg had a presence just by nature of his height. I tried to assess whether Sloan appeared anxious, which he surely must have been if he'd killed Claudette. His face was shiny with sweat, but the temperature and humidity had both risen over the day, so it was unfair to judge him on that. And he was pumping Brandenburg's hand and grinning like a monkey.

"Good afternoon, and welcome to Key West," said the chief to the waiting crowd. "On behalf of all of us at the police department, we wish you a happy holiday week. It's a very busy time in our town, and we ask for your cooperation in helping the island stay safe. Please obey traffic rules and be courteous to visitors, and if you see something out of order or need assistance, let one of our officers know."

His face grew more serious. "We are also asking for information regarding the recent death of pastry chef Claudette Parker. As you may have read online or in our local newspapers, she was found murdered on her front porch several days ago." He shifted his sunglasses to the top of his head and glanced around to make eye contact with some of the people watching.

"Anyone who has any information about her death or who might have seen something unusual in her neighborhood that evening, please come forward. Feel free to approach me this afternoon, call the help line at the department, or message us on Facebook. We appreciate your assistance in advance—as talented as our department and officers are, we cannot have eyes everywhere. That is why we need you, both visitors and members of our community, to be our partners. Thank you, be safe, and don't eat too much pie!"

He grinned, shook hands again with David Sloan, and disappeared into the crowd.

"He comes across as both friendly and deadly serious," Helen said, nodding her approval. "Every once in a while, a plea like that garners some interesting information. But more often the keys to cracking open a case emerge from a suspect or a witness whom the police already know. Somebody they've already interviewed remembers a bit more. Or decides that holding back on details only makes them look guilty."

I studied her face, wondering how she knew so much. And how I knew so little about my own husband's family history.

"I know you have work to do," she said. "I'm going to walk around and see if I can chat up Paul and Bee, and even Sloan, if he has a minute. When shall we meet up?"

I glanced at my watch. Midafternoon already. "Say, in an hour? I'll have captured the highlights by then."

As I walked around the lighthouse grounds, I reminded myself of my mother-in-law's advice—not to constrain my thinking about murder suspects to the baking community. And also to remember that if we were considering someone from Nathan's past, we probably should be looking for a Key West newcomer.

I took pictures of the chefs with their pies and their fans for the *Key Zest* social media accounts, noticing that the Blue Heaven pies were there but Bee was not. Did this have something to do with our earlier conversation?

Next I videoed five men diving face first into the cream-covered pies on the table in front of them. The pie-eating contest was a crowd favorite, but also sort of disgusting. I wondered whose pies they'd used—I suspected they came from a half-price grocery store sale—and what this said about our island's tendency to gluttony. Maybe it was just a mood, but I decided not to post pictures of the contest. Besides, the pie-laden faces reminded me of Claudette's attack on David Sloan. And the horrible death that followed.

As I moved away from the pie gluttony table, I ran into my friend Jennifer Cornell, a chef with a catering business who sometimes shared the industrial kitchen with my mother. As we greeted each other and chatted, I remembered that she had gone to the same culinary school as Claudette, the Auguste Escoffier School of Culinary Arts. And had they also both interned in Paris? We discussed the tragedy of Claudette's death, and then I asked, "How well did you know her? Were you in the same class?"

Jennifer shook her head. "Not well. She was coming in as I was finishing up. Back in those days, she was kind of touchy-feely. Meditating to the sound of brass Buddha bowls ringing while counting rosary beads as feverishly as an Italian grandmother."

"Beads?" I asked, suddenly on high alert. "Can you remember what they looked like?"

"No," she said, after thinking for a minute. "The intensity of French chefs shrieking at her for tiny mistakes snuffed those tendencies out quickly, and she quit wearing them. I think she almost dropped out—which, considering her talent, would have been tragic."

She stopped talking to stare at me. "No, on the other hand, she probably wouldn't be in the morgue on a slab if she'd quit and taken another path."

David Sloan came to the microphone again and announced that tasters had fifteen more minutes to complete their rounds and cast their votes. I said goodbye to Jennifer and made another sweep around the grounds, chatting briefly with the pastry chefs and taking more photos. Bee had still not shown up at the Blue Heaven table. All I could think about was the beads Jennifer had mentioned. And what Tony from the gym had said. Were those beads the same as what I'd seen Bee wearing earlier today? I thought they might be similar, and I wished I'd paid closer attention.

Then I noticed that Christopher was again serving Sloan's key lime martinis. He'd told me the other night that he had a busy schedule in this high season, and he hadn't exaggerated. I wasn't going to consume something that sweet and alcohol laced, not this afternoon, even if it was calling to me. But I stopped to say hello.

"You may be the busiest guy on the island," I said.

"I've got a lot of competition," he said, grinning. "You, for example, are always working. Can I get you something?"

"No thanks, I—"

My words trailed off as we watched Chief Brandenburg and two uniformed officers approach Paul Redford's table. We weren't close enough to hear what they said to him, but he objected fiercely. Chief Brandenburg kept talking, looking calm but poised for whatever chaos might break out.

Paul dropped the silver pie server he was holding onto the table, picked up the pie he had been about to cut, and slammed it to the ground at the chief's feet, where it splattered green goop over his polished black shoes and blue serge pant legs.

"If you're finished with your tantrum, let's go," said the chief in a loud voice. Then they marched him off across the grass toward the exit, Brandenburg ahead of him and the two officers at each elbow.

"Wow," I said.

"Wow is right," said Christopher. "I'm glad they finally figured out who had it in for Miss Parker. Maybe we can all relax and enjoy the New Year."

I turned back to him and pointed at the little cups of light-green liquid on the table. "I'll have one of those after all."

Chapter
Twenty-Three

Things are still a little tense between them, still lumps in the batter that they need to whisk out.
      —Jennifer Gold, *The Ingredients of Us*

As I dropped Helen off in the Truman Annex, I noticed that my mother's catering van was in the driveway. I should pop in to say hello. We found Mom and Sam relaxing on the back deck, looking drained and happy to have time at home.

We described the excitement at the lighthouse. "I suppose anyone is capable of murder, but Paul didn't strike me as a murderous kind of guy," I said. "His pie was so good."

Everyone laughed. "You never want to believe that a great cook—or especially a baker—has a mean streak," my mother said.

"Maybe he was just wound super-tightly with the pressure of the new business, and he snapped and crossed over the line?" Sam asked.

I nodded slowly. "According to Sigrid, he may have been an investor in her shop as well as Claudette's second-in-command. Maybe something she did or said caused him to believe that everything was slipping away."

"Is Nathan off duty tonight?" my mother asked. "We are thinking of throwing some steaks on the grill and making a big salad for dinner. Would you like to bring Miss Gloria and your gorgeous husband along?"

"But you've been working nonstop," I said, frowning. "You should take the night off."

"We have to eat," she assured me. "And it won't be one bit fussy or fancy. Steaks, salad, garlic bread, done! And besides, we want to catch up."

I glanced at Helen, who shrugged. "A night at home sounds good to me. We've been awfully busy since I arrived."

I texted Miss Gloria and Nathan to explain the plan and then headed home for a shower. While Miss Gloria was showering and dressing, I searched on the locals' Facebook page to see if the news about Paul's arrest had gone public. Of course it had. There were multiple blurry photos published, including a close-up of the pale-green spatter on the police chief's shoes. The eyewitness accounts varied widely, from watching Paul get handcuffed and dragged off kicking and screaming to Paul spitting in the face of the new chief. None of which I'd seen.

And there was lots of chatter about whether people believed he was a murderer, and why or why not. He was having a hot affair with Claudette and she spurned him . . . she stole his recipes and refused him credit . . . he'd siphoned off the money she had set aside for creditors and she found him out . . . Nothing I hadn't already heard or imagined, having been on the front lines of the key lime crime for the last few days. And most of it probably fiction.

Now on a roll, I couldn't resist Googling another enigma: my new mother-in-law. I typed in *Helen Bransford, Atlanta*. Pages and pages of links loaded, detailing her expertise in forensic science, close psychological observation during witness examination, and the psychology of police departments.

Miss Gloria emerged onto the deck, her white hair wet from her shower. "What are you looking at? You look like you saw a ghost."

"My mother-in-law's curriculum vitae. Why didn't Nathan warn me? She's some kind of well-known forensic scientist. She's got to have over a hundred articles published," I said to Miss Gloria. "She's brilliant. I had no clue she was so important. What could we possibly have to talk about? We have nothing in common. No wonder she didn't want to come to the wedding."

Miss Gloria clucked and chirped. "First of all, you're too tired to think straight. Second, this is a mistake we all make. I think the scientists call it an attribution error. We all think our influence is bigger in the world than it actually is, at least in the eyes of the people around us. You assume Nathan's mother didn't come to the wedding because she hated the idea of you. But she had her own reasons to stay away from the wedding. And none of them had to do with you because she doesn't know you. And as she gets to know you, she'll fall in love exactly the way the rest of us did."

I zipped across the room and gave her the biggest hug. "I don't know what I ever did without you."

She grinned. "I don't know either. And here's one more thing: do not forget that you have something huge in common. Nathan. You both love him to the moon and back. And as long as that love continues, it's a powerful bond between the two of you. That's how I feel about my daughters-in-law, anyway. Most days." She snickered.

We drove back down the island to the Truman Annex, a path that was beginning to feel deeply grooved. The others were already gathered on the back deck, sipping cocktails and nibbling on cheese. Nathan got up to hug Miss Gloria and give me a kiss on the lips.

"All my favorite girls in one spot," he said. "Mark this down as a perfect night." He turned to his mother. "I am so sorry we haven't gotten to spend much time together at all. This week could not be crazier. And add a murder on top of the New Year's Eve shenanigans and the fact that half of our hired security people seem to have come down with the Keys flu . . ." He sighed and rubbed a hand over his eyes. "Anyway, I'll try to make it up to you. And somehow thank my in-laws for their incredible hospitality." He saluted Sam and blew a kiss to my mother. He put his arm around his own mother's shoulders. "I hope my mother's been behaving herself."

"We've hardly seen her; she's the easiest houseguest," said my mother.

"And your Hayley's like a mad hummingbird," said Helen. "She flits around the island, barely stopping to sip a bit of nectar."

I laughed. "I never pass up nectar." I raised my glass of white wine to all of them. "Here's to a quieter New Year. And may Claudette Parker rest in peace."

Sam stood to put the steaks on the hot grill as three texts in succession hit Nathan's phone. He glowered and went down the steps to the dipping pool area to read them.

"I suppose with Paul behind bars," my mother said, "there's not a chance that Claudette's shop will survive."

"I don't see who would have the nerve to carry that forward," I said. "She had the chutzpah to imagine she could compete with anyone and come out ahead. And she had the talent too. With someone less gifted in charge, that store could end up as just one more key lime shop, only with a pretentious name."

Nathan returned to our group. He glanced at his mother and then me, looking distressed.

"We've developed more holes in our schedule, and they have to be filled. Every one of us is taking an extra shift or more over the next two days, including Steve Torrence, me, and even our new chief. They're expecting me at the station in thirty minutes for my four-hour stint. And I'll be working all day tomorrow too. My apologies, Mother. I was planning to take the day off and show you around, but the timing is dreadful."

"I understand," she said. "And your wife and Miss Gloria and your in-laws are absolutely delightful and welcoming. And I will never eat another piece of key lime pie again." We all laughed.

"Do you want to take a steak for the road?" Sam asked. "We could make you a sandwich. I have some nice arugula and spicy mustard in the fridge. And a loaf of French bread from Old Town Bakery. It would make a fantastic—"

Nathan shook his head. "No thanks. Not meaning to be rude, but I've lost my appetite. Don't wait up," he told me. "Four hours probably means six. I hope to be home by midnight." He looked tired, gray half circles under his beautiful green eyes and a few wrinkles radiating from frown lines that I hadn't noticed before. I imagined his stomach would be churning with the latest bad news.

"I'll be there," I said, rather than voicing any of the other admonitions that ran through my mind. *Be careful. Can't someone else do it? I miss you. Be so very careful.*

When the steaks were finished and resting on a platter by the grill, I set the table outside while Sam tossed a gorgeous green salad with a mason jar of homemade dressing and crumbles of blue cheese. The flames in the hurricane lamps flickered in the breeze, and I could hear the sound of water slapping against the cement walls of the Navy pier on the Truman Waterfront. This truly was a slice of paradise, if anyone in my family circle could slow down enough to enjoy it.

"That dressing looks and smells amazing," I said to Sam.

"I tried my hand at a knockoff version of Baby's salad from Clemente's," he said. "I know how much you love it." He grinned at me as I sliced the oven-hot bread, drenched in melted butter and crushed garlic. "Dinner's ready," he called to the others.

"You are such a treasure," I said. "Thank goodness my mother didn't blow it."

"That sounds like a story," said Nathan's mom, as she took a seat next to me.

"I'll tell it," said Miss Gloria, piling her plate high with sliced steak and a big helping of salad. "I love this story. Poor guy proposed right in front of everyone, and instead of graciously accepting, she walked out without saying a word."

My mother buried her face in her hands. "That's so embarrassing."

"It was my mistake for surprising her," said Sam. He reached for her fingers and squeezed. "Tell Nathan's proposal story instead. I bet Helen hasn't heard that one."

And so Miss Gloria did, embellishing the details of Nathan arranging for Robert Albury to sing "Try a Little Tenderness" on the Pier House pier, and giving me a box containing a key to the houseboat next store to Miss Gloria's, and then dropping to one knee in front of the crowd—all as if she'd lived through it herself.

"I never knew he had such a romantic streak," said Helen, her smile wide.

My mother looked completely beat, so as soon as we'd cleared the dishes and helped Sam load them into the washer, I gathered my belongings to take Miss Gloria home. "Remember, we have Cooking With Love tomorrow morning," I told Helen, to remind her of our date to help with the soup kitchen work. "Eric likes me to be there no later than eight. Seven thirty is even better. You're not obligated, of course."

"Why not?" she asked, laughing a little. "What else would I do?"

* * *

Once home, I walked the dog and fell immediately into a deep sleep.

Nathan woke me up two hours later getting into bed.

"The world's gone crazy out there," he said. "We had to break up a situation at the Garden of Eden—the clothing-optional floor of the Bull and Whistle," he added with a weary sigh. "One crazy drunk stole the clothes belonging to another and ran off across Duval Street lickety-split. Wearing only a T-shirt and waving the other guy's shorts in his hand like a flag. I'll be so glad when the New Year arrives and things slack off a little."

I nudged Evinrude to the side and snuggled next to my husband's chest.

"How's it going with my mother? She seems to like you," he asked tentatively.

"I learned some interesting facts about her today. On a random Google search."

"A random Google search?" His eyebrows furrowed in the sliver of street light that trickled in through the slats of the blinds that the cats had bent during one of their races through the houseboat.

"I wanted to get to know her a little better. You don't talk about your family much, so I had to use the tools at hand." I sighed. "The Internet doesn't help me understand what's going on in her mind, though. It's like she runs hot and cold. One minute she's telling me how much she appreciates the fact that I saved your life. The next minute, she's describing your first wedding in great detail."

A look of horror crossed his face. "Tell me she's not talking about my first wedding."

"Oh yes, I know all about the eleven attendants and the monkey suit." I snickered but then got serious. "She obviously loved your first wife. I don't know if I can ever live up to her image of what a daughter-in-law is supposed to be."

"There's a lot you don't understand," he said quietly. "It's a long story."

"I'm waiting. We have all night."

He pulled away from me, arms crossed over his chest, staring at the ceiling. "You know that I have a sister. And that we aren't close because she lives in Scotland."

I remembered him explaining this to me when I asked him about inviting his family to the wedding. I'd thought we ought to invite her anyway, but he'd demurred.

"There's a little more to it. She was kidnapped."

I waited in silence, feeling horrified, but not wanting to say or do anything that might discourage him from talking.

"You probably remember seeing those lost kids on milk cartons?" he asked grimly.

My eyes went wide with horror.

His next words came out in a rush. "Yup. One of those was our Vera. Obviously my parents never got over it, and neither did their marriage. You can understand, then, why my mother freaked when Trudy was attacked. And why she doesn't want to get close enough to you to care enough to ever get that worried again."

"I am so sorry, Nathan. Your sister. That's tragic."

"We're over it," he said, convincing no one. "We did get her back eventually, but we never got her back emotionally, if you understand what I'm saying."

I didn't really understand. Even Evinrude, my gray tiger, blinked at him askance.

"I'm not sure I do; do you mind saying more? I can tell it's a painful subject for your whole family." Grand understatement, but he obviously wasn't in the mood for a joke.

"Vera—my sister—didn't die, so don't think the worst," he told me. "But she was never the same carefree girl. She didn't feel safe in our town, and she got the idea of going to school abroad. My parents agreed because she was so freaked out. And frankly, so were they. I've not seen much of her since. It put a lot of stress on our family, and my parents' marriage finally shattered."

He heaved a big sigh, and I squeezed his arm for comfort. And waited.

"They never caught the guy who took her, and my mother blamed my father. If a high-ranking police detective can't track the man who ruined his daughter's life, what's the point of putting himself and his family in danger day after day after day? What's the point of anything?" He sounded both angry and sad. "Mother went back to graduate school, and she's been working on solving impossible cases ever since. It's personal for her."

I was beginning to see so clearly why her fears for Nathan's safety had mushroomed. And also why he acted weird when I did something that he felt put me in danger. "Where is your sister now?"

"She's living in Scotland. She talked my parents into letting her go to St. Andrew's for college. While she was there, she met and married a Scottish man, and I doubt she'll ever come back."

"How did I not know more about this? We should have put her on the guest list for our wedding."

"She wouldn't have come," he said firmly. "She's only been back to the U.S. once since she left. And that was so hard for her. Why pressure her and set you up for disappointment in the likely event that she refused?"

This was messed up—I wished he'd felt he could share all this with me before I forced it out of him. I'd married a complicated man.

"I'd like to meet her one day," I said. "She's your sister. Think of all the things she knows about you that I might entice her to share." I started to snicker, and he finally smiled.

"We'll see."

I felt his breathing even out, meaning he'd dropped off to sleep, leaving me with a world of questions. For instance: on what occasion had his sister come back to the country? I had a sinking feeling it was for his first wedding—she would have been one of the eleven bridesmaids in pink ruffles. I knew I should not take any of this personally, as Miss Gloria would be quick to remind me. And I understood that it took a while to get to know someone in a deeper way. As you grew to trust each other, you let the other person in on the secrets that might not have felt safe with a new acquaintance. But I might spend a lifetime with this guy and still not understand half of what was in his history and his head. From now on, I swore, I would ask more questions. Even if he clammed up. Especially if he clammed up.

Chapter Twenty-Four

No one who cooks, cooks alone. Even at her most solitary,
a cook in the kitchen is surrounded by generations of
cooks past, the advice and menus of cooks present, the
wisdom of cookbook writers.

—Laurie Colwin

My mother arrived at the church at the same time I did, with Helen in tow.

"Here's your assistant," she chirped.

From the strain in her voice, I suspected she was probably feeling as worn down as I was by the busyness of the week in combination with entertaining a full-time visitor. Although they'd insisted that hosting Helen was no trouble, having someone stay in the house, and worrying about whether she had what she needed for breakfast, or was annoyed at being left alone so many hours—it had to be a strain. They were not the kind of hosts who could slap a box of cereal and some instant coffee on the counter and call it hospitality.

I squinted to look at her more closely. Or had something else happened?

"I'll be with you in a minute," I called to my mother-in-law. "There are some unusual tropical flowers two houses up the street worth looking over," I told Helen. She stared at me for a minute—she'd not said one word about interest in tropical vegetation. But then she looked at my mother's face, nodded, and walked to the house I'd pointed out near the church and pretended to admire their lush garden.

I circled around the car to chat with Mom. "What's up?"

She whispered, "I know you're strung out, but is there any way you could help me late this afternoon serving at a party at the Hemingway Home? Of course you can bring Helen, but I didn't want to commit her until I knew if you were available." She was practically wringing her hands in desperation.

"Of course," I said. "Just tell me when, and one or two or three of us will be there."

"Oh, don't worry Miss Gloria; she's got to be exhausted," said Mom.

"I'll ask anyway, because she'd feel left out if we acted like she couldn't handle it."

"Of course," said my mother. She grabbed my hand and planted a big kiss on the palm. "It's not really fair to pull you into my catering world, but I had no idea that three of our temporary staff would bail out. Call in sick, I should say, aka the dreaded Keys flu, aka too much fun the night before. And no one really wants to work New Year's Eve. I suspect it's the same disease that's running rampant through the police department." She hopped back into the van, slammed the door, and called out the window as she drove away, "Thanks a million. I'll text you later about when to show up."

I led my mother-in-law into the church, where the small vestibule fed into the worship area upstairs, with the church office on the bottom floor to the left and the kitchen and community room at the back. For a small bare-bones place, an amazing amount of wonderful work got done here.

"Cooking With Love happens every Saturday, with one set of volunteers doing all the cooking. And then a second crew packs up individual lunches to take to our clients. We usually feed around a hundred and sixty people, mostly lower-income and housebound senior citizens," I explained.

"I work with my friend Eric once a month, and he's in charge of the menu." I grinned. "So today we're the grunts, which usually involves a ton of chopping. But I think he said he's planned a chicken-and-stuffing casserole for today."

"Chicken and stuffing for a hundred and sixty people?" Helen asked, looking overwhelmed. "Out of this kitchen?" She peered into the galley kitchen again, with its oversized eight-burner gas stove, industrial-sized refrigerator, and three sinks. Small, blistering hot, and low-tech.

"It's kind of like magic," I said. "Magic made by people and love. That sounds goofy, but I mean it."

I introduced her to my friends, Eric and Bill, who were already at work. "Eric is a psychologist with a private practice, and Bill is a superstar guide at the Harry Truman Little White House. They love to cook and eat and drink lemon-drop martinis, and they have two adorable dogs and a darling house."

"And that is probably more than you wanted to know about us," said Bill with a laugh. He came over to shake her hand. "Welcome to chaos."

"What shall we do first?" Helen asked. "I will warn you, my knife skills are probably not up to your standards."

I looked at Eric and we both giggled.

"No knife skills needed for this recipe," he said. "This is like no cooking you've done before." He directed her to the industrial can opener that was attached to one of the countertops. Next to that were dozens of cans of soup, broth, and evaporated milk.

"Hayley and I will lay out the chicken and stuffing in the casseroles, if you don't mind opening cans. Then we mix all those liquids together, pour it over top of the dry ingredients, and poke around to make sure everything is saturated. When we're finished with that and have the pans in the oven, we'll be making a little coleslaw. We will serve frozen strawberries for dessert. We try to keep things easy; otherwise the quantities would be overwhelming."

From the size of my mother-in-law's pupils, I suspected she was already feeling overwhelmed. But she began to gamely open can after can after can. I ripped open jumbo bags of dried stuffing and spread the contents over the shredded chicken that Eric had tackled. When everything was ready, we popped the pans into the ovens.

While we were waiting for the casseroles to cook, we prepared large bowls of shredded cabbage and carrots, mixing the vegetables with mayonnaise, cider vinegar, and celery seeds. I heard the buzzer of the front door, then male voices in the vestibule. Steve Torrence and Chief Sean Brandenburg came into the hall. Both were dressed in polyester blue uniforms, which didn't happen that often for Steve because he spent more time at the station and attending community meetings these days than on patrol.

"Good morning, everyone," Steve called out to the room of workers.

"Oh good, I can introduce you to our friend," I told Nathan's mother. "He often works with Nathan on special projects, and if that's not enough to keep him busy, he serves as the pastor for this church and he does weddings, including Nathan's and mine."

The two men came over to us, wide grins on their faces.

"I couldn't resist the opportunity to meet the woman who produced Nathan Bransford," Steve said. He shook her hand and then gave her a kiss on the cheek and turned to introduce us to the chief. "Please meet Helen Bransford, and Hayley Snow, everyone's favorite gadfly." He pulled me into a hug.

I wriggled away and punched him in the arm. "If you came for lunch, you're a little early," I said to the chief. "We'll be happy to save something for you, and send a box along for Nathan." Although I very much doubted he'd be interested in hot chicken casserole during the heat of the day.

"Not eating today. Just wanted to stop and say hello," said Steve. Then his face grew serious and he lowered his voice. "And let you know that Paul Redford was not charged or detained."

"What does that mean?" I asked. "Did you discover he wasn't the killer?"

"We didn't have enough evidence to hold him," said Steve. "The investigation is ongoing, and we're pursuing many leads."

"Meaning he has a very clever lawyer?" Nathan's mother asked. The frown on her face deepened. "Is he still under investigation, or have you moved on to another suspect?"

Both of the men turned to look at her. "He is a person of interest. That's as much as we can say," said the chief in a genial voice. "I'm sure Nathan will keep you informed as he's able."

Steve added, "So please keep your eyes open, and even more importantly, stay out of trouble. That's a direct quote from Nathan."

"Always," said Nathan's mother, smiling warmly as she returned to stirring a gigantic jar of mayonnaise into the bowl of vegetables.

"What do you make of that?" I asked her, once the men had left our station.

"The police can't hold someone overnight if they haven't charged them. You probably know—or you should know—that you don't have to answer any questions unless you've been charged with a crime." She peered at my face, looking for confirmation that this advice was familiar. "Even then, you can clam up and demand a lawyer. I hope Nathan is telling you the basics in case you end up on the wrong side of the law."

Did she know I'd been a suspect in a poisoning case a few years back? That in fact I'd actually had an excellent motive for the murder? And had Nathan told her about the way he and I met—across an interview table, not in a bar or on a tennis court or on Match.com or Tinder like normal people?

"He tells me what he thinks I need to know," I said, to end the possibility of an awkward discussion. "Sounds like they're saying Paul is off the hook and the real murderer is still out there."

She nodded in agreement.

While Steve and the chief visited with the other cooks, the delivery volunteers began to trickle into the church basement. Soon the space was alive with their cheerful banter, and the two men circled the room shaking hands (the chief) and giving hugs (Steve) and chatting.

"For the final part of our job, we serve up the food into individual portions as they come through the line with the containers," I explained to Helen. "These volunteers load them up into giant coolers and deliver them around town."

As we dished out casserole and coleslaw, Eric asked, "What did the police want?"

I explained that Paul Redford had been released after questioning last night. "As usual, Nathan wanted them to warn us to butt out. To be fair, the murderer's still out there and he wants us to be safe." I tipped my head toward Helen and sighed. "But since we found the dead woman, we can't help feeling like we're in the middle of the case, like it or not."

He shoveled a big scoop of chicken casserole into the take-out container held in front of his station. "That reminds me, you remember Jai who works at Project Lighthouse?"

"Of course," I said, feeling a little shiver of gratitude and relief at the sound of her name. As if I'd forget the woman who'd helped us locate my stepbrother when he'd gotten mixed up with a troubled crowd and gone missing in the spring-break-crazed streets of Key West.

Eric nodded. "You know I'm on the board for the Florida Keys Children's Shelter. They had a planning breakfast yesterday, and Jai mentioned she was super-disappointed that their

Santa didn't show up for their post-Christmas, it's-always-Christmas party for teens. It made me wonder . . ."

"Oh my gosh," I said, as one of the most perplexing pieces of the murder dropped into place. "The missing Santa was Claudette, wasn't it? That totally explains why she was dressed in a Santa outfit when we found her."

"And it means the outfit was probably not related to the murder," Helen added. "She must have been on her way to the party wearing that costume."

Eric nodded again. "And it explains why she was a no-show. Jai told me that Claudette was especially interested in her project for traveling teens because her own sister disappeared years ago."

I glanced over at Nathan's mother, whose expression had frozen. After what Nathan had told me about his sister last night, I understood that Helen would want me to keep probing, and that if I didn't, she'd jump in. "What exactly did Jai find out about the girl's disappearance?" I asked.

Eric looked apologetic. "I'm not sure what happened. We didn't really get into the details." The line of volunteers in front of us began to move too fast for further conversation, and we spent the next fifteen minutes working at top speed.

By the time we'd finished cooking the lunch and serving it into the containers wielded by the multitude of volunteers, it felt like we'd been working all day. But it was only eleven thirty. The delivery people dispersed and we set about cleaning up the kitchen.

"I need to get back to the houseboat to help Miss Gloria acclimate the new kitten. I think Cheryl said she's bringing him from the SPCA around noon. But I have time to run you down the island and drop you off at Mom's first," I said to Helen, once we'd finished. "Or if you'd rather, we can run home to check in with Miss Gloria and get a bite to eat."

I lowered my voice so as not to hurt anyone's feelings. "We're invited to take some of the leftover casserole home, but honestly, after I've worked on a meal like this, I usually don't find it very appealing. But I could throw together a chef salad in no time."

"I'm not really hungry," she said. "But I'd appreciate it if you'd take me to the Project Lighthouse on the way home. I want to talk with the woman who said Claudette had a sister."

I'd had the same thought. But (a), I didn't see how I was going to jam visiting Project Lighthouse into an already crazy day, and (b), the chief of police had made a special trip to the church to warn us to stay out of the murder case.

"But you heard Steve and the chief," I said. "They asked us—no, they begged us, not to take on anything on our own."

"No problem," she said, her gaze leveled straight at me. "I can call an Uber."

I stared back. She was one tough cookie. I had to wonder whether she imagined that Claudette's sister's disappearance—and maybe Claudette's death—were related to her own family tragedy. That couldn't be—too much coincidence. But at least talking to Jai might provide a clue to Claudette's past that we didn't yet understand. In that case, I couldn't possibly say no.

"I'd be happy to take you."

Chapter
Twenty-Five

Tell me what you eat and I'll tell you who you are.
—Jean Anthelme Brillat-Savarin

I texted my friend Jai to make sure she was on duty and that it would be convenient for us to stop and chat about Claudette. I thought she would be there—New Year's Eve was a perfect time to have a safe space available for drifting teens. On the few blocks across town to Truman, I explained to my mother-in-law the basics about Project Lighthouse.

"It's a drop-in center for homeless kids and runaways. They try to provide a place where kids can get support, and maybe apply for an ID, because nothing happens without that. No ID, no job, no school, no nothing. And she helps them think about the next step in their lives—when they're ready. Sometimes it's finding a place to live or a job or school, and sometimes having someone who will listen to them is all they need. Or even simply hold them in place while the world spins around them. That can mean a lot. Jai and the other staff call these kids 'travelers,' because they're usually on the way to something. They don't always know what that something is."

I parked a block away from the storefront. Usually this end of Truman was not so busy in the daytime, but all bets were off in the days leading up to New Year's. There was a small gaggle of teenagers clustered outside the Project Lighthouse door, several of them carrying brindle puppies. One strummed a guitar and sang a Bob Dylan song; others joked and laughed together. They looked like normal kids, but I knew their stories were more complicated. Someday I would tell my mother-in-law about my stepbrother Rory, but it had a sad ending for one of his friends, and now was not the time to get into that. I waved her inside.

We stepped into a chaotic open space. A washing machine gurgled at the back of the room, and I could smell a pot of chili cooking. Two more puppies were wrestling on a rug with a few kids watching and laughing. There was a set of drums on one side of the room, and bookshelves containing books for GED classes, SAT preparation, and a full set of Harry Potter books and Nancy Drew mysteries.

Jai, a thin woman with tattoos on her arms and long red hair pulled back into a ponytail, waved hello from behind the desk, where she was talking to one of the travelers. "I'll be with you shortly," she said. "Have a look around."

We perched on the edge of a sagging brown couch that had seen much better days, Nathan's mother watching everything. I remembered the first time I'd visited the center; the chaos had felt a bit overwhelming. But I'd learned that for the kids who dropped in, it felt safe and homelike, but without the restrictions and complications and painful memories their real homes might have had.

When Jai had finished talking with the girl in front of her, she came over to greet us. I introduced her to Helen and explained our interest in Claudette Parker's murder.

Her face darkened. "We're going to really miss her. This is so tragic. Especially considering what happened to her sister years ago."

"Will you tell us about that?" I asked her.

"I don't suppose it's confidential at this point," Jai said, and heaved a big sigh. "I think she felt comfortable here and wanted to help because these kids reminded her of her sister, Lorraine. Lorraine was a little bit troubled and liked to live on the edge, flouting her parents' rules at every opportunity. Claudette said she spent a lot of time skipping school and hanging out with other kids who weren't walking a traditional path."

Nathan's mother smiled. "That sounds like a kind way of putting it."

"I suppose," said Jai, "but who am I to say what's right for each kid? Here we try to focus on providing a place where they feel accepted and not judged. Because there's too much of that out in the world."

"For sure," I said. "And if you don't feel sturdy when you face all that outside judgment, it can throw you for a loop."

Jai leaned over to pat the puppy that wandered closer to us and was nosing around her feet. The little dog squatted as if to pee on the rug, and Jai called for one of the kids to whisk him outside.

"Maybe Claudette felt badly that she wasn't able to help her sister find her way, and then it was too late," she said. "And maybe these kids reminded her of Lorraine. Anyway, she brought in tons of homemade cookies and day-old pastries from her shop. Which, I have to say, tasted better than most people's day-of baked goods." She patted her stomach. "I'm sure I put on a couple pounds over the past few months. She sat with the kids when she had time, and tried to chat with them. They're usually not inclined to talk with grown-ups, but she was good at listening." She paused, thinking about how to phrase what came next. "Though she was intense, and that sometimes scared the kids off."

"Intense in what way?" I asked.

"Maybe she pushed a little too hard to learn their stories? She really wanted to help them understand how to be safe. A couple of times kids backed away from her, and didn't show up here for a day or more."

"What happened with her sister?" Nathan's mother asked.

"She accepted a ride from a guy who was cruising the streets in downtown Atlanta in an old Pinto. The other kids saw her get in, but no one seemed to know the guy who took her, and they never could nail down a good description. Maybe he had blond hair? Sunglasses? A black ball cap? A checked shirt? He was probably no older than twenty, but the kids reported that he looked like an adult. They were too vague to help the cops find him."

"And so what happened?" asked Helen, leaning forward toward Jai, a look of anguish on her face.

"No one saw her alive after that," Jai said. "They found her body a week later in a ditch near the city dump. It did a number on her family. I could tell how much it marked Claudette's life, too. That's why I encouraged her to keep coming. For her, I think it was therapeutic."

"Understandably," I said. "That is so tragic." I glanced at my phone, which was buzzing like crazy—eight texts from Miss Gloria on the screen—and raised my eyebrows at Helen. "Sorry to rush you, but I need to get home. Miss Gloria seems to be flipping out."

She exchanged phone numbers with Jai, then followed me out to the scooter, completely silent. The shadow of Claudette's grief hung thick between us. I couldn't think of a thing to say, so I stayed quiet, and we zipped home to Houseboat Row. On our way from the parking lot to our boat, we followed Mrs. Renhart, who wore a gigantic stuffed hot dog on her head and encouraged her bedraggled and hot-dog-costumed Schnauzer, Schnootie, up the finger.

"What is that all about?" my mother-in-law asked in a low voice.

"She's coming back from the dachshund parade. It's a kind of flash mob for wiener dogs and their owners, and everyone wears costumes and they march about two blocks because the dogs have such short legs. She's crazy about the event and so happy to have her rescue dog participate. Last year she invited me to go along, and I felt as though I couldn't refuse. It brings her so much pleasure. I went dressed as a hamburger." I suppressed a snort of laughter.

Helen leaned in close to whisper, "Does she realize that her dog is not a dachshund?"

Now I burst out laughing. "I'm pretty sure she does."

Although Miss Gloria had skipped Cooking With Love in order to wait for the little cat to be delivered, he still hadn't arrived by the time we boarded the houseboat. My roomie was pacing from the kitchen, through the living room, and out to the deck and back.

"Do you think they've changed their minds and given him to someone else?" she asked, wringing her hands. "I'm so nervous. I couldn't even concentrate on my favorite *Outlander* rerun."

"That's serious," I said. She was a huge fan of the Scottish time-travel show and had gotten the rest of the household sucked into it—except Nathan, who proclaimed the plots ridiculous. To be honest, I thought his refusal had more to do with his embarrassment about watching steamy sex scenes alongside Miss Gloria than it did weak plots.

At that moment, we heard the sound of an unfamiliar engine rumbling from the parking lot. And then a door slammed and Cheryl appeared, walking up the finger of the dock carrying a pet crate. The sound of frantic, high-pitched kitten mews emanated from inside.

"I bet you never thought you'd see me again!" she called out cheerfully as she got closer. "The person who was desperate to adopt the kitty was told by her husband that it was one more cat or him. It wasn't an easy decision, but she went for her husband." Cheryl's laugh boomed out across the bight. "Then we had five applications to choose from. But once I explained the story about how Miss Gloria had found the kitten shivering under the porch on the night of the murder, we all agreed she was the rightful owner."

We invited her to board the boat, and she hopped across the small gap and set the cat carrier on the deck. All three of our animals rushed over to investigate. Evinrude backed away almost immediately, raising his handsome gray striped body into Halloween cat shape, followed by a low growl and a full-throttle hiss. Miss Gloria's Sparky danced around the perimeter of the crate, batting at the little kitten inside. And Ziggy ran quivering through the doggy door that Nathan had installed and headed toward Miss Gloria's bedroom.

"Hello, T-Bone!" crowed Miss Gloria, kneeling down to peer into the crate. "Welcome to our nuthouse. It's a little bit chaotic here, but I bet you'll feel like part of the gang within twenty-four hours."

She winked at Cheryl, and I could tell she was nervous about whether we'd be judged as overwhelmed with animals, unfit for another adoption. And then watch the new kitty get whisked away to the next cat lover on the list.

"Come, sit down and take a load off," she told Cheryl. She sat back cross-legged on the deck and pointed our guest to her own chaise lounge. "We'd love to hear your tips."

Cheryl sat, pulling the kitten's crate closer to her. "When you are introducing a new family member, we always advise not mixing the established animals too quickly with the new kitten. Everybody needs time to acclimate." She patted the crate with the kitten inside. "Even though T-Bone has been living with a bunch of cats at the shelter, your furry fellows are new to him. And I'm not sure he's ever met a dog. We recommend starting the kitten out in a safe room—meanwhile, they can adjust to each other's scent, but with a door securely separating them. They will tell you when they're ready to mix it up. It might take a week or more. And then be sure to treat them all equally." She plucked at her white T-shirt that had three black cats painted on it, and below that the words *This is why we can't have nice things.*

She looked hot, so I offered everyone a cool beverage. As I got up to get a glass of ice water for Cheryl, I couldn't help bugging my eyes out a little bit at Miss Gloria on the way to the kitchen. We did not have the patience to keep the kitten in a separate room for a week while everyone adjusted to his odor. Nor did we have the space. And treat all the animals equally? Ha! Around here, the winner was whoever shoved onto your lap or into the feed bowl first.

By the time I returned, Helen, who'd been mostly quiet since our visit to Project Lighthouse, had taken the floor. "Are you absolutely certain you didn't see anyone leaving Claudette Parker's home the night of the murder?" she asked Cheryl.

Yikes, how had this conversation evolved into an inquisition? Or *devolved* might be the better description.

Cheryl's face colored a deep crimson. "Are you working for the police?" she asked.

"Not a bit," said Helen. "As I'm certain we told you, we feel like we have a personal stake in bringing the killer to justice, since we were the ones who found the woman. You can imagine how that felt," she added, patting her hand over her heart.

"Awful," said Cheryl, shifting uncomfortably in her chair.

Helen leaned forward. "So are you certain you didn't see anyone leave Claudette's house that night? Apparently the police took Redford in for questioning yesterday—in fact, Hayley here saw it happen. And then we heard this morning that he was released; *apparently* there wasn't enough evidence to charge him. Do you know anything about any of this?"

Cheryl's face colored again, and she cleared her throat. "I did see Paul that night. He came by to talk with me, super-upset. I've known him for years and years, and I know he's no murderer. He went to talk with Claudette about a promotion, and about getting some acknowledgment that he'd invested in the business and provided some of the recipes. She was adamant that this wasn't happening. He didn't know what to do next, so he came to me to blow off some steam. Maybe he thought I knew her well enough that I could put a word in with her? I advised him to sit tight and show her how indispensable he was." She sighed. "Of course he panicked when he heard the news that she'd been murdered right around the very time he was at her house."

"Was she dead when he went to speak with her?" Helen asked. She had crossed her arms over her chest and looked very fierce.

"Of course not!" Cheryl yelped. The hand holding her water glass trembled. "He would have reported that instantly."

"Did you tell the police about his visit?" I asked, stunned that this was the first we'd heard of it. I glanced over to meet Helen's eyes. We'd sat right in Cheryl's yard and ate her cookies and sipped her tea and talked about that night until we all thought we'd covered every possible angle.

"Yes. After he called me in a complete panic about all the news of her murder. I phoned the cops yesterday and confessed that I'd skipped over that conversation," she said. "I told them that he could not possibly have killed her and been so calm—I assured them that he was only concerned about his job. And then exactly what I worried about happened—they arrested him for a murder he didn't commit." She looked close to tears.

"First of all, they didn't arrest him—they only talked to him. He's definitely back home now," I said. "We heard that from the chief of police this morning. And second, it was absolutely the right thing to call the cops. They can't find the real murderer if people are holding important information back."

She nodded. "I'm glad they know everything I know now. But you have to understand that he's been a dear friend for a long time. I didn't feel it was my place to throw him under the bus. After speaking with the police, I called Paul and told him to tell everything he knows, too." She got to her feet and said her goodbyes. "You should feel free to call us if you have any trouble with Mr. T-Bone, anything at all."

Miss Gloria hugged her and walked her down the dock to the parking lot to get last-minute advice about the kitten's diet.

"I can't believe she didn't tell us those details right away," I said to the others when Miss Gloria was back. "That could make a huge difference about who the cops arrest. And maybe Paul saw something that will help the police solve the case. Sheesh."

At that moment, a text came in. My mother was on the way home, driving by Houseboat Row, and would happily take Helen with her for a couple of hours if that suited. It did suit. My mind was boggled and I felt drained and stressed. I'd need to rally in order to summon the energy to work my mother's party.

I walked Helen up the dock, where my mother and Sam were waiting in the catering van. "Thanks so much for the ride," Helen said. "It's been a very hectic day."

"Hectic on our end, too," Sam said, "and it doesn't look as though things are slowing down anytime soon."

We agreed to meet at the Hemingway Home at four, and I returned to our boat to take a little rest. Before I could voice my concern or physically stop her, Miss Gloria unhinged the cat carrier and let the orange kitten out. He stood in the sunlight, blinking, as though he'd landed in Oz or on the moon, maybe. From inside the boat, Ziggy began to bark sharp shrieks of alarm. Evinrude, with his tail hoisted hard like a flag in a stiff wind, marched off our boat, jumped to the dock, and headed up the finger to Connie's house. This was where he went when he was annoyed with me. Though lately he had gone less often, since Connie's toddler, who loved grabbing ears and tails, was not all that appealing to him either.

Sparky approached the kitten and tapped him with one black paw. The kitten hissed and bolted past me through the doggy door and into the houseboat, Sparky fast on his heels. Like a train out of control, the two cats leaped onto the kitchen counters, knocking over coffee mugs and bottles of herbs and spices as they ran. Then the kitten disappeared into my room with the bigger cat in hot pursuit. We heard crashing and howling.

"Good thing Cheryl isn't here to see our cat-acclimation technique," I said with a laugh, and hurried in after them. The kitten had disappeared into a narrow space underneath my chest of drawers, and Sparky, not quite slim enough to follow, lay on the floor next to the furniture and swatted at him.

"Okay, pal," I said to the black cat, "Time for you to clear out. You're traumatizing the new recruit." I picked Sparky up, dropped him out in the hallway, and closed the door. Then I turned to inspect the source of the crashes. The cats had knocked over the family photographs I had displayed on the bureau, along with the blue pottery bowl I used to store my rings when I was cooking. It had shattered into a dozen pieces. I got down on hands and knees to gather them up. No point in getting mad—he had panicked, and for good reason. I heard a small rattling noise, and then one orange-and-white paw batted a blue bead out from underneath the chest. It looked exactly like a piece of the necklace I'd found on the sidewalk outside Claudette Parker's home, the same necklace I'd brought home and photographed for Tony the jeweler. I searched my room for the rest of the beads but came up empty-handed. So much had gone on in the past few days that I hadn't realized the beads were missing. Could they have been stolen by the intruder the other night?

This reminded me that I'd forgotten to follow up with Tony. I took a picture of the single bead and texted it to him, followed by, *Did you ever find any information about the owner of this?*

He answered right back. *Checked my records. Did not work on this necklace. But this is part of a mala or prayer necklace, I can confirm that. Because of its size, this bead is possibly the sumero or head bead where the meditation or chanting cycle begins.*

Then, feeling guilty about all the secrets being kept about the murder and uneasy on top of that, I forwarded this information to Steve and Nathan. *From my jeweler friend Tony. And FYI, please don't jump to the conclusion that I went looking for clues about the murder. This is a stray bead from the necklace that must have been stolen in the break-in—I found it on the sidewalk outside Claudette's home. Then the new kitten discovered this under my chest of drawers.*

Oops, this was the first Nathan would have heard about a new cat in our family.

I went to the kitchen to pour myself a glass of iced tea, then collapsed on the bed to rest for a few minutes, clucking reassuring nothings to the kitten in hiding. I felt unsettled by the discovery of the bead and the realization that the necklace had gone missing the night of the murder. And to be honest, exhausted.

It was hard to imagine revving myself up to help my mother with her New Year's Eve wedding party later this afternoon, but she had done me a huge favor by absorbing Nathan's mom the past few days. This was the least I could do to repay her. From her description, they needed someone to put finishing touches on platters of food and deliver them from the van to her and Sam. They would do the hard work of interacting with the guests at the party. At least Helen and I would be spared the task of making pleasant chitchat with drunken party guests in addition to the actual physical labor.

A little paw reached out and tapped a piece of the blue bowl that I'd overlooked. T-Bone followed the pottery out from under the bureau and sashayed over to me, his orange stripes dulled by dust.

"We may have to call you our living Swiffer," I said, leaning over to scoop him up and rub his neck and chin. He settled in next to me, purring a rough kitten purr. Was there any sound more soothing? My mind flitted back to the murder. The necklace could have belonged to Claudette and she might have dropped it at some point near her home. In that case, finding the bead meant nothing.

On the other hand, if the necklace belonged to the killer—a big if—they were either someone religious or, more discouraging, someone who simply liked those colors. Would it make sense that this person had strangled poor Claudette and then dropped the necklace in her haste to get away? I couldn't help thinking of Bee Thistle. Both times I'd seen her this week, she'd been wearing beads. And she had strong arms from doing such physical work in the kitchen. Not every woman would be strong enough to kill someone with her hands, but she might be. And she'd certainly been nervous about something.

Although I shouldn't assume the necklace belonged to any woman. Because really, in Key West, there were no rules. Even on an ordinary day, men wore tutus, for heaven's sake—adding a necklace to the look would be nothing.

Chapter
Twenty-Six

She tried to imagine Mr. Ross, sitting at their kitchen table while her mother hacked at the overcooked meat and picked away at him with her questions.
—Ann Cleeves, *Raven Black*

It took me half an hour to drive from the dock to the wedding venue—a distance I usually managed in ten minutes. Truman Avenue aka Route 1 was jammed with honking cars and tourists on bicycles and scooters weaving carelessly through the traffic as the New Year's Eve party headed for its crescendo. I was glad that Miss Gloria had decided to stay home to supervise the cats. It was going to be a harrowing, exhausting night.

Eventually I worked my way the two blocks over on Whitehead to Olivia Street, which ran one way alongside the red-brick wall surrounding the home formerly inhabited by Hemingway and his family. I parked a block north of my mother's van and walked back to the side gate where workers and caterers entered the grounds near the small cat cemetery. By now, the kittens and older cats that were nervous in crowds would have been shut away in the screened-in cat houses built for that purpose. Sometimes party guests got a little too enthusiastic about greeting the cats, or even got the urge to set them free from what they imagined was a prison sentence behind the brick walls.

Sam, Helen, and my mother were in the back of the van, organizing trays of food, wearing aprons covered with white sequins that sparkled in the overhead light.

"Nice outfit," I said to Sam. "Besides looking sharp, it might repel spills, right?"

He shrugged and grinned. "The bride insisted. She read in some silly magazine that the more bling the better for a New Year's Eve wedding. We're doing our very best to manage a wedding that's out of control."

My mother rubbed her eyes with her fists. "Now they want the party to run up to almost midnight; then they'll get married, and then the whole party tears off to celebrate Sushi dropping in the red shoe at midnight."

"Is serving fish in shoes traditional in this town for New Year's Eve?" Helen asked, her expression perplexed.

"Sushi's one of the drag queens who performs at 801 Bourbon Street," I reminded my mother-in-law. "At midnight, they lower her down from the second floor in an outsized red-sequined slipper. It's the Key West version of the ball drop in Times Square."

My mother nodded. "And afterward, they come back and we're to serve a second meal."

"Who in the world is going to officiate a wedding at midnight?" I couldn't imagine a normal pastor agreeing to that schedule.

"Someone on the groom's side of the family got one of those temporary certificates," my mother said. She sucked in a big breath of air. "If you don't mind, I'll start you on the food for the after party. Thank goodness you mentioned Christopher at the library. Our usual bartender is one of the no-shows and Christopher agreed to bartend for the entire night—the bridal couple insisted on having an open bar for six hours, plus a champagne tower." She clutched her head between her hands. "Paul Redford is here to help too. And Bee from Blue Heaven."

"You hired two possible murder suspects to cater a wedding?" I asked, sort of joking. But not really. I was beginning to feel nervous about spending time with either of them. Especially now when I needed to be focused on the work, not watching our backs.

"Paul was working at our shared industrial kitchen all week—he's a real professional. I have a feeling he was tweaking his own recipes and didn't want to unveil anything until they were perfect," my mother explained.

She tried to smile, but her lower lip was wobbling like she might weep instead. "I posted a note to the Facebook locals page saying I'd pay double for tonight. And that was who answered—Paul and Bee. They're both professionals," she repeated. "One of them is out of a job and the other needs the extra money, and they both have lots of experience. I've got Bee on desserts and Paul on hors d'oeuvres, so they shouldn't get in each other's way."

"Sounds like a good arrangement," I said, beginning to worry about how rattled she sounded.

"And since the silly bride insisted on key lime pies for the after party, they are the ideal help because they were able to bring pies with them," said my mother. "I would have suggested your key lime cupcakes if they hadn't come up with this additional demand yesterday. Instead I hired David Sloan to make up individual servings of key lime parfait to go with the pies. He'll help with the serving at the second party—he's very good at handling drunk people," she added. "Or so he said."

I felt instantly relieved that she hadn't asked me to help. I'd baked several hundred key lime cupcakes for Connie and Ray's wedding a few years back—that quantity was a big production. I couldn't imagine taking that on this weekend. For someone I'd never laid eyes on and who sounded like the worst kind of diva. But now, unfortunately, my mother had added a third murder suspect to her employee roster: David Sloan.

Mom lowered her voice to a whisper and pulled me a step away from the others. "I think your mother-in-law is beat. I don't believe you'll have to worry about another visit soon. We've completely worn her out."

I grinned. It had been chaotic—we were all beat. "Tell me about the menus."

"Sam is going to grill tenderloins—that's where most of the cats are congregating," said my mother, pointing across the cemetery to the spot where Sam had set up his grill. A circle of polydactyls clustered at his feet. "And this afternoon I made huge vats of mashed potatoes loaded with butter and sour cream, and those are in the warmer. If that doesn't stop their hearts, nothing will. And we made a beautiful tropical salad with mangos and walnuts. And we bought the most glorious wedding cake from Key West Cakes. It looks like a fairy-tale castle with make-believe sand and turrets—simply stunning."

"Sounds like you've got everything under control," I said.

"Not the after party," said my mother. "That's where I really need you ladies to pitch in." She showed us a huge pile of croissants that filled the van with their buttery scent. "I've made up chicken salad with pecans and dried cherries from the bride's great-uncle in Michigan. So I'll have you stuff the croissants and arrange them on platters, and then make up the fruit salad.

"But first, if you could, I'd love for you and Helen to finish up the croissant corsages." She pointed to a separate pile of baked goods.

I wasn't sure I'd heard that correctly. "Croissant corsages?"

"You heard me—this is what they want to give the guests when they return for part two of the party. An edible wedding favor."

She showed me the sample corsage that the bride and wedding planner had given her. On the bottom was a small arrangement of tropical flowers and ferns to which a real croissant had been attached. "The guys at Gourmet Nibbles and Baskets have provided the flower part, so your job will be to work the craft wire through the pastries so they're attached to the corsages. Glue them down if necessary," she added forcefully, handing me a craft gun. "Eating a little glue won't kill anyone after midnight. They'll be too intoxicated to notice or care."

"This is a first," I said.

Helen's mouth had fallen open as my mother described our assignment.

"You didn't have these at your wedding to Nathan?" she asked.

My mother and I looked at each other and burst into hysterical laughter. "Can you imagine if I'd come down the aisle wearing one of these? First of all, you'd attract all kinds of insects in the dark, not to mention birds. Second of all, Nathan would have hated it. And third, it strikes me as over-wrought to the point of grotesque."

My mother shook her head. "Young people getting married don't understand that it's not the frills and the most unusual sideshow that makes the wedding great—it's choosing the right life partner and having the people you love most around you to help you celebrate and launch your married lives." She held up the white aprons studded with sequins that we were to wear when doing anything public. "When you've finished the corsages, put these on and come have a look around. The grounds look magical, even if this whole production must have cost them a bloody fortune."

Two hours later, when dark had fallen, Helen and I had finished the sandwiches and made one hundred croissant corsages, some of them more polished than others. It was not that easy to sew baked goods to flowers. We'd ended up using the glue gun liberally.

"Let's take a spin around the grounds," I said. "And I need to text our notes about Claudette's sister to Nathan, along with anything else we can think of."

"Happy to help," Helen said, tying the sequined apron she'd been issued around her waist. "I'm feeling a little claustrophobic in this space."

We left the van and circled around the cream-colored house with its lemon-drop shutters and covered porches. As my mother had described, the property had been turned into a fairyland of light and glitter, including a huge disco ball that pulsed over the dance floor.

As we walked, admiring the stunning flower arrangements and the twinkling lights everywhere, I dictated notes into my phone for Nathan. I'd decided to spill everything out and let him decide if any of it was new or important. Starting with the tragedy of Claudette's sister as revealed by Jai, Helen and I reviewed the conversations we'd had and stops that we'd made over the last few days.

"Cheryl," I dictated, "told us that Paul Redford had in fact visited Claudette's house on the night of the murder, which you already know by now. We wonder if someone else was there too at the same time, who may or may not be the murderer." I reminded him about how the kitten T-Bone had retrieved a bead from under my bureau, and how Tony the jeweler had identified it as a mala bead. We stopped in front of the dessert table to admire the arrangement of pies and parfaits.

"It's . . . it's extravagantly stunning," Helen told David Sloan, who was dressed in a starched white chef's coat, not a spot of food on it.

"The mala beads are used while chanting or praying, sort of like a rosary," I added to my dictated notes. I turned to David. "Thanks for helping my mother out. I know you've had a crazy week too." He nodded. "We never did hear who won the pie contest. My bosses are going to kill me because I got distracted by the police brouhaha and didn't stay for the end."

"The Key Lime Pie Company's double-creamy pie won the pie drop—I think it must weigh a little more because of the extra whipping cream," he said. "And Paul Redford's pie was the dark-horse winner in the overall tasting. Though I don't suppose he'll be selling a lot of them from his jail cell." A wicked smile spread over his face.

I didn't bother to correct his assumption about Paul as murderer. The truth would be in the paper and online soon enough. And of course, if Sloan himself was the killer, he would certainly know that Paul's arrest was a red herring. And he would feel enormous relief—hence the grin.

We paused to admire the champagne fountain, the golden sparkly liquid pouring over an ice sculpture that had been carved to look like a fairy princess's castle to match the theme set by the wedding cake.

"Are you beginning to get the idea that no one ever said no to this girl?" Nathan's mother asked.

Christopher, the bartender who was standing nearby, began to laugh. He wore a crisp white shirt and a black bow tie. "Have you met her?" he asked. "You hit the absolute dead-center bull's-eye with that theory."

I introduced myself again to him—he remembered—and also introduced him to Nathan's mother.

"Helen came here to relax for a couple of days, but it's not worked out that well, with the murder and all," I said.

"Haven't they arrested someone?" he asked, his forehead furrowed into worry lines.

"Apparently they let him go," I said. Not wanting to get into the details of what we knew and didn't know, I turned my attention back to the phone.

"Which kind of work do you prefer," Helen asked Christopher, "your work at the library or bartending at special events?"

"It's actually a perfect combination," he said. "And between the two jobs, I can make a go of this island." They continued to chat about the cost of living in Key West.

"In case you hadn't heard, Paul Redford was the big winner at this afternoon's contest, for what that's worth," I said into my phone. "Will you take a look at this before I send the notes off to Nathan?" I asked my mother-in-law once Christopher had returned to making drinks for party guests. "A pie contest hardly makes sense as a motive."

My mother-in-law took the phone from me to look over the notes I'd made. She shook her head. "I'm not seeing other patterns that really jump out. You keep talking about how this town struggles with newcomers versus old-timers. Do you see any trends like that here?"

"Conchs, that's what the natives are called."

"Will I ever get that designation?" asked Christopher, after he'd served two girls dressed in skintight sparkly sheaths. "Looking good, ladies," he told them.

"Probably not. You have to have been born here to be a conch," I said.

The wedding guests were beginning to stream onto the lawn through the front gate. And then the bridesmaids swept in, wearing diaphanous gowns fluttering with gold and silver strips and bejeweled tiaras on their heads and giggling loudly. They made a beeline for Christopher's bar.

"Excuse me, princesses incoming," he said, winking as he pivoted away and began mixing drinks at warp speed.

We headed back toward the catering van. "Christopher mentioned that the cost of living has gotten so high that ordinary working people can be driven out by the prices," Helen said. "Is it possible that someone became unreasonably enraged about that? Someone who saw Claudette as an example of the changes? Or who felt their job and their business were threatened by her success?"

"Yes, possible." I couldn't help adding my thoughts about the Key West high season. We were seeing the results of that right here at this wedding. "And some people tend to dread the influx of tourists and visitors—at least the ones who treat the island as though it was their personal playground—and yet we can't survive without them. When the island is so crowded, as it will be through March, sometimes you have to fight for a restaurant reservation. Or even a seat at the movies. And it took forever for me to even drive here tonight."

"So who's been around forever and isn't thriving? Might that be a good question?" Helen mused.

I thought she had a point. I had been talking all week about who owned Key West: who should own Key West versus who was going to own it, whether that was fair or not. I had been super-lucky when I came down here on the spur of the moment because I'd been able to live with Connie. And I was super-lucky after that, landing Miss Gloria as a roommate. Our living arrangement worked because we enjoyed each other's company, and I felt like I could do almost as much for her as she did for me.

And then I was lucky a third time, meeting Nathan, the man I'd fallen for, who wanted to stay right here on the island and had the kind of job that could make that happen.

"Although I would think there must also be a specific personal connection to Claudette. And the specifics of the person are most important, like did they wear mala beads? And were they angry or disturbed enough to leave her in that terrible pretend Santa position? Let's check in with Bee Thistle," Helen said, and began weaving through guests on the brick pathway where I imagined the ceremony would take place. I hurried to catch up with her.

Bee was manning a second dessert station, attempting to prevent guests from stripping it bare of pie and key lime macaroons before the party had even officially started.

My mother-in-law steamed up to her. "Are you absolutely certain you did not visit Claudette Parker's neighborhood the night of her murder?" she asked, before I could advise her to approach with caution.

Bee's eyes got wide, and darted from Helen's face to mine. She slid out from behind her table, ran toward the Whitehead entrance of the property, and disappeared onto the street.

"That went well," Helen said. "She obviously saw or even did something. Maybe we should follow her."

Fortunately, she was distracted from what I thought would be a terrible idea when my mother texted that they were ready to start serving, and could we please ferry the potatoes and salad out to the tables nearest the grill? *Be careful, the potatoes are super hot,* she'd added. *We think there's something wrong with that warming oven.*

I sent another quick message to Nathan about Bee, and we headed to the back of the Hemingway Home, past the little cat cemetery and out the side gate to my mother's van. I couldn't keep the vision of the pie that had been thrown in our houseboat from flashing to mind. Even if Bee seemed an unlikely killer, she had to be involved somehow. Otherwise, why would she be so nervous? My stomach clenched with tension, but I tried to focus on getting the work done for the party.

"Maybe you should arrange the platters and I'll start carrying them out," Helen suggested once we were inside the van. "I don't have an artistic bone in my body."

I handed her the first bowls of salad, and she put them on the rolling cart that my mother had provided and went rattling off on the bumpy sidewalk in the direction of Sam's grill. In the way back of the van, I opened the warming drawer. I'd never seen mashed potatoes boiling, but these were bubbling hard around the edges, where the hot butter had pooled. Suddenly the van's overhead light flickered and then went out, leaving me in the pitch-dark. I pushed the drawer closed so I wouldn't accidentally burn myself.

Dammit. This was not the time for equipment malfunction. Maybe a loose bulb needed tightening? I felt around for the fixture on the van's ceiling. Before I knew what was happening, my hands had been yanked behind my back and a piece of tape slapped over my mouth so I couldn't yell. A voice whispered harshly.

"If you fight, you'll get hurt. And so will your family." More tape was slapped around my wrists and my ankles, and then I was shoved into the small cabinet underneath the sink. Some minutes later, a second person was shoved in with me, and then the doors clanged shut. I heard the rough noise of the engine firing up and we lurched away from the curb.

Chapter Twenty-Seven

I leaned over and opened a drawer to grab my French rolling pin. Using both hands, I whacked her over the head as hard as I could. She wobbled for a few seconds and then fell to the floor.

—Krista Davis, *The Diva Sweetens the Pie*

I t was hot in the little cabinet and extremely uncomfortable, and I felt scared and shocked. The tape that had been slapped over my mouth also covered one nostril and I was having trouble breathing. A wash of fear rushed over me, so strong I could smell it. I was going to suffocate.

Nathan and I had talked months ago about what I should do if I was ever taken hostage. I'd tried to laugh his concerns off, but he was dead serious. And honestly, I'd seen enough crimes over the past few years to accept this as a distant possibility.

"The main thing is not to let the panic take over. You will feel panicked and terrified; that's perfectly normal. Even professionals in law enforcement panic sometimes. Acknowledge the fear, then set the feelings aside and get to work. Your brain is your biggest asset. Breathe slowly and absorb all the details of what's around you. Try to be logical and not let emotion take over. Notice everything, even if you can't see. You'll smell things, you'll hear things."

He'd cupped my face in his hands, and from the pain in his eyes, I knew this conversation had to be as hard for him as it was for me. "How many captors? How old? What do they sound like? What is their emotional condition?

"Do you understand what I'm saying?" he'd finished.

I could only nod because I knew he needed me to.

Now the thought of Nathan and how much he loved me, and the possibility of never seeing him again, nearly brought me back to hysterics. I forced myself to breathe—count to five on the way in, hold for two, count to seven on the way out. I concentrated on feeling the warm whoosh of air in and out of the uncovered nostril, and began to feel a little calmer.

First question: who else was in the van?

I'd have known if it was my mother—she was on the petite side like me, and she always used a lotion from Alaska that left the sweet scent of lavender in her wake. And wouldn't she have tried to tuck herself around me for comfort? It wasn't Mom. But this person was too small to be a man, and I could feel curly hair tickling my neck. Maybe Helen?

Second question: who was driving the van? Pretty much everyone we'd suspected of Claudette's murder had been at the party. Bee, Paul, David . . . That thought got my heart racing again. *Breathe, Hayley. What else do you notice?* My captor's voice was not exactly deep but rusty sounding, and she or he'd been strong and fast. I'd had no time to react or try to protect myself or even see who'd taped me up. Those characteristics made it less likely to be Bee, although she'd gotten spooked when Helen asked her if she'd been on the scene of the murder. If it wasn't her, that left the possibility of David Sloan or Paul Redford. Or any other man who'd been at the crazy party.

Third question: Nathan had also instructed me to try to visualize where I might be taken. I was pretty sure we were heading north, because all major roads eventually headed north on this island. North to oblivion—that's where we were going. I couldn't help feeling sorry for Nathan, who would be losing both of the important women in his life. He'd blame himself; I knew he would. Because the hideous person driving this vehicle was most likely his enemy, not ours. We were either collateral damage, or about to be knocked off for being too nosy. I tried not to think more sad thoughts, because then I'd start to cry and my nose would get all stuffed up, and it was hard enough to suck air in through the duct tape without that.

Somehow, while my mind was spinning in a hundred directions, Helen had worked off the tape over her mouth. "Hayley," she whispered, "are you okay?"

How could a person with duct tape slapped over her mouth, riding in the back of a van, jammed into a cabinet that wasn't really big enough for one woman let alone two, and headed to a pretty certain annihilation answer a question like that? But I eked out a muffled grunt to let her know I was still alive.

"I'm awfully sorry about this. It's a bit my fault for coming down and pursuing this scumbag. But I was afraid not to. If you'd called and told me Nathan had been killed and I never did anything about it, I couldn't live with myself." She was quiet for a moment. "I have a confession. I didn't come down because I was worried about Nathan. I was concerned about Claudette." Her voice broke.

My mind was spinning with the possibilities, trying to absorb the idea that she had actually known Claudette prior to this visit. That she had lied to me all along. We bumped along in silence for a while, while I worked the tape with my lips and teeth. By the sounds of the traffic and the van's tires clacking on pavement, I could tell that we had turned off the island and were headed north on Route 1 toward the mainland. About fifteen minutes later, I'd chewed a hole in the tape and I could whisper back.

"You knew Claudette was in danger?" I said in a low voice, feeling like I'd finally pulled the string of the lightbulb that had been hanging right in front of me all along. "And you said nothing? And then we found her murdered and you pretended to know nothing about it?"

"I'm sorry. It's so complicated."

I waited in silence, determined not to bail her out.

"I can see why you'd be annoyed, but I'll try to explain. You know how Jai said Claudette was missing a sister who never came home? Claudette went wild with grief exactly as we did when our daughter Vera went missing.

"Did Nathan tell you about Vera?" Her voice was low and packed with sadness.

"He did, last night. He didn't want to, but I kind of forced it out of him."

After a long pause, she said, "I always suspected the same man took both of them. The similarities were too striking. There is a private Facebook group for victims of crimes who don't feel justice has been done. I found it after Vera came home and the police were unable to solve the mystery of her kidnapping. Both Nathan and my ex-husband believed it was unhealthy to stay involved with those bitter people online. In fact, my ex forbade it. Which is exactly why he's an ex."

"Claudette was a member of the same group," I said flatly.

"She was. We all had pseudonyms, but it was pretty easy to match crimes with people. For ten years, she'd been doing her own research, and she told the other members she was very close to breaking the case. And that caused me to be deeply worried for her safety. Imagine if you'd murdered a girl almost a decade ago and got away with it. And then found out someone hadn't forgotten, that in fact she was doggedly on your tail?"

She was silent for a few moments, and I figured she was reliving the agony of losing her daughter. Or feeling a press of guilt about Claudette—she hadn't come in time to help her. Or maybe most important at the moment, trying to sort out who was driving the van and how we were going to get out of this alive.

"I suspect you have found me to be a cold fish," she finally said.

With the tape still over my most of mouth, and the fact that it was dark in this cabinet, I hoped I could get away with a grunt that neither confirmed nor denied.

"If you don't mind, I'd like to explain."

I grunted again. If this was the end, I might as well know whatever she felt pressed to say.

"After Nathan married Trudy, for a while it was almost like having my daughter back. She was so bubbly and so girly and she called me all the time to chat, and I'd missed that so much. And then she suffered that awful home invasion and we all freaked out. It felt like a repetition of the absolute worst time of my life. Nathan went crazy—he felt that he should have been home to prevent this. And the guy who broke in was someone he'd arrested previously. He felt he was to blame and he wanted to hold Trudy closer so that nothing else would happen to her, and she felt suffocated. She pushed back. And I felt helpless to help them. Nathan's not the kind of man to want marital tips from his mother—especially since I had divorced his father not long before. All I could do was watch the problems unspool."

I hated hearing about the pain they'd suffered. "I'm so sorry about all that. Your family has suffered a lot of loss. What finally happened?"

"In self-protection, he started pulling away from her, which made her cling to him like Saran wrap. They couldn't break the cycle. And finally he could see the relationship was over because with each round, they got angrier and further apart. There was too much damage." She sighed. "And I understood their process completely because the same thing happened with me and Nathan's father after Vera was taken. There comes a point where the relationship is in tatters and can't be patched. There are gaping holes where trust and love used to be . . ." Her words trailed off.

I made a noise that I hoped sounded sympathetic. I was sorry that she and Nathan's father had not been able to figure a way out of the darkness. Not so sorry about Nathan and Trudy.

"And then last fall Nathan made his announcement that he was marrying again. I hope you can see why it was hard for me. The truth was, I couldn't get past all the pain. And I didn't try hard enough, I'm sorry. It was so hard losing Trudy, almost as if Vera had gone missing again. And so I kept my distance from you."

"I understand," I said. "It's okay."

"Not really," she said. "I'm truly sorry if I've made you feel like something's wrong with you. Because there isn't. You're warm and lovely and so is your family. And my son is lucky to have you."

At first I felt like crying. But my next thought was that we should not take this kidnapping lying down. We should fight to the bitter end or die trying. To use every awful warrior cliché.

I felt around with my bound hands to the inside corners and edges of the kitchen cabinet. As I'd hoped, one serrated metal edge had been left exposed. I began to saw at the duct tape, pulling away when I accidentally rubbed my skin on the sharp edge instead of the tape. It was painful and it was slow and the muscles in my arms began to throb with the effort, but eventually I felt the tape begin to give. I yanked hard and the tape ripped so that I was able to slide my left hand out. And then I worked the tape off the rest of my mouth and nose, feeling a great whoosh of relief.

"Stay still," I whispered to Helen. "My hands are free. Now I'll work on yours."

Within minutes, she too was free of the tape binding her wrists. And we'd both managed to ease the tape off our ankles.

"We better make a damn good plan before we burst out of here," she said, cracking the cabinet door open so we could breathe more easily. "He's liable to be desperate enough to shoot us on the spot if he sees us loose."

"He?" I asked. "I'm pretty sure it's Bee."

"No," she said. "It's a man. Sloan."

Sloan? But why? Our questions would have to wait.

"What do you suggest?" I asked.

My only idea was opening the back door and flinging ourselves out onto the highway. At the speed we appeared to be going, this would be suicide. Especially since the traffic on the Overseas Highway was so busy this week. Even if we survived slamming into the road surface without killing ourselves, we'd risk getting run over by the person right behind.

"Nathan once said try to make a connection with a kidnapper so you become a human being in his eyes, not a faceless victim," I said.

"But you already know this guy, right?" asked Helen. "That hasn't seemed to help so far." I thought about David Sloan and the interactions we'd had this week and what I'd observed during the course of the pie competition, beginning with the scene at the library. This summed it up. He wanted what he wanted, and he'd do what needed to be done to get that.

And then I thought about Claudette's side of the equation. If she had figured out that he'd killed her sister, she'd have been enraged. She'd have been waiting for the right moment to take him down. The pie in the face suddenly made perfect sense. Not that she meant it as an even exchange for her sister's murder, but perhaps as a shot across his bow.

Helen pushed the cabinet door open wider so we had enough light to see the van's interior. The detritus of my mother's wedding catering job lay all around—on the floor, the counters, and on the little gas stove. I could smell mayonnaise and stale bread and overripe melon and pineapple. Gallons of chicken salad and hundreds of petite croissants and croissant corsages and fruit salad had been scattered everywhere.

My mother must be distraught by now, since we hadn't returned with more trays of mashed potatoes and bowls of salad. Maybe she'd already rushed outside the walls of the Hemingway Home, steaming with annoyance. Maybe she'd seen the van missing and immediately called the cops? Or would she still be working inside, imagining I'd gone on some poorly considered errand or gotten entranced by one of the cats and distracted from my assignment? In that case, she'd be sending me dozens of texts. And she'd be furious that I wasn't answering. Before long, she would storm off the grounds, then find the van gone.

"Maybe if we bang pots and pans, he'll pull over to the side to see what's making the racket. And then we burst out of the back and run," said my mother-in-law.

"Do you have a gun?" I asked her. "Because he probably does. I'm not sure it's better to die by getting shot down than by throwing ourselves out on the road and bashing our heads on the concrete."

She sighed. "I did have one, of course. He took it away."

Of course she did. She was from a law enforcement family in which owning a gun did not feel more dangerous than not owning a gun, as it did in my family. Nathan had asked if he could buy me a weapon after we'd gotten engaged, but so far I had refused.

"Let's think through how he would react if he heard a lot of banging back here," she suggested.

"At first, he might just look through the little window from the cab," I said. "So if we either stay in the cupboard or press against the wall, he would see nothing. Except maybe he'd notice all the stuff that's been knocked to the floor. Though we didn't do that—his erratic driving did."

"You know your mother's kitchen," said Helen. "Is there anything in her drawers we could use as a weapon?"

I closed my eyes and tried to visualize what I'd seen when Mom and Sam gave me a detailed tour—delighted with their purchase and proud of the improvements they'd made. "She's got a couple of serious carving knives, unless she already took them into the party. Which I'm afraid she might have, because Sam had to use them at his carving station, didn't he?"

"Beats me," said Helen. "I tune out when there's too much discussion about food."

I grinned, but it hurt my lips where I'd ripped the tape off. I tried to picture each of the drawers and cabinets around us. "There is a rolling pin," I said suddenly. "It's a whopper. The kind a serious pastry chef would use on pie crust if she's rolling out a lot of dough. And we have an endless supply of piping-hot mashed potatoes."

We quickly settled on a plan: I'd wield the rolling pin while she grabbed a pan of potatoes. When the door opened, she would smash the hot vegetables in his face, distracting him enough that I could knock him down with the rolling pin. It sounded ridiculous, but it was all we had.

We crawled out of the cabinet and grabbed the biggest pots and pans hanging from hooks in the ceiling, then took two large metal spoons from one of the drawers.

"He's going to be frantic about getting to the mainland," I said. "Because every burglar and bad guy knows there is only one way off the Keys. Once my mother realizes the van is missing and makes one call to the police and they alert the sheriff's department, then he gets pulled over and dragged off to jail."

"He may be frantic, but we are determined," she said, and I could see the intensity in the grim set of her lips. She nodded, and we began to bang the pots and pans and spoons against the steel of the van, the places my mother had asked Sam to cover with corkboard. Lucky for us, he'd been too busy to make any further cosmetic changes. We flattened ourselves against the wall between the passenger cab and the cargo area and banged and banged and banged.

I could feel the van slow, then take a sudden turn to the right and begin to bump across an unpaved surface.

"Ready?" she asked. "We are strong, we are brave, and there are two of us and one of him."

We picked up our weapons and I gave her a quick nod of reassurance, ignoring the pounding, hammering, throbbing of my heart.

Chapter Twenty-Eight

"You think someone killed her to keep her quiet?" Vera licked her fingers to pick up the crumbs from her plate and the surrounding table.

—Ann Cleeves, *Silent Voices*

We crouched low on either side of the back door of the van, me wielding the rolling pin and my mother-in-law with a large foil tin of hot potatoes. The van jerked to a full stop. Helen stumbled, and the pan of potatoes flew out of her hands and splattered across the floor and the wall. She froze where she'd landed on her knees, probably thinking the same thing I was: with only one rolling pin between us, we didn't stand a chance against a man with a deadly weapon.

I finally noticed that the tool we'd used to distribute hot glue on those silly corsages was still plugged in. "Grab the glue gun," I hissed.

When the door was thrown open, I was so surprised not to see David Sloan that I almost forgot to swing my makeshift bat. But Helen didn't hesitate, shooting a stream of hot glue into Christopher's eyes. He screamed, and I gathered my wits and walloped him with all my strength. He sank to the pavement, clutching his head, and I hit him again, this time on his right forearm. The gun in his hand skittered across the road, discharging a round into the scrub palmettos on the other side of the ditch. He fell to the ground, moaning with pain.

"You make one move and I'll bash your head in the next time." I brandished the rolling pin, practically growling with anger so he would realize I meant every word.

While I stood guard over him, Helen scrambled back into the van and emerged with the roll of duct tape.

"Put your arms behind your back," she told him.

"She broke my arm," he squawked. "It's killing me."

I gave him a light whack on the back, and he did what she'd told him. Each time he tried to squirm away, I rapped him again with the rolling pin to let him know we meant business. Within minutes, he was hog-tied exactly the way he had left us. Helen slapped an extra piece of tape over his mouth.

"There is nothing we care to hear from you," she said in a fierce voice. "I have half a mind to jam him in that little closet," she said. "See how he likes that claustrophobic space. Meanwhile, where is his phone?" She sorted through his pockets until she found his cell phone.

"Call 911 and tell them where you think we are." She handed the phone to me, and I called. Then we stood guard, waiting for the authorities to arrive and take over. Finally my mind slowed down enough to react to what I was seeing.

"Christopher?" I said, feeling puzzled. "What the heck is he doing here? I was sure it was David Sloan or even Paul. Or for that matter, Bee. This guy never crossed my mind—he was so polite and helpful." His eyes were wide and wild and he was trying to talk through the duct tape I'd slapped over his lips.

Helen's face looked stony and she kicked at him. "If he killed Claudette, he's also the one who took my daughter and ruined her life. We wondered if it was someone who moved down here recently. I bet he followed her here, planning to keep her from revealing his identity if needed."

Christopher struggled on the ground, grunting through the duct tape. It sounded like he was trying to say, "I can explain . . ."

"You keep your mouth shut unless you want Hayley here to bash your brains in with that rolling pin," Helen barked at him, then scrambled into the ditch along the road to retrieve the gun he'd lost. Once back on the side of the road, she parted Christopher's hair with the barrel of the gun to show me the dark roots. His eyes went wide as she pressed the barrel of the gun against his temple.

"I have half a mind to shoot you dead right here," she said. "I know for sure that Hayley, being married to a cop, understands the Florida stand-your-ground statute: a person is justified in using deadly force if she reasonably believes such action will repel imminent death to herself or another."

She glanced over at me, and though I felt sick to my stomach, I nodded. I couldn't imagine not telling the truth when the police turned up—I doubted that shooting him when he was trussed up like a spring lamb would fit the stand-your-ground bill. But he deserved to be terrified. Nor was I going to argue with my mother-in-law in this kind of a mood. If she shot him here in cold blood, I was sure Nathan would find her the best lawyer in the state.

I heard the whine of sirens in the distance, and several cars had begun to pull over behind us, their occupants running up to see how they could help. Helen kept the gun trained on Christopher and instructed the bystanders to stand back until the cops arrived. I saw several of them using phones to film Christopher on the pavement, who was wild-eyed, flopping from side to side, and trying to yell through the duct tape.

A sheriff's department SUV screamed to a stop alongside us, and two deputies leaped out with weapons drawn.

"Ma'am," said one to Nathan's mom, "put the gun on the ground and step back with your hands in the air."

She did as she was told, I dropped the rolling pin and raised my hands too, and the deputies patted us both down. While we were explaining what had happened, a fire department ambulance screeched up behind us, and finally the vehicle I'd been waiting for—Nathan's. He darted over to us with a look on his face that I hoped to never see again: fear, rage, and anguish. He had pulled his gun out of its holster as he ran, and now he trained it on Christopher.

"If you hurt either one of them, I swear I will shoot you dead on the spot."

"We've got this," said the sheriff's deputy. He held a beefy hand up to my husband and stared at Nathan hard until he holstered his gun.

I ran over and flung myself into Nathan's arms. "I'm okay. Your mom is okay."

He hugged me so tight I could barely breath, and then walked over to hug his mother, and then pulled both of us into his strong embrace. He rocked us, back and forth, whispering soothing words. "I'm so sorry. You're okay. He'll never hurt anyone else."

Chapter
Twenty-Nine

A party without cake is really just a meeting.

—Julia Child

It was late when the hospital staff finished checking us over and the cops wrapped up our initial interviews. Nathan drove me home to the houseboat, where I slept like the dead for seven hours. I heard nothing—not Nathan leaving before dark after grabbing a few hours of rest, not Evinrude clamoring to be let out in the early morning, not the caterwauling of a cat fight with our new kitten facing off against the other two, Ziggy yapping on the sidelines. Miss Gloria had left a note on the counter describing all that, and added that she had gone off to a New Year's Day brunch but would be back midafternoon.

Your mother texted to say that she and Sam are bringing dinner over here at five. She couldn't wait any longer to hear the whole story. She's bringing your mother-in-law, of course. And Nathan insists he'll be here too.

That left a couple of hours of free time. I desperately needed a large café con leche, and something to eat. I drove my scooter to the Cuban Coffee Queen near the harbor and put in my order for coffee and cheese toast. Too restless to eat on the bench by the water, I gobbled half of the sandwich as I strolled down Greene Street. This neighborhood was again packed with tourists, some bleary-eyed from their New Year's Eve celebrations. I paused in front of Claudette Parker's little bakery, Au Citron Vert, intensely curious about what I'd find. More than likely a *Closed* sign, and possibly even one that read *For sale or rent.*

The shop was not open, but the lights were on and I could see a man working at the counter. I cupped my hands around my eyes and leaned against the glass to look more closely. It was Paul. I tapped on the window. He shook his head and pointed to the *Closed* sign on the door. I tapped again and held up my index finger to show that I only needed a minute. His shoulders drooped, but he crossed the room, unlocked the door, and let me in.

"Thank you so much for opening—"

He cut me off. "I have nothing to sell today."

"Oh, I understand," I said. "I just wanted to be sure that you knew they arrested Claudette Parker's killer."

His eyes went wide.

"Christopher. He worked at the library. It's a long story, but he kidnapped me and my mother-in-law last night, and we were able to get away, and then the police and sheriff's department showed up and all is well." My voice was a little shaky. "I felt bad about pressing you about her death. You had enough trauma working here." I paused for a minute, wondering how much to say. I didn't suppose it mattered. "Cheryl told us that you stopped by Claudette's house the night of the murder."

"I wish we'd ended on a better note," he said sadly. "I hate for an argument to be the last thing I remember. The good news is, I found another investor and it looks like I'll be able to buy the shop and continue her work." He sighed. "And show off some of mine."

"Wonderful! Do you mind saying who?" None of my business, but I was intensely curious.

"David Sloan," he said, watching my face for a reaction. "Obviously he and Claudette were oil and water, but he's willing to try to work with me. And he knows a lot about Key West and certainly knows a lot about selling key lime pie. And this is where I want to be, and I'm sorry it all happened because she died, but I don't suppose it matters to her now."

"I don't suppose it does," I said. "I wish you all the best. There's likely to be lots of publicity about this shop when this latest news hits the papers."

"I'm planning to open tomorrow morning," he said, flashing the first smile I'd seen.

"Maybe someone from *Key Zest* can stop by and report on the new owner's plans," I said, matching his grin.

* * *

I went to the office to work for a bit, tweaking my article about key lime pie in Key West and drafting a teaser about the new chef-owner of Au Citron Vert. I returned to the houseboat by four. Nathan was already there, along with Helen and Miss Gloria and my mother and Sam. They buzzed around me for a few minutes, insisting I take the best lounge chair and bringing me a lap blanket and a glass of wine.

"I'm fine," I finally said. "All this attention is lovely but completely unnecessary. Let's all sit down and hear about the murder case. Who was Christopher, really, and what was his connection to Key West? And why did he kidnap those girls in the first place?" I threw an apologetic look at Nathan's mom, but hoped she wanted to sort out the rat's nest as much as I did.

"I'll take the easy part first. He didn't come down with any plan in mind. The draw wasn't Key West per se," said Nathan. "He was watching Claudette. He managed to get accepted into your private Facebook group under an alias." Here he cast a fierce look at his mother. "He must have gotten worried about how much she knew about him and that she had planned to take her information to the police. He talked enough this morning that we can put some of the pieces together."

He glanced at his mother for reassurance—did she want to hear all this? She nodded for him to continue.

"From the spreadsheets we found on her computer, we believe that Claudette had spent years tracking him down. And finally she figured out that he was her sister's killer. We don't know whether she'd figured out that he followed her to Key West."

"So he killed her because she knew too much?" I asked.

"So it appears," Nathan said.

"How could he possibly have known ahead of time that not only would we take that Conch Train Tour, we would go back and look more closely and notice Claudette's body?" Miss Gloria asked.

She had the little orange kitten on her lap, and he was purring so loudly I could hear him from across the deck. Sparky watched balefully from behind a potted plant.

"I don't think the connections match that perfectly," Nathan said. "I think it was an ugly coincidence that you three discovered Ms. Parker's body."

"It wasn't coincidence," I protested. "It was your mother's Spidey sense. She felt in her gut that something was terribly wrong."

He rolled his eyes a little.

"Claudette hacked into some DNA databases that weren't available back when her sister was murdered," said Helen. "And she made the mistake of talking in the group about how she was on to him."

"We'll know more details when we finish sorting through both of their phone records and computer logs," Nathan added.

He squeezed my hand and kept talking. "He was a lethal killer intent on not being found out and put in jail or executed. So when he understood that Claudette was on his heels, he had to kill her. I suppose he thought he'd gotten away with it, because we had so many good suspects." He let go of my fingers, frowning. "Once he realized that Hayley and Helen were close to figuring out the murder, he had to kidnap them as well."

"But how in the world did he know they knew?" Miss Gloria asked.

I looked at Nathan's mom and gulped. "Unfortunately, he overheard us talking about whether I'd told Nathan about all our theories." I glanced at Nathan. "I'd been meaning to send you a text earlier, but the past few days were insane. We talked everything over while we were working on the wedding— that was the first time I had the chance to think things through. And he overheard some of what I dictated in my text to you."

"Maybe he hoped we hadn't told the police what we knew yet," said Helen. "If that was true, he would still be in the clear. *If* he got rid of us." Her voice trailed off. We were all quiet for a minute, listening to the slap of water on the hull and the tinkle of Mrs. Renhart's wind chimes.

"Do we know why he killed that poor teenager in the first place?" asked Miss Gloria. "Why he kidnapped your daughter?"

Helen focused a steady gaze on my roommate's face. "He was an angry, sociopathic young man, overindulged by doting parents who could not believe there was a problem. My Vera managed to get out of the situation alive because he shut her in his trunk and she was smart enough to pull the tab that popped the lid."

"Claudette's sister was not so lucky," Nathan added.

"But why take another girl?" Miss Gloria asked.

Nathan shook his head, his expression steely. "We may never know. He may not understand it either. But he won't do it again. I'll make sure of that."

"Cheryl finally admitted to seeing Paul in Claudette's neighborhood the night of the murder," I said. "I wouldn't be surprised to hear that David Sloan had been there too."

"We knew Sloan didn't kill her," Nathan said. "He had a dozen witnesses confirming that he'd spent the late afternoon and early evening drinking beer at the General Horseplay Bar. Most of them were intoxicated, but all the regulars saw him, so he was off the hook."

"When we heard that Cheryl hadn't told everything she knew about that night and figured out that the blue prayer bead I found on the sidewalk probably belonged to a woman, I was almost certain the killer had to be the Blue Heaven pastry chef," I added.

Nathan grimaced. "We had Bee in the station early this morning for a long chat. She admitted that she came to Claudette's home the night of the murder to talk about getting hired as her second-in-command at Au Citron Vert."

"She didn't want to talk about any of that when I visited," I said.

Nathan rolled his eyes. "And that is why we beg civilians to leave interviewing to the professionals. Anyway, she pumped herself up that night to tell Claudette that she was the best pastry chef in town. Instead of having that conversation and coming away with a new job, she found Claudette dead on the porch. She panicked and ran off, sure that police would conclude that she was the killer. In her haste, she caught her necklace on a palmetto branch and it broke. Partway down the street, she realized the necklace was gone. This discovery would confirm that she'd been at the scene of the crime, so she came back to find it. Unfortunately, you and Miss Gloria and my mother had arrived at the house, and she saw you picking up the beads."

I gulped. "So she was the one who tossed our houseboat?"

Nathan nodded. "She really panicked once the police talked with her the first time, and came to the houseboat hoping to retrieve the necklace. She found the beads in the bowl on your bureau, although she must have dropped one in her hurry."

"And the kitty found it!" crowed Miss Gloria. "I knew he was a winner the minute I saw him in the bushes."

"What about the pie smashed on the window?" I asked, frowning.

"She apologized for that," Nathan said. "She hoped to throw us off the scent. Apparently she spent some time thinking about which piece of pie it should be. Should she throw her own pie in order to prove she wasn't the one who did it, because no chef would throw her own pastry? Or should she throw Claudette's version?"

Nathan wrinkled his nose as if to say he'd never truly understand the minds of the food-obsessed.

Then he heaved a big sigh. "Hayley, do you remember that you were worried about someone you saw on the Florida website who had been released or escaped from prison?"

"Of course I remember. And it wasn't one person, it was hundreds. It makes my blood run cold to think about people out there that you put away that are waiting all through their prison terms to pay you back when they are released."

"Here, here," said my mother-in-law. "And I have access to more material than you do. Which I am, by the way, not intending to share."

"I should hope not," said Nathan. "As you can see, this case has nothing to do with my work. It does nobody any good to worry about consequences of this job. Either you do it or you don't. And if I'm going to do it, I'm going to do it well. And that means I will solve ugly cases and hopefully put some bad people in jail." He shrugged his big muscular shoulders. "It's part of the job. It's part of the deal. It's part of being in a cop's family."

Sam came to the door of the houseboat. "Soup's on," he said. "If everyone wants to come grab a plate, we'll serve supper inside and eat out here. We've got platters of caprese salad with mozzarella, tomatoes, and slices of grilled steak, along with a watermelon salad, and a basket of baguette slices from the Old Town Bakery. And I made a chocolate cake, figuring all of you are sick to death of key lime pie."

"That sounds amazing," I said, realizing I hadn't eaten last night. And had only nibbled at the cheese toast from the Coffee Queen. "You never told us what happened to the wedding party. We ruined both of the menus by driving off in your van. When did you figure out we were gone? How did the bride react?"

"The groom's father came running over to tell us that the bartender disappeared and the guests were going crazy without any cocktails. I was so annoyed, because we were paying Christopher top dollar," said my mother. "And by then Sam noticed that you ladies weren't delivering any of the stuff we'd asked you for. So we both left our posts and came over to see what was up. The van was gone, and I had the worst feeling that something terrible had happened to you. I called Nathan and Steve and then dialed 911 for good measure."

"Meanwhile, with the plans for the wedding party shattered, the groom took the opportunity to announce to the bride that he'd had cold feet for ages. He finally got up the nerve to tell her the wedding was off. Then he and his attendants bolted for Duval Street," said Sam. "The whole night was a disaster. But in the end, your kidnapping probably saved them from years of unhappy married life and an expensive divorce." He chuckled. "And a couple of our helpers had the good sense to wrap up some of that beautiful filet, and we stashed it in our fridge. So dinner tonight is on the father of the un-bride."

"Your dinner sounds so good," said Miss Gloria, dislodging the kitten from her lap and heading inside. "I can't wait another minute." Helen and my parents followed her into the kitchen.

"Save a little for us," I called after them, then turned back to my husband. "I do understand that danger comes with being part of a cop's family. It's part of loving a great big lug like you, but it's not the part I am happy about. And I'll probably never get used to it. And I'll certainly never stop worrying."

He cupped my face in his hands, gently, so he wouldn't press the sore patches where the adhesive had torn the skin, and looked deeply into my eyes. "I understand that. I have another question," he said.

I nodded to let him know I'd answer anything.

"Why in god's name did you insist on investigating this murder when I asked—or rather, begged—you not to? It's not that I want to control you. Really." He ran a finger along my jawline, stopping at the bandage below my ear that covered the rawest patch of skin. "I was terrified you would get hurt. And you did. Can you understand how devastating that feels?"

I closed my eyes, blinked them open. "I wanted so much for your mother to like me. More than Trudy. And she felt desperate to protect you by solving this murder. So I went along. I know that wanting her to love me is not a good reason, and not a fair hope, but you asked."

Nathan put a hand to his forehead. "Sweetheart, can't you see it? She's falling for you, hard. Exactly the way that I did." He planted a sweet kiss on my lips. "You don't need any more crazy shenanigans to make that happen, okay?"

"One more question," I said. "Since I'm realizing I don't know everything about you like I thought I did. And realizing it's not fair to make assumptions."

A pained look flitted over his face, as though he was expecting a topic he'd rather not discuss, but he smoothed it away quickly. "Hit me," he said.

"Here goes: would you mind if I hung something on our kitchen wall that said *You Are the Icing on My Cupcake*? Maybe with a couple of kittens playing with the cupcakes?"

Nathan began to laugh, his shoulders shaking. "You *are* the icing on my cupcake. You're the batter and the cake and the cupcake liners, too. You are everything to me, Hayley Snow. If you want to decorate our place—assuming we ever move in—in cat lady cute, and adopt all the felines at the shelter, that's fine with me. As long as there's a little room for me in your bed and at your table."

He grabbed me into a big hug, squeezing so hard I could hardly catch my breath. "And I plan to take you on a fabulous honeymoon later this year," he added, holding me away so he could see my face. "Absolutely anywhere you want to go."

"Hmmm. Ever since Miss Gloria and I started watching *Outlander*, I've been itching to see Scotland."

Miss Gloria came out onto the deck with her plate. "Oh my word, are we going to Scotland? That is at the very tip top of my bucket list!" She set her plate down and picked up a magazine from the end table to fan her face. "I can't wait to see all those redheaded men in skirts . . ."

Recipes

Cheese Puffs With Fig Jam

These puffs are super-easy and always a big hit at parties. You may need to tell guests they are appetizers made of cheese, not cookies! If you prefer a zippy filling, use hot pepper jelly instead of the fig jam.

Ingredients
½ pound sharp cheddar cheese, shredded
½ cup (1 stick) butter, unsalted
1 cup flour
Fig jam
Preheat oven to 400.

Mix first three ingredients thoroughly in food processor or by hand. Chill ½ hour. Roll into small balls and place on a cookie sheet covered with parchment. Bake five minutes.

Remove pan from oven and make a depression in the top of each puff with the back of a spoon. Fill each depression with fig jam and continue baking until golden, about five more minutes.

Alvina's Crumb Cake

My father did not cook much, but he was proud of the two recipes in his repertoire: a pie crust made with oil, and this coffee cake. I made a few tweaks to his recipe, including using cake flour, which makes a finer crumb. I also added butter and brown sugar to the topping, and reduced the oven temperature (I remember the cake often coming out crispy).

Ingredients

2 cups granulated sugar
1 cup (2 sticks) unsalted butter, softened
4 cups flour, cake if you have it
1 teaspoon cinnamon
½ cup brown sugar
¼ cup (½ stick) unsalted butter
⅓ cup additional flour
4 heaping teaspoons baking powder
3 beaten eggs
1 cup milk
1 teaspoon vanilla

Preheat oven to 350.

Pulse the sugar, 2 sticks of butter, and flour together. (I used a stand mixer—small lumps are acceptable, even encouraged.)

Remove one cup of this mixture for topping and place in another bowl. Into that mixture, using either a pastry cutter or a fork, cut cinnamon, ½ stick of butter, and brown sugar. Set aside.

To the original batter, add baking powder and eggs. Mix well.

Mix in the milk and vanilla—do not overbeat.

Pour the batter into a well-buttered 9 × 13–inch pan and sprinkle the reserved cinnamon crumbs over top. Bake 35 or so minutes, or until a toothpick stuck in the middle comes out dry.

This is also delicious with a handful of fresh blueberries folded in before baking.

Cheryl's Chai Snickerdoodles

Cheryl served these in her backyard when Hayley and Helen and Miss Gloria came by to interview her about the murder. The chai spice gives them a special kick.

Ingredients

¼ teaspoon salt
1½ cups sugar
2½ teaspoons baking powder (low-sodium works fine)
2¾ cups flour
1 cup (2 sticks) unsalted butter, softened
2 eggs, room temperature

For the topping:
2 teaspoons cinnamon
1 teaspoon chai spice
3 tablespoons additional sugar

Preheat oven to 375.

Sift dry ingredients (salt, sugar, low-sodium baking powder, and flour) together. Set aside.

Using either a beater or a stand mixer, beat the butter until light and fluffy. Beat in the eggs one at a time, about 1 to 2 minutes after each addition.

Slowly mix in the dry ingredients—don't beat too long or the cookies will be tough.

Divide dough into two parts, roll into logs, and wrap with parchment paper. This isn't a beauty contest, so no need to be too fussy about your logs, as you'll be rolling the cookies too.

Refrigerate two hours or freeze one hour.

Mix the cinnamon, chai spice, and remaining sugar on a plate. Cut the logs into one-inch pieces and form them into balls. Roll the balls in the cinnamon mixture and place them on 2 parchment-covered baking sheets. You should end up with about 2 dozen cookies—big ones!

Bake 8–10 minutes, removing them from the oven as soon as the first cracks appear.

Knockoff Baby's Salad With Italian Dressing a la Clemente's Trolley Pizzeria

This dressing is based on a salad Hayley is mad for at her favorite pizza place in Key West, called Clemente's Trolley Pizzeria. She always orders Baby's salad to go with her pizza, and so do I. The secret to the salad is homemade Italian dressing.

Ingredients

For the salad:
Romaine lettuce (or mixed greens with arugula)
Tomatoes
Carrots, shredded
Red onions
Garbanzos, drained and rinsed
Blue cheese
Avocado
Cucumbers

For the dressing:
1 teaspoon dried parsley
2 teaspoons dried minced onion
1 teaspoon dried basil
½ teaspoon dried oregano
½ teaspoon garlic powder
¼ teaspoon freshly ground black pepper

½ teaspoon crushed red pepper or to taste, if you want a
  little zip
¼ teaspoon salt
2 tablespoons grated Parmesan cheese
1 teaspoon honey or sugar
¼ cup white wine vinegar
2 teaspoons fresh lemon juice
¾ cup extra-virgin olive oil

Chop and combine the salad ingredients to form a salad. For the dressing, mix the spices, salt, and cheese with the honey or sugar, vinegar, and lemon juice in a glass jar and shake well. Add the olive oil and shake until well mixed. Dress the salad and toss well.

Store any leftovers in the refrigerator.

Eric's Chicken and Stuffing Casserole for 160

Cooking lunch for 160 people is not so easy, as I learned in the basement of the Metropolitan Community Church, helping my friend Eric Nichols at Cooking With Love. This is the first meal on which I worked as sous-chef.

40 pounds cooked diced chicken
16 pounds stuffing mix, such as Pepperidge Farm or Stove Top
16 pounds condensed cream of chicken soup
16 pounds condensed cream of celery soup
40 cups chicken broth—can be unsalted
24 12-ounce cans evaporated milk
Preheat ovens to 350.

Layer diced chicken in eight large (12 × 24-inch) greased foil pans. Spread stuffing mix over top. Mix together the two soups, broth, and evaporated milk. Distribute this liquid over the eight pans of chicken and stuffing. Stir lightly so that the liquid mixture saturates the chicken and stuffing layers. Bake 35 to 40 minutes until casseroles are bubbly.

David Sloan's Key Lime Martini

The fictional David Sloan served up these little gems at his book signing at Key West Island Bookstore. The recipe can be found in the real David Sloan's cookbook *The Key West Key Lime Pie Cookbook*. I've reprinted it here with his permission.

2 ounces Stoli Vanil
1 ounce Licor 43
1.5 ounces heavy cream or half-and-half
1 tablespoon fresh key lime juice, plus a little extra

Crushed graham crackers

Add the first four ingredients into a shaker filled with ice. Dip a martini glass into a plate containing key lime juice and then into the crushed graham crackers. Strain vodka mixture into the glass. Enjoy!

Lucy Burdette's Decadent Key Lime Parfait

This dessert can be made in one glass bowl, or if you prefer individual servings, use martini glasses or small mason jars. Either way, the layers will show through the glass and your guests will swoon!

Ingredients

5 whole graham crackers, crushed, to make about 1 cup
2 tablespoons butter, melted
1 tablespoon brown sugar
2 cups whipping cream
¼ cup powdered sugar
1 teaspoon vanilla
½ cup key lime juice (about 1 pound key limes)
14-ounce can sweetened condensed milk
key lime zest (optional)
Preheat oven to 350.

Crush the graham crackers. (Easy tip: place the graham crackers in a ziplock bag and roll them to crumbs with a rolling pin.) Mix the crumbs with the melted butter and brown sugar. Spread this on a baking sheet covered with foil or parchment paper and bake 10 minutes or until golden. Let cool, then break into crumbs again.

Meanwhile, whip the cream with the powdered sugar and vanilla. Set half of this aside for the topping.

Juice the limes and strain out any seeds.

Mix the condensed milk with the lime juice. The citrus will cause the milk to thicken. Gently stir in half the whipped cream mixture.

Layer some of the baked crumbs into eight parfait or martini glasses, then add some of the key lime mixture; repeat, setting aside a few crumbs for topping. When all ingredients are distributed, top with dollops of remaining whipped cream. Sprinkle with remaining crumbs and zested lime if you want a stronger flavor.

Caprese Salad With Grilled Flank Steak

Sam serves this light but delicious supper at the end of *The Key Lime Crime*. He used leftover grilled filet from the ruined wedding, but you can grill your own steak—or use leftovers. Flank steak or filet is probably the best choice.

1 pound flank steak
Salad dressing of your choice
1 bunch butter lettuce, or mixed greens if you prefer
1 box fresh cherry tomatoes or 2–3 ripe large tomatoes
8 ounces fresh mozzarella balls, such as bocconcini
8–10 leaves fresh basil
1 ripe avocado, sliced
Olives of your choice

Marinate steak in the dressing of your choice 2–4 hours. The knockoff Baby's Italian salad dressing would be delicious, or try a balsamic vinaigrette.

Grill steak to medium-rare, let rest a few minutes, then slice on the diagonal.

Wash and dry lettuce; arrange on a pretty platter. Top with sliced tomatoes, mozzarella balls, basil, olives, and avocado. Place steak on top and serve more dressing on the side.

Acknowledgments

I'm very grateful to the talented staff at Crooked Lane Books—Jenny Chen, Ashley Di Dio, Matt Martz, Chelsey Emmelhainz, Rachel Keith, and many others who nurtured this book to life and then launched it into the world. Thank you all! I am crazy about my cover artists, Griesbach and Martucci. And what a joy to work with editor Sandy Harding again—an unexpected pleasure! Thanks always to my persistent and smart agent, Paige Wheeler.

My Facebook friends are so generous when I need help. They are instantly willing to brainstorm what to name a character or a book or a bakery—or even murder motives. This time out, Ann Mason came up with the name Au Citron Vert (French roughly translated as "at the key lime") for Claudette Parker's pâtisserie. Perfectly chichi! And Tammy Werking Hiday cleverly described T-Bone the cat as "the living Swiffer." Thanks to Mike Brady for suggesting the next book should include the Conch Tour Train.

Thanks to the real David Sloan for enthusiastically endorsing the idea of becoming a character in *The Key Lime Crime*, and for giving me permission to share his decadent recipe for a key lime martini. Thank you to Eric Nichols for including me on his Cooking With Love team, and to all the volunteers who show up at Metropolitan Community Church every Saturday to make sure hungry folks in Key West receive a delicious hot meal. Many thanks also to Amber Debevec, Steve Torrence, Suzanne and Paul Orchard, Michael Nelson, Tony, Lorenzo aka Ron, Eric and Bill, Leigh, and Cheryl, who are real people and not responsible for the actions of their fictional characters. Steve is generous about correcting my police procedure errors and assures me Chief Sean Brandenburg will be watching too. By the way, I did get stopped by a real Key West cop—on a bicycle, not a scooter. I'm grateful they are out there looking for troublemakers. And Michael Nelson, I'm sorry for making such a fictional mess in your library.

My friends and amazing writers at Jungle Red Writers are a source of constant support and encouragement. Thank you, Hallie Ephron, Hank Phillippi Ryan, Deborah Crombie, Rhys Bowen, Julia Spencer-Fleming, and Jenn McKinlay— these gifted women are exactly the kind of posse you want for your team. Thanks especially to Hank this time for her suggestions on the cover copy.

As Hayley, Miss Gloria, and Mrs. Bransford did, I attended a pie-making class at the Key Lime Pie Company. It was made so much more fun by the three women who joined me, Lori Tedesco Singley, Judy Monahan, and Louise Procida, and by Sigrid, who taught the class with humor and enthusiasm.

The character of T-Bone is based on the kitten I adopted while writing this book. I had a lot of help choosing him— with wonderful results! Thank you to my friends Stan Duprey and Bunnie Smith and Cheryl and Renee and my sister Sue for advice and encouragement, and to the Florida Keys SPCA for keeping T-Bone safe until I was ready for him.

I couldn't possibly sample all the key lime pies in Key West, but I made a good-faith effort. I can sum up my research by saying I never had a bad bite. Thanks to everyone who helped with this job—especially John, who tried every piece I brought home. And reported at the end of the pie-tasting season, "You know, I'm really not that crazy about key lime pie." He's my number-one supporter and always game for the next adventure.

Angelo Pompano and Chris Falcone, my longtime writing buddies and good friends—I could not do this job without your thoughtful comments and good humor. Thank you!

Sometimes a little independent bookstore sells the Key West mysteries with incredible enthusiasm and should be mentioned by name. Thank you to Jean Lewis and all the staff at Copperfish Books in Punta Gorda, Suzanne and Paul Orchard at Key West Island Books, and the staff at both Books and Books in Key West and R.J. Julia in Madison, Connecticut.

And that brings me to my readers. Thanks for following Hayley's Key West adventures, for writing to let me know your reactions, and for spreading the word about the series. You make all the hard work worth it!

Lucy Burdette
December 27, 2019

Read an excerpt from

A SCONE OF CONTENTION

the next

KEY WEST FOOD CRITIC MYSTERY

by LUCY BURDETTE

available soon in hardcover from
Crooked Lane Books

CROOKED
LANE

NEW YORK

Chapter One

Whoever said cooking should be entered into with abandon or not at all had it wrong. Going into it when you have no hope is sometimes just what you need to get to a better place. Long before there were antidepressants, there was stew.
—Regina Schrambling, "When the Path to Serenity Wends Past the Stove," *The New York Times*, September 19, 2001

The phone rang, and I felt a shiver of worry as my guy's name flashed on the screen: *Nathan Bransford*. A ghost walking on your grave—that's how my grandmother would have described the shiver. I tried to shrug that off as an old wives' tale, but . . . My new husband, Nathan, was a detective with the Key West Police Department and utterly serious about fending off disruptions to his work. Texts were tolerated. Calls not so much. And that meant he never called without an utterly serious reason.

"Hi, sweetheart," I said. "What's up?" I couldn't help worrying about him, always. Considering that we had reservations to fly to Scotland tomorrow, where we'd be staying with his sister and her husband, now I was also concerned about a police emergency interfering with our long-delayed honeymoon trip. But I was learning the rules of married life, one of them being don't instantly show him that you're worried because that makes him feel weak or something even worse. And definitely don't show that *you're* worried that *he's* worried.

He cleared his throat and his voice came over the line a little more rumbly than usual. "I heard from my brother-in-law today while at work. Honestly, my sister sounds a bit"—there was a pause—"unhinged, is the only way to describe it." He was again quiet for a minute, and I could hear him cracking his knuckles, echoing Evinrude the cat, who was crunching on the dog's kibbles. "To make things worse, he insists that I play golf. In fact, he's already made three reservations. At one of the fanciest courses in the world, where duffers and hackers like me don't belong. I'll be in the deep end, way over my head. Plus, a round of golf lasts a lifetime, and that will cut into my time with you."

Nathan had grown up in a family where golf was a given. As part of his teenage rebellion, he'd dropped it cold as soon as he left home for college. "It'll come back to you, like falling off a horse. Oops, sorry—mixing my metaphors. Don't worry about me—I know I'll love your sister. How bad could she be if her husband's planning all that golf? And besides, Miss Gloria makes everything a party." I paused. "Sounds like you're getting cold feet about the trip," I said, keeping my voice light.

"No cold feet, but this sure isn't turning into much of a honeymoon."

I snickered. "We gave that up when we asked Miss Gloria to join us. And she's going to make the trip so much richer. She's so excited—she's researching her family tree on Ancestry and she's made a little map marking where all her relatives might be buried."

We were all headed to Scotland, a delayed honeymoon for Nathan and me, and the first trip abroad since her husband's death for Miss Gloria. Nathan had offered to take me anywhere I wanted to go. I chose Scotland because of *Outlander* and *Shetland,* natch, and because I wanted to meet his mysterious sister, whom I'd only recently learned about. When I'd broken the news to Miss Gloria, my fellow fanatic *Outlander* watcher, she'd said mournfully, "Scotland was the next trip Frank and I were going to take. And then—poof—he was gone. Dead of a heart attack and not traveling anywhere but to the morgue. I'm so happy for you, Hayley," she added. She really meant that, but she had a shimmer of tears in her eyes.

Later that night, Nathan suggested that we should invite her along. I was shocked. "It's our honeymoon," I reminded him. I would have loved to have her travel with us, but I was afraid my new husband would regret it once we were on the road. Traveling with an old lady might be a challenge. Not that anyone who knew her would describe Miss Gloria as old. Some days she showed more zip than me—and I was fifty-something years younger. And if she did happen to droop, the tiniest catnap brought her roaring back to life.

"We're already spending most of the week with my sister," he said. "Miss G would only be an improvement."

On the phone, Nathan heaved a big sigh. "Now the plot's gotten thicker. My mother's coming."

I almost choked on the swallow of water I'd just taken. I'd gotten to know Nathan's mom right before New Year's. We'd survived a harrowing situation that left us filled with respect for one another. However, she was tall, formal, and super-accomplished, and she still scared the pants off me.

"She's worried about my sister too," Nathan continued, "but she hasn't seen her in a couple of years, so she figured our visit would be an easy way to work herself into the mix. I assured her that you wouldn't mind." I could hear him taking a big breath. "I'm sorry."

"We'll figure it out," I said briskly. "I'm sure it will be fine. I've got to run. I've got scones in the oven and only the barest bones of an article on the computer screen."

I'd wheedled a week of vacation out of my bosses at *Key Zest* magazine but then felt guilty about dropping the ball and offered to write a special section on Scottish food and music for the next issue—*Hayley Snow, traveling correspondent*. In addition to the article I was committed to send by tomorrow—a roundup of restaurateurs' opinions about the Mall on Duval Street, I'd promised a couple of scone recipes. I've always been and probably always will be an overachiever, once I get my compass aimed at the right point. And my bosses weren't going to turn me down, even if it was my so-called honeymoon.

The Mall on Duval had been a brainstorm from our new-ish mayor. It involved closing several blocks of the busiest strip in Key West to car and truck traffic on weekend evenings, in order to increase foot traffic and attract locals as well as visitors. The jury was definitely out on whether it was a raging success or the worst mistake since the harbor dredging that opened the gates to the influx of giant cruise ships.

I got up from my lounge chair on the teak deck and walked into our new houseboat, our home. Nathan and I had been living here two weeks and I still had to pinch myself to believe it was real. Though we'd spent months pouring over plans and many more months waiting for workers and materials to show up, the outcome was, in a word, stunning—without a whiff of flashy.

Our builder, Chris, had managed to secure Dade county pine lumber from a demolition project that now found a new life as my kitchen counters and drawers. He'd also managed to find Dave Combs, an amazing contractor and woodworker, who helped to execute our dream to polished reality. At the deep end of the counter, he had built shelves where I lined up my pottery containers holding baking supplies; and above that, vertical slats for my prettiest plates; and a little higher, a glass-fronted cabinet for the flowered blue china mugs and teapot that had been handed down from my grandmother's kitchen. There was a separate shelf for my cookbooks, and a gas stove on which every burner worked without coaxing or danger of explosion, and even a special cabinet that exactly fit the mammoth food processor that my mother-in-law had given us as a wedding present. From a wrought iron rack on the wall and ceiling over the stove hung an assortment of pots and pans, whisks, cheese grater boxes, and the other tools of my trade.

313

Though I wrote food criticism for a living, I lived for feeding my family and friends. The new kitchen made that activity almost purely pleasurable. There were, of course, trade-offs that came automatically with living on a houseboat—neighbors were close by, and the water all around us amplified every sound. That meant we shared our neighbors' music, no matter the genre. And we heard every woof and meow from every furry resident. And space was at a premium. That meant that our bed, three steps up from the double oven at the end of the kitchen, was built into the wall of the bedroom, with reasonable walk-in space only on his side, and a smaller mattress than a well-muscled man might prefer. As newlyweds, we did not find this close proximity to be a drawback. And we loved waking up in the morning and looking out on our aqua-blue watery world. On nice days, we opened the sliding doors so the whole world became part of our bedroom.

We had no room for houseguests aside from a berth on the living room couch, but since the people I loved most also lived on this island, I could easily survive with that restriction. I had a small built-in desk in the living area, and pale green walls that set off the rich woodwork and matched the color of the sea on a stormy day, and a special slot for Evinrude's litter box, and room for a bed for Nathan's dog, Ziggy, too. I couldn't believe that I lived here, married to a sweet and sexy hunk of a guy, with Miss Gloria, one of my best friends, next door, and my old college roommate and dear friend, Connie, right up the dock.

I heard the sound of a cowbell ringing, the system we had set up to alert me that Miss Gloria was out on her deck and available for conversation. She insisted I should feel free to ignore the call, but so far I had not failed to respond. It wasn't an easy transition for either of us, my moving out along with two members of our furry menagerie. Easy access with the toll of a bell made the change go more smoothly and feel less draconian.

I poked my head out the door and called over.

"Are you ready for a tea and scone break? I have some banana date scones coming out of the oven in five minutes."

"Are you kidding?" she asked. "I'll set the table. Bring the guys with you."

She didn't need to mention that, as both—Evinrude, my cat, and Ziggy the dog—had already gotten acclimated to the sound of the bell. Bell equals treats plus fun with old friends.

I pulled the fragrant scones out of the oven, the air now scented with the aromas of pastries browned just right plus the richness of bananas and a pile of butter. I transferred three of them to a yellow gingham plate, another wedding present, this time from Connie. I added the butter dish and a little bowl of freshly whipped cream and another of raspberry jam to the tray. Then I poured hot water into the blue flowered teapot and covered it with a tea cozy in the shape of a sheep that had been a gift from Nathan's sister. Following my gray tiger and Nathan's exuberant min pin, I started over to Miss Gloria's place, navigating the gap between the deck and the sloshing bight with care. Next time I should remember to heat the water in her kitchen.

Miss Gloria's two cats, handsome black Sparky, and adorable and mischievous orange tiger T-Bone, were waiting on her deck. She snatched the orange kitten up so he wouldn't wind between my legs and trip me.

"Are you working?" she asked. "I hate to bother you when you have so much—"

"You never bother me," I said patiently. "Remember what we agreed on after Nathan bought the boat?" I settled the tray on the table in between the two lounge chairs and gestured to the place next door.

"Friends and family first," she said, her eyes twinkling. "Your mother and I taught you well, didn't we?"

I'd spent a good part of the last few years here on this deck, talking with my friend and absorbing the life rhythms of Houseboat Row. "The recipe called for banana nut, but I changed out the nuts for dates," I said. "There's a ton of Irish butter already in the mixture, but I thought we might need a little melted butter on top too." I split open one of the scones, watching the steam drift up, and slathered it with Kerrygold butter. We each grabbed a half, doused it in whipped cream and jam, and tucked in.

"Heavenly. Maple syrup?" she asked, quirking her white eyebrows into peaks.

"Your palate is getting so sophisticated," I said with a big smile. "What else is up this morning?" I removed the sheep cozy, poured tea into each cup, and stirred in a tablespoon of honey. This was mango honey, with a hint of ripe fruit, that I doubted you could get anywhere outside of the Florida Keys. And it was the second week of June, ushering in the hot and sticky summer season, not hot tea weather at all. But both of us had gotten so excited about the impending trip that we couldn't let a day go by without practicing taking a proper Scottish tea.

"Two things," she said. "I want to go over my packing one more time. And I need you to remind me how to get into my Ancestry account. I fell asleep last night while I was looking at my family tree, and Sparky walked on the keyboard, and now I can't remember how to get back there."

"Easy yes on both," I said, popping the last of the sweet and buttery scone into my mouth. I cut the third confection in half and buttered that too. As we ate, I described the phone call with Nathan. "He's worried that his sister is flipping out," I said.

"What are the symptoms?" she asked, stroking Evinrude, who had pushed onto her lap and was eying the bowl of whipped cream.

I reviewed the conversation in my head, coming up with not much detail. "I didn't even ask. He was so busy telling me that his mother's joining the trip, that question never even came to my mind. I'll find out more tonight."

"Helen is coming too? This doesn't sound like much of a honeymoon. I could bail out—maybe your mother should be going instead of me, since Nathan's mother will be there."

I cut her off before she could work herself into a lather. "Don't be silly—she's too busy to go on a trip right now. And we love that you're coming. We wouldn't have it any other way."

Forty-five minutes later, we'd polished off every crumb of our tea and gone through everything in Miss Gloria's suitcase, which she had laid out on the bed in my former bedroom. I wondered how it was possible to feel so thrilled with my new home and new husband and yet sad about leaving this cozy little space. Evinrude, who had followed us in, circled around several times on the pillow, appearing puzzled, then curled up for a snooze while we inspected the suitcase.

I advised Miss Gloria to remove the shorts and bathing suit and add another sweater and a raincoat. Early June in Scotland was rumored to be both chilly and wet. And being petite and thin, she tended to feel cold in even the warmest weather. And as she hadn't gone swimming in Key West for the past decade—too nippy for her tastes—I doubted she'd be paddling about in the cold lochs of Scotland.

"Besides, they do have clothing stores in Scotland, I am told," I said with a wink. "We can buy anything we've forgotten." Then we went to her computer, where I restored her access to her family tree with a few quick strokes of the keyboard and watched two videos of Scottish bagpipers, admiring their music and their swinging kilts and well-muscled calves.

"Thanks so much," she said, hugging me warmly. "Are you going downtown this afternoon?"

"Yes, I need to spend at least an hour wandering Duval Street and interviewing a few of the restaurant owners and diners. Somehow I have to get this article finished before we leave."

"Would you mind running me over to Sunset? I feel like I need to touch base with Lorenzo before we go to your mother's for supper."

Lorenzo was our Tarot card-reading friend who set up every night at Mallory Square to advise visiting tourists about their lives. Some people dismissed him as a fruitcake, but I knew better. He had a deep spiritual connection with the universe around him. And he understood the unconscious motivations of the world and the people he met better than anyone I'd ever known, with my psychologist friend Eric Altman running a close second.

We agreed that Miss Gloria could spend the time while I was interviewing people having a little tipple of wine at happy hour, and then we would both buzz over on my scooter to talk with Lorenzo. And after that, run to my mother and Sam's place for a pre-trip going away dinner.

We clipped on our helmets, Miss Gloria grabbed my waist, and I fired up my scooter and pulled out onto Palm Avenue. The traffic was light, a welcome change from the hordes that flooded Key West in the high season from December through March. I enjoyed all the seasons of our island but a break from the partying crowds was welcome. I took White Street to Southard, and parked my bike in the assigned area at the corner of this one-way road, which would leave us very near to the blocks designated as a pedestrian mall.

Each week, in the local papers, I'd read articles assessing the effects of this pedestrian mall project. The restaurants along these blocks were thrilled with the opportunity to expand their space to outdoor seating right on the street. Others, retail places without that same option, insisted that their sales were dropping. And restaurants outside the three-block mall often complained that they weren't allowed the same outdoor open seating, and suggested that their sales were being siphoned off by the lucky few. The dispute appeared to be coming to a head soon.

I settled Miss Gloria on the couch outside the art gallery Duval Destiny and brought her a tiny glass of complimentary chardonnay. She had not an inch of room for new art on her walls, and these psychedelic roosters and orgasmic naked women certainly wouldn't be her style even if she did, but the owners didn't seem to mind her occasional appearance. To my mind, she was an asset, as she never let a tourist pass by without chitchatting with them about supporting local businesses and artists.

As I walked closer to the Italian restaurant where I planned to start my research by questioning my waiter acquaintance Cheech (so nicknamed for his spacy appearance), I heard a loud noise—the crack of a gun?—and then a panicked voice yelled, "He's got a gun! Help! A gun!" Then all around me people began shouting and crying and running and pushing—both ways, toward the noise and away from it.

I froze for a moment, with my heart pounding. The spate of mass shootings in the news had us all in terror that we would experience this kind of event firsthand. No matter where you were headed or what the event might be, the bad guys could find you. Churches, movie theaters, schools, shopping centers—nothing was sacred. Nothing was safe. Which definitely put a damper on the Key West party mood.

Nathan had insisted on drilling the entire family on how to behave in the case of an active shooter: First, you should look for the exits when you arrive at any destination.

Second, if you are caught in an incident, evacuate and run if at all possible. If escape is not possible, drop, roll, hide, and call it in. In that order. And silence devices so beeps and messages won't give you away to a killer intent on hunting victims.

If there is no other option, fight.

It must have killed him to tell us all of that, especially the fighting.

I sorted quickly through the possibilities. If I headed to the teeming sidewalk, I was afraid I'd be crushed by the panicked crowd. Running down the less-crowded middle of the street was out too. If there really was a crazy person shooting, I'd become the perfect target. As Nathan advised, I dropped to my knees on the pavement and rolled into the gutter. Too late, I froze, wondering whether I'd gotten the rolling bit mixed up with a fire emergency.

Chapter Two

Everything depends on the moment the spice hits a hot pan: whether it sizzles with a mouthwatering fragrance or turns to ash.

—Sasha Martin, *Life from Scratch*

My face ended up smooshed near the white-stenciled words on the curb above the drain, warning potential litterers, "Anything discarded here will wash into the ocean." The gutter smelled of stale beer and cigarette butts and pizza, but strongest of all was the stink of my own fear. I curled into the smallest human ball possible, knowing that I could still be an open target for a crazed shooter. Should I get up and run to help Miss Gloria? Nathan had drilled the same safety information into her head as he had mine, with great patience. I had to think she'd be hunkered down behind the art gallery furniture. Or maybe she'd been smart and quick enough to run inside.

Hearing more muffled shouts but no gunshots, I crab-walked toward better cover—a nearby trash can. I peered around the edge to see what was going on. I heard the sound of footsteps pounding and two different voices yelling, "Drop the gun! Hands above your head! Police!"

Then I heard the clatter of metal on pavement and saw two hands stretched high above the heads of the crowd. Tourists and bystanders had begun to push toward the scene while two fierce police yelled at them to move back. More officers came running down the street, some with guns drawn and some with police dogs loping beside them.

"Stand back," a tall officer shouted to the crowd. "You need to clear the area."

Miss Gloria came up behind me and tapped my shoulder. "I think you're okay to come out from behind the trashcan now. The only bad guy they seem to have trapped is Ray."

"Ray?" I stood up and brushed the grit off my knees, realizing I had scraped them raw in the flurry of activity. Ray was my dear friend Connie's husband, father of the adorable baby Claire, and a very talented and peace-loving artist. I could not imagine him getting into an altercation with the cops, especially over a gun.

She took my elbow and we moved to the sidewalk, close enough that we could hear the men talking. Shouting was more like it.

"I panicked," Ray was explaining. "I heard gunshots and got spooked. I would never shoot anyone, I swear. My gallery manager was there—she saw everything—"

"You'll need to come to the station," said the biggest cop, the same man who had stopped me for running through a stop sign on my scooter after Christmas. He was intimidating because of his size and his bald head, but he seemed like a nice enough man. If you liked tough police personas. Which, being married to one, I suppose I did. Before migrating to Key West, I didn't know one single policeman. I'd never imagined I'd end up with so many police officers in my life.

"You can't brandish a weapon in a public space. It's a crime," the cop said.

"But it was self-defense," Ray told him. "Or it would have been." His voice trailed off weakly, as though he recognized he was in deep trouble. The crowd around him had gotten louder, offering their own opinions and observations.

I caught Ray's eye and shouted above the din. "Do you need anything? Do you want us to come with you? Call Nathan?"

He shook his head, the expression on his face bleak, then marched down the street with a cop at each elbow. Should I text Connie? Or butt out and assume Ray would call her? I decided to text Nathan instead and ask him to check up on Ray. Better not to terrify my friend until we had some facts. I also needed to let Nathan know that although we had been on the scene, we'd suffered nothing more than a few scary moments.

The tourists who had gathered around to see the cause of the commotion were encouraged by the police to move on with their evening activities while the authorities continued to investigate the incident. I felt a little shaky and not at all interested in writing this "woman on the street" article that I had promised my bosses. As usual, I had loaded too much onto my plate. But this time I wasn't going to try to choke it all down. Interviews about the Duval Mall experiment were not going to be possible under these circumstances anyway. Everything would still be here when we got home from our trip. I sent a quick text off to my two bosses, explaining that Duval Street was a disaster following a possible shooter incident and that I'd do the Mall article on my return. Which was all true. But most of all right now, I needed to see Lorenzo and then share a meal with my mother and Sam, and then, finally, check in with Connie and Ray.

* * *

Ten minutes later, we parked the scooter in the lot off Mallory Square. With sunset not due until after eight, the crowds were light on the plaza. The sun was still blazing high in the sky over the horizon, and the air felt hot and still and smelled of yesterday's popcorn. Even the seagulls were quiet, perched on the edge of the pier, facing in toward the square, on the lookout for a breeze or a handout. We found Lorenzo free at his booth near the edge of the water.

"What happened?" he asked, getting up to greet us. You both look upset."

Miss Gloria explained the incident on Duval Street. "It was enough to rattle the sturdiest of souls. All those people running and shrieking, and us with no idea what was really going on."

"The world's gone mad," he said in a somber voice. "We're all at sixes and sevens." He gave us each a hug and then sat back down and reached for his deck of cards.

We perched on the two folding chairs across from him, our hands clenched on the blue tablecloth. "You know what isn't helping?" I added. "I think we're both nervous about traveling." I glanced at my friend, and she nodded her agreement.

"We want to go, we're so excited. But at the same time, it's a little scary too," said Miss Gloria. "I haven't been out of the country in many years, and Hayley's never been abroad. And Key West is comfortable. It's home."

"And we like being able to check in with you when we feel like the world's rocked off its rails," I said. "You're our security blanket."

A wide smile lit up his face, and he pulled the deck of colored Tarot cards out of our reach. "I don't need to read any cards to tell you that this will be the trip of a lifetime. Everybody feels a little anxious going somewhere new. You can let that stop you, or you can acknowledge the feeling and then go anyway. It's so wonderful that you're sharing this trip together. And if you need to talk with me while you're away, your mother can come over with her phone and we'll FaceTime." He reached across the table to gather a hand from each of us, and then squeezed. I felt his warmth spread through my fingers, and that made me feel the tiniest bit teary.

"Should we bring you back a redheaded man in a kilt?" asked Miss Gloria, once he'd let go of our hands. Lorenzo had had a longtime partner in his life, but no new fellow recently. And he loved the Jamie character from *Outlander* as much as we did.

"Perfect!" said Lorenzo, and we moved aside for his next customer, a large woman in a bright purple shirt, who was pacing behind us.

"I read about you in a mystery book," I heard her say. "I still can't believe you're here and you're real."

He chuckled. "Very real."

Then we motored over to my mother's home, located on a street a block from the waterfront in the Truman Annex. We could smell something delicious before we even got inside the house.

Mom met us at the door. "I wasn't sure what kind of cuisine you'd have in Scotland," she said on the way to the kitchen. "But we made a shepherd's pie and a nice, light lime sponge cake for dessert. There was no point in trying to replicate fried fish and mushy peas—we can't compete with what they do with a deep fryer!" She gestured at the big center island, where they'd set up bottles of wine, one red and one rosé, beaded with cool droplets. "Pour yourself a glass of wine and then we'll eat."

"I was so excited at the thought of making Scottish rumbledethumps," said Sam as he pulled a bubbling casserole from the oven. "That would have involved leftovers and no meat—not proper for a send-off meal. But I still love the name."

"This dinner sounds amazing," I said. "And we could use some comfort food about now."

While Miss Gloria explained the gun incident at Ray's gallery, I went to the sink to blot the blood oozing from my knees and wash the scrapes off. No telling what organisms might lurk on the Duval Street pavement.

"Poor Ray was having an absolute fit," I said. "I couldn't even believe he had a gun with him. But I'm sure I'll hear the full story once we get home to Houseboat Row tonight."

We took our seats out on the porch and inhaled every bite of Sam's ground beef and veggie casserole, which swam in a thick gravy and was topped with mashed potatoes and turnips. "The Scottish people are going to beg for this recipe," said Miss Gloria to Sam. "Do you mind writing it down so Hayley can make it?"

Sam began to scroll through his notes, to send the recipe to Miss Gloria's phone. I got up from the table to help my mother clear the plates.

"Nothing from Connie or Ray?" she asked, as we loaded dishes in the dishwasher.

"Not a peep." I brought out my phone and navigated to the Key West police Twitter account. "Let's see what the authorities are saying."

I read the most recent tweet aloud. "'No active shooter was discovered on the Duval Street mall. One individual has been taken in for questioning. Police searched the area and found no credible threat. Visitors are advised to take caution and report suspicious activity.'"

The tweet further down their page from earlier in the afternoon reported a possible shooting, with police on the scene. "Anybody in the area should shelter in place and evacuate when cleared."

It seemed pretty clear that they had determined there had been no gunshot before Ray's panicked reaction, and that perhaps visitors to the area had also panicked, including Miss Gloria and me. This was the good news and the bad news about social media. Important information could be spread quickly, but often it was inaccurate and sometimes inflammatory. I reported this latest news to my family while Sam cut us wedges of a light and lovely lime sponge cake.

"I've read about other incidents like this," Sam said, passing the plates around. "Even in Times Square, people heard what they thought were gunshots, and the noise turned out to be the backfiring of a dirt bike. And in Boca Raton, a panic was started by popping balloons."

"I hate that the world has come to this," said my mother, looking sad. "I'm glad you'll be getting away for a bit. Is it true that they don't allow guns in Scotland?" She gulped and threw a worried look at me. "Do you think Nathan is planning to bring his handgun? I wonder if that would be permitted?"